Library of
Davidson College

RUDIMENTS OF MUSIC

RUDIMENTS OF MUSIC

A NEW APPROACH WITH

APPLICATION TO THE KEYBOARD

By John Castellini

New York · W · W · Norton & Company · INC ·

COPYRIGHT © 1962 BY W. W. NORTON & COMPANY, INC.

Library of Congress Catalog Card No. 62-7973

ALL RIGHTS RESERVED

Published simultaneously in Canada by
George J. McLeod Limited, Toronto

ISBN 0 393 0 09573 8

PRINTED IN THE UNITED STATES OF AMERICA

This book is dedicated to
ANNE
*my wife—devoted, patient, and **wise**.*

CONTENTS

1 Some Characteristics of Sound   3
    Pitch—dynamics—timbre · *The harmonic series* · *Temperament*

2 Location of Pitch   8
    Meaning of staff lines and spaces · The G and F clefs · The grand staff—ledger lines · *History of the staff*

3 The Piano   16
    Names of white keys · Names of black keys—chromatic signs · The sharp · The flat · The octave · The pedals · *History of the piano*

4 Playing the Piano   22

5 The Staff and the Keyboard   33
    Writing a melody on the staff · Use of letter names · The staff and the keyboard

6 Rhythm   43
    Metrical patterns in poetry · Metrical patterns in music · *History of rhythm*

CONTENTS

7 Notes and Rests — 49

Notes · Rests · The tie and the dot · *History of notation*

8 Meter — 55

Measure and bar line · Time or meter signature · Rhythmic representation of a melody · Measure *vs.* bar · Rhythmic patterns of pieces in triple and quadruple meter · Syncopation · Simple and compound meters · Metrical groups within the measure · *History of time signatures*

9 Written Music and the Keyboard — 68

Hints for practice · Counting · Tempo · Fingering · A Melody played by two hands

10 Role of Right and Left Hands in Keyboard Music — 77

11 Transposition — 86

12 Origins of Our Scales — 90

Greek modes · Church modes · Pentatonic scale · Modal songs

13 The Major Scale — 96

Names of the scale degrees · Major scale pattern · The written scale · Use of the sharp · Use of the flat · Accidentals · The natural · Double sharp and double flat · Enharmonic change · Playing the major scales · Major scales with suggested fingerings · Summary of suggested fingerings for major scales · Order of sharps and flats (major scales) · Circle of fifths (major scales) · Key signatures · Hints · *History of accidentals*

14 Minor Scales — 114

Natural minor scale · Relative major and minor · Order of sharps and flats (minor scales) · Circle of fifths (major and minor scales) · Playing the natural minor scales · The major and relative natural minor scales with suggested fingerings · Summary of suggested fingerings for natural minor scales · Harmonic minor scale · Playing the harmonic minor scales · The major and relative harmonic minor scales with suggested fingerings · Summary of suggested fingerings for harmonic minor scales · Melodic minor scale · Playing the melodic minor scales · Major and relative melodic minor scales with suggested fingerings · Parallel major and minor · Summary · Miscellaneous scales · Chromatic scale · Whole-tone scale · Other scales · *History of harmonic minor scale* · *History of melodic minor scale*

15 Intervals   139

Melodic and harmonic intervals · Compound intervals · Inversion of intervals · Classification of intervals · Kinds of intervals · Consonances and dissonances · Intervals altered chromatically · Summary · Tritone · Enharmonic intervals · *History of intervals*

16 Chords   149

Triads · Triads of the major mode · Triads of the minor mode · Summary · Seventh chords · Additional chords

17 Inversions   156

Root positions · Inversions of a triad · Inversions of a seventh chord · Figured bass · Triad in root position · Seventh chord in root position · Figured inversions of a triad · Figured inversions of a seventh chord · Summary · Figured bass illustrated

18 Basic Chords and Cadence Patterns   165

Cadence · Authentic cadence · Plagal cadence · Cadences in the major mode · Voice leading · Cadences in the minor mode · Authentic cadence including the IV chord · Authentic cadence including the I_4^6 chord · Authentic cadence including the II_6 chord · The secondary dominant · Cadence including the V_7 of IV · Cadence including the V_7 of V

19 Chordal Patterns and Accompaniment figures   173

Accompaniment figures for two hands · Accompanying by ear · Select your own accompaniment · Teaching a song · Accompaniment figures for left hand only

CONTENTS

20	**Extended Chordal Patterns**	**189**
	Using the IV chord · Using the II_6 chord · Using secondary dominants · V_7 of IV patterns · V_7 of V patterns	
21	**Use of the Damper Pedal**	**208**
22	**Suit the Accompaniment to the Tune**	**213**
23	**Indications of Tempo and Expression**	**219**
	Tempo markings · The metronome · Other tempo directions · Directions for both tempo and dynamics · Terms indicating dynamics · Terms indicating expression · Terms indicating tonal production · Miscellaneous terms · Auxiliary words · Abbreviations · Signs	
24	**You—the performer**	**230**
	Appendix I Table of Pitches	234
	Appendix II The C clef	235
	Index	237

FOREWORD

This book stems from a course called "Rudiments of Music," which has been given for many years with marked success in Queens College, New York. The syllabus of the course was fashioned primarily to fulfill the needs of education students who had had no earlier musical training whatsoever. This book, also entitled *Rudiments of Music,* deals with notation, rhythm, scales and keys, intervals, chords (triads and seventh chords with emphasis on the dominant seventh), and their inversions. It also gives the student sufficient knowledge of the piano to enable him to play melodies and simple accompaniments. Though the book, like the course, is designed for the nonmusic student, it contains much of value for students majoring in music, and particularly for those who are to use music in their work with children and older groups.

    The materials of the text are related to four areas: (1) an exposition of what is often called "the language of music"; (2) the historical background of this; (3) an introduction to the technique of piano-playing; (4) a body of songs that can serve for work with school children and with various community groups. The melodies of the songs are presented with a variety of accompaniment figures which also have application to innumerable songs not included here.

    Ideally, the student should pursue the entire content of the book. However, because of insufficient time or other limitations that often attend courses in rudiments of music, it may be that one or more phases of the study will have to be passed over or given only brief consideration in class. Recognition of such possible limitations is manifest in the organization of this text. The historical sections are set in different type from the rest of the text, and with one exception are placed at the end of chapters. The exception is the whole of Chapter 12, "Origins of Our Scales." While the historical material need not be made the subject of class work, it should be read by the student so that he may have a basis for understanding the very thing he is anxious to learn. The *why* is often as interesting as it is important.

A special feature of this text is the immediate application of knowledge of the rudiments of music to the playing of the piano. Nonmusicians often express a wistful desire to be able to play the piano; actually, piano-playing is no more difficult than typing. Careful study, application, and practice of the instructions in Chapter 4 have given many nonmusicians the feeling of extraordinary accomplishment with the thrill of discovery that they *can* play the piano. One can hardly expect to play a complicated piano piece after one's first lesson, but fingers can be taught to strike the right keys of a piano as easily as those of a typewriter. One needs only a good measure of self-confidence, the resolution to succeed, and practice.

The piano is a most effective accompanying instrument. In Chapter 19 we are introduced to a variety of practical accompaniment figures for nursery, game, "community-sing," and folk songs. These patterns can be mastered by the student even before he achieves the independence of hands that is needed for playing piano pieces of medium difficulty. Chapter 19 can be introduced immediately after Chapter 11, "Transposition," if it is synchronized carefully with the study of scales, intervals, and chords and their inversions as given in Chapters 13 to 18. This procedure, enabling the student to acquire a practical skill early in the course, is strongly recommended.

The author wishes to acknowledge his indebtedness and gratitude to the colleagues and friends who gave counsel and help in the preparation of the manuscript: Robert Farlow, Harold and Helen Folland, Gabriel Fontrier, Konrad Gries, Charles Haywood, Donald Kirkpatrick, Paul Henry Lang, Joseph Machlis, Saul Novack, Mary Ranney, Haskell Reich, Curt Sachs, Oliver Strunk, and Evelyn Switzer.

A signal expression of appreciation is due Margaret Lowry, who made invaluable suggestions as to the content and organization of the material, and Robert Higgins, who gave so generously of his time and talent to the refinement of the text.

JOHN CASTELLINI

RUDIMENTS OF MUSIC

CHAPTER 1

SOME CHARACTERISTICS OF SOUND

"How wondrous is the work of God,
How glorious His creation . . ."
        Haydn—*The Creation*

It is the disposition of man to take for granted much of nature's handiwork, of which one of the most unquestioningly accepted phenomena is that of sound. Sound manifests itself in many ways but *musical sound* is special because it is ordered and controlled. Sing a tune such as "Mary Had A Little Lamb," "Frère Jacques," or "Three Blind Mice." As you sing, listen. If you really *listen* and concentrate on the listening experience you will become increasingly conscious of the impression the melody makes upon the ear. This is musical sound. But what is sound itself? What are some of its physical aspects?

For a number of years we have known that everything—literally everything (even everything which goes to make up this book)—is in a state of motion. This motion, called vibration, is not motion in the sense of advancing location but, rather, it is a to-and-fro process, a fluctuation within fixed limits. Sometimes it can be seen by the eye, as in the waves created by a stone thrown into a calm pool of water. Here the waves advance from the center of the pool to the bank but the water does not. It rises and falls in an oscillating movement until the energy has been expended.

Some such motions can be heard by the ear; for instance, those which are made by the voice, the piano, and other musical instruments. There are

SOME CHARACTERISTICS OF SOUND

others that can be both seen and heard, such as the vibrations of a stretched rubber band or the string of a bass viol when plucked. There are still other manifestations of vibrations; for example, those in the telephone, radio, and television. These can be neither seen nor heard, but they can be "captured" electronically and transformed into sound and picture.

To hear sound we need:

1. *A vibrating object.* Almost anything can serve as a vibrating object. Strike a drinking glass, a piece of metal, or blow through your lips.

2. *A transmitting medium.* With a few exceptions, almost any solid, liquid, or gas is a good medium for transmitting sound waves. For humans, air is obviously the most common carrier. The to-and-fro motion of the vibrating object is passed on from one molecule of air to the next until, eventually, the vibrations reach a point some distance from the original source.

3. *A receiver.* Finally, a receiver, the ear, absorbs the energy which has been passing through the transmitting medium and converts it into sound.

Thus, when someone sings, his vocal cords are set into motion, the vibrations produced pass through the air, and they are received by the ear and sent to the brain, which interprets them as sound.

Sounds differ in *pitch, dynamics,* and *timbre.** Let us examine these characteristics because they are of prime importance to musical sound.

PITCH, *the highness or lowness of sound,* is dependent on the frequency of vibrations. (Frequency is expressed in cycles per second.) The faster the vibrations the higher the pitch; the slower the vibrations the lower the pitch. The human ear is sensitive to pitches ranging from approximately 20 to 16,000 cycles per second.

DYNAMICS in music refers to *the loudness or softness of sound.* This depends upon the intensity of the vibrations. Without regard to the sensitivity of the individual ear (which varies from person to person) the degrees of dynamics can be measured. The yardstick for this measurement is called a *bel,* after Alexander Graham Bell, the inventor of the telephone. Because it has been found useful to deal with units of one-tenth of a bel, the common term employed to measure the level of loudness is the *decibel.*

TIMBRE, *the quality of sound,* is conditioned by the nature of the vibrating object and its medium of transmission. At this point we must digress to explain the physical phenomenon that determines quality of

* The word retains its French pronunciation. *tahm'br.*

sound.

A sound can be produced which is pure as to pitch, that is, where there is only one frequency present. To produce such a sound, special equipment is necessary. A natural musical sound is not pure; it is complex. There are many frequencies present in the vibrating object because it is in motion in its different parts as well as in its whole. For example, a string or a column of air vibrates not only in its entirety but *simultaneously* in its halves, thirds, fourths, fifths, and so forth. The sounds created by the vibrations of these fractional lengths are called *partials,* or (less correctly) *overtones.* These partials are sounds which are higher in pitch and much softer in dynamics. What we hear and identify as a tone is the composite sound of a *fundamental* pitch and its *partials.*

The phenomenon of a fundamental and its partials can be demonstrated by the following experiment. Go to the piano and strike the C two octaves below middle C.* The sound is low in pitch because the full length of the string vibrates at the rate of 65.4 cycles per second and these fundamental frequencies are the most prominent ones. Listen to this low pitch; try to remember it. Now, with the left hand, slowly and *without making a sound,* depress the same key. If you do this very gently, the hammer will not strike the string and there will be no sound. But the damper will be raised off the string, with the result that it will be free to be set in motion, that is, to vibrate. While continuing to hold down this key with the left hand, use the right hand to strike *hard* and *sharply* the C one octave above the depressed key. Quickly release the key struck by the right hand. Notice that you will continue to hear the pitch of the C just struck, but, inasmuch as the key has been released and the damper has rested again upon the string and stopped it from vibrating, it is obvious that the sound cannot be coming from that string. In fact, you are now hearing the pitch of this upper octave (130.8 cycles) emanating from the string of the lower C. This occurs because the vibrations of the fundamental of the upper octave, reinforced by the resonating sounding-board, have set into sympathetic vibration the halves of the longer string. The sound you hear comes from these halves, which vibrate twice as fast as the entire length of the string. Release the key held down by the left hand, and the sound will stop. Repeat this experiment and observe it carefully.

In like manner depress the lower C key again. This time strike *hard* and *sharply* the G just below middle C. Quickly release the G and listen to the sound. Notice that the pitch of the G continues, but again, it is not coming

---

* If you are not familiar with the keyboard and do not have the help of one who is, this experiment may be deferred until you have studied Chapter 3, "The Piano."

SOME CHARACTERISTICS OF SOUND

from the shorter, higher string but from the longer, lower one of the low C. This pitch of 196.2 cycles per second is the result of the independent and simultaneous vibrations of the thirds of the string.* Release the low C and the sound of the higher G will stop.

Similarly, the 4th, 5th, 6th, 7th, 8th, and 9th segments of the string may be put into sympathetic vibration by holding down the low C and striking, as before, middle C and, in ascending order, the next E, G, B♭, C, and D. (Each time release the low C and depress it silently again before proceeding with the next higher note.)

For additional material on The Harmonic Series, see the end of this chapter.

The following final experiment with a fundamental and its immediate partials demonstrates an exciting acoustical marvel. Again, depress the key of the C two octaves below middle C. While the damper is off this string, strike hard and sharply *and in quick succession* the following keys: C below middle C, the next higher G, middle C, the next higher E, G, B♭, and the C above middle C. It is quite a sound you will hear from the string whose fundamental is the C two octaves below middle C. And mind you, all of the various pitches you hear are being produced by one and the same long string.

A knowledge of secondary vibrations is necessary to the understanding of *timbre*. Every instrument, whether it be the voice, a flute, or a bell, accentuates, in its own peculiar way, different partials. This accounts for the fact that every sound has a quality, or timbre, all its own. For example, in relation to the human ear the French horn seems to accentuate the upper partials in the harmonic series; therefore, the fundamental tones themselves *sound* higher than they really are. This is not as true of the trombone. By regulating the accentuation of different partials, it is possible to imitate the quality of all musical instruments. This is, in fact, the principle underlying certain electronic organs.

What we call a *musical sound* is produced by an instrument which clearly emphasizes a fundamental and certain of its natural partials. *Noise*, on the other hand, is a complex sound which includes no clearly defined fundamental and many unrelated partials.

The reader interested in the physical nature of sound can pursue the subject further in books on physics and acoustics, or in the general and music encyclopedias under the headings of *acoustics, harmonic series, overtones*, or *temperament*.

---

* Just as the halves of the string vibrate twice as fast as the entire length, so the thirds vibrate three times as fast. This proportion continues throughout the entire series of partials.

SOME CHARACTERISTICS OF SOUND

Up to this point the discussion has been directed to the differences in sound: pitch, dynamics, and timbre. A composer can easily specify dynamics and timbre. Any language offers sufficient words to indicate the degree of loudness or softness desired; and it is simple enough to name a certain instrument if the tone quality of that instrument is wanted. But the representation of pitch goes beyond the language barrier. This demands special signs and symbols. For this a whole system has been invented.

THE HARMONIC SERIES

The experiment proposed near the beginning of this chapter does not show all the partials associated with the fundamental C two octaves below middle C, but it does show the principle of what is called the *harmonic series*. The following table shows the harmonic series as it occurs beginning with a fundamental (also called the first partial) C two octaves (Latin *octava*, the eighth) below middle C and extending upward four octaves to the C two octaves above middle C.

Frequency	65.4	130.8	196.2	261.6	327	392.4	457.8	523.2
Segment	1	1/2	1/3	1/4	1/5	1/6	1/7	1/8
Pitch	C	c	g	c′ *	e′	g′	−b♭′	c″
Frequency	588.6	654	719.4	784.8	850.2	915.6	981	1046.4
Segment	1/9	1/10	1/11	1/12	1/13	1/14	1/15	1/16
Pitch	d″	e″	f″–f♯″	g″	−a″	−b♭″	b″	c‴

* See Table of Pitches in Appendix I, page 234.

This table starts with a tempered C where a′ = 440. It progresses, however, according to the harmonic series as it occurs in nature. Thus, some of the tones in the table are not quite in tune with respect to the piano because of the difference between the natural harmonic series and the tempered scale.

TEMPERAMENT

The piano is tuned according to a *tempered* system, in which the octave is divided into twelve equal degrees, called *half steps*. For these half steps to be equidistant, the same ratio must exist between each one of them. The ratio for the octave is 2 : 1; the ratio for each of the 12 half steps of the octave is $\sqrt[12]{2}$: 1, or 1.059463 : 1. Thus, if we start with middle c′, whose frequency is 261.6 cycles per second, we can find the next of the half steps in the octave by multiplying 261.6 by 1.059463—a pitch, called c♯′, whose frequency is 277.2 cycles per second. Continuing this process of multiplying each new frequency by 1.059463 twelve times we arrive at the octave c″ whose frequency is approximately 523.2 cycles, or double that of middle c′.

CHAPTER 2

LOCATION OF PITCH

Melody—the most important element in music—is a meaningful succession of single pitches. We can learn a melody by having someone sing it for us, and then, through imitation and repetition, make it our own. For the most part, this is the way we learn the songs of our youth: nursery tunes, church hymns, and game songs. As we grow older and listen more carefully to other music at the theater or concerts, on the phonograph, radio, or television, we are able to aquaint ourselves with a very large number of pieces without any formal training in music. This is the way in which folk music has been handed down from generation to generation.

In learning a melody the basic problem is that of distinguishing the various pitches. You can observe differences in pitch in a melodic line by singing the familiar tune to "Mary Had A Little Lamb."

> Mary had a little lamb,
> Little lamb, little lamb,
> Mary had a little lamb,
> Its fleece was white as snow.

The first three tones of the melody fall in pitch with each syllable:

LOCATION OF PITCH

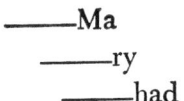

The following graphic representation can aid you in distinguishing the approximate location of the various pitches.

```
5                                    tle lamb,
4
3   Ma      lit   tle lamb,             lit
2     ry  a              Lit   tle lamb,
1       had
```

```
5
4
3   Ma         lit  tle lamb, Its      white
2     ry   a              fleece was        as
1       had                                    snow.
```

In the French song "Frère Jacques," * the first three tones of the melody go in the opposite direction. A graph of this tune would have a different appearance. Now, sing this song and follow the direction of the syllables.

```
6
5                            vous?        vous?
4                       mez          mez
3   Jac       Jac   Dor          Dor
2     re        re
1   Frè    ques, frè   ques,
2
3
4
```

* English text: Are you sleeping? Are you sleeping,
Brother John, Brother John?
Morning bells are ringing, morning bells are ringing:
Ding, ding, dong, ding, ding, dong.
Literal translation: Brother James, are you asleep? Ring the bell for matins [morning prayers] din, din, don.

LOCATION OF PITCH

```
6      nez              nez
5  Son  les      son    les
4           ma                ma
3           ti                ti
2
1                  nes,           nes: Din,    don, din,    don.
2
3
4                                          din,         din,
```

"Three Blind Mice" has still another pattern. Again, follow the graph of the melody as you sing this song.

```
8
7
6
5                             See             see
4                                  how they        how they
3  Three         three                       run,         run!
2      blind         blind
1          mice,         mice,


8      all ran         far         cut off their
7          af      the                     tails    a
6            ter                                    with
5  They               mer's wife, She
4
3
2
1


8  carv              ev  er you         sight
7                        see      a
6                              such
5      ing knife; Did              in your life,
4                                          As
3                                              three
2                                                  blind
1                                                       mice.
```

LOCATION OF PITCH

This kind of representation of the melodies is only an approximation, because merely placing the words or syllables higher or lower in relation to each other does not locate definite pitches. In order to locate exact pitches we use symbols which fix definite pitches within a system of five parallel lines and spaces called the *staff*. The staff, as we know it today, is the result of centuries of evolution.

For the History of the Staff, see the end of this chapter.

MEANING OF THE LINES AND SPACES

In order to understand what staff lines represent and how they locate the position of exact pitch, let us look at the parallel found in the familiar radio dial. Its general pattern is this:

```
|||||||||||||||||||||||||||||||||||||||||||||||||||||||||||||||||||||||||||||||||||||||||||||||||||||||||
55  60    70    80    90    100   110   120   130   140   150   160
```

These markings and numbers indicate that the set is capable of receiving broadcasts of waves where the frequencies range from 550 kilocycles (550,000 cycles) per second to 1600 kilocycles (1,600,000 cycles) per second. Certainly, the average listener never thinks what the 70 on the dial means; he uses it only as a point of reference to show where he may tune in a particular station.

The lines and spaces which we use in printed music have the same function as the markings on the radio dial. They indicate the location of pitches instead of radio stations, but the principle is the same. The difference lies in the speed of the vibrations. Whereas the radio dial represents extremely high frequencies, the music staffs locate those which we can hear. We can represent the heart of the complete musical range with eleven lines and spaces.

```
———698+———
            659+
———587+———
            523+
———493+———
            440
———392———
            349+
———329+———
            293+
———261+———
            246+
———220———
            196
———174+———
            164+
———146+———
            130+
———123+———
            110
———97+———
```

As the radio dial enables us to signal out the various broadcasting stations, so this system of lines and spaces makes it possible for us to locate different

LOCATION OF PITCH

musical pitches. However, since the use of numbers to represent the frequencies of the complete musical range is unnecessarily cumbersome we name the lines and spaces after the first seven letters of the alphabet. Seven letters suffice because every eighth degree of the system is the octave of the first and has the same letter name. Therefore, the same seven letters can be used over and over again.

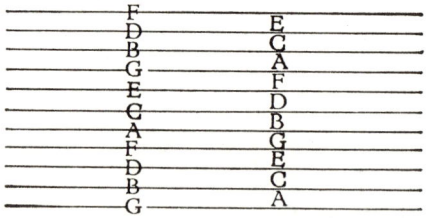

In order to make it easier for the eye to distinguish the lines and spaces, the sixth or middle line of the eleven is omitted and the upper and lower groups of five lines are separated slightly. Each set of five lines is called a *staff* (pl. staffs or staves).

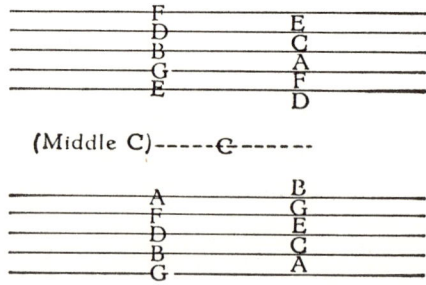

The G and F clefs

Although this separation makes it easier to distinguish the two staffs, there still would be confusion in knowing the pitch of any line or space if each staff were used individually without relation to the other. In that arrangement, the lowest line of a single staff might represent either the G of 97+ cycles per second or the E of 329+ cycles per second.

To overcome this difficulty, one line is given identification by a special symbol. Because this symbol acts as a key to reveal the names of the lines and spaces of the staff it is called a *clef* (French, from Latin *clavis*, key). The two clefs most commonly used today are the G and F clefs.

The symbol on the staff used to indicate the pitches above middle C was originally the letter G. Usually placed at the beginning of the staff, it fixes the pitch of the second line above middle C. With the second line (G)

LOCATION OF PITCH

as a point of orientation, it is now easy to locate the other pitches above middle C. The symbol currently used (𝄞) still resembles the letter G, but it has undergone obvious changes. Notice how the end of the scroll curls around the second line (G).

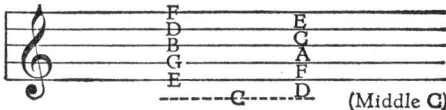

The symbol on the staff used to indicate the pitches below middle C was originally the letter F. Placed at the beginning of the staff, it fixes the pitch of the second line below middle C. This line (F) is the fourth line of the staff counting upwards. The F clef is composed of the letter and two dots (𝄢). The letter starts on the F line and the two dots are placed on either side of the same line.

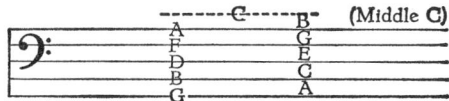

The grand staff

When the two staffs are joined by an extended vertical line and brace the resulting figure is the *Grand* or *Great Staff*. The grand staff is used in writing music for the piano and other keyboard instruments.

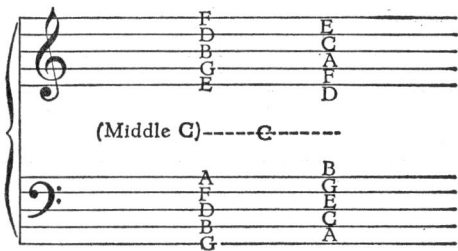

The upper staff employs the *G* or *Treble Clef* and locates the higher pitches; it is called the *Treble Staff*. The lower staff employs the *F* or *Bass Clef* and locates the lower pitches; it is called the *Bass Staff*. The word "treble" is derived from the Latin *triplum*, the third and highest voice of the medieval motet. The word "bass" is pronounced like and has the same meaning as the adjective *base*. Its spelling has been influenced by its source (late Latin), *bassus*.

LOCATION OF PITCH

Ledger lines

To indicate pitches which are higher or lower than the confines of the staff, the process of the staff is continued above and below by the addition of short lines, called *ledger,* or *leger lines.* Ledger lines were introduced in the seventeenth century. The term *ledger* came into use about 1700; its derivation is unknown.

Ledger lines should be spaced equidistant from the staff and from each other.

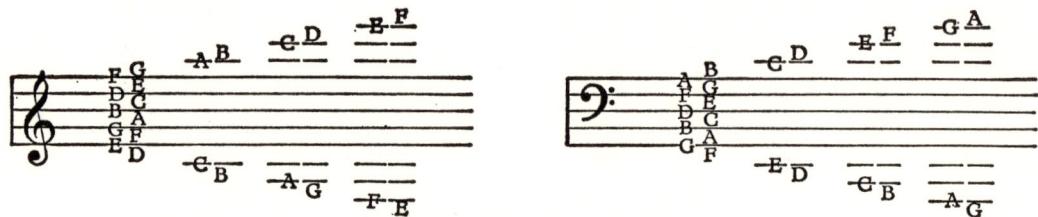

Very high or low pitches can be represented in another way. Instead of using many ledger lines above or below the staff, the sign 8va⎯⎯⎯⎯⎯⎯⎯⎯⎯ (Italian, *all'ottava,* at the octave) is employed. When placed above the staff, 8va⎯⎯⎯⎯⎯⎯⎯⎯⎯ indicates pitches which are an octave higher than written; when placed below the staff, 8va⎯⎯⎯⎯⎯⎯⎯⎯⎯ indicates pitches an octave lower than written.

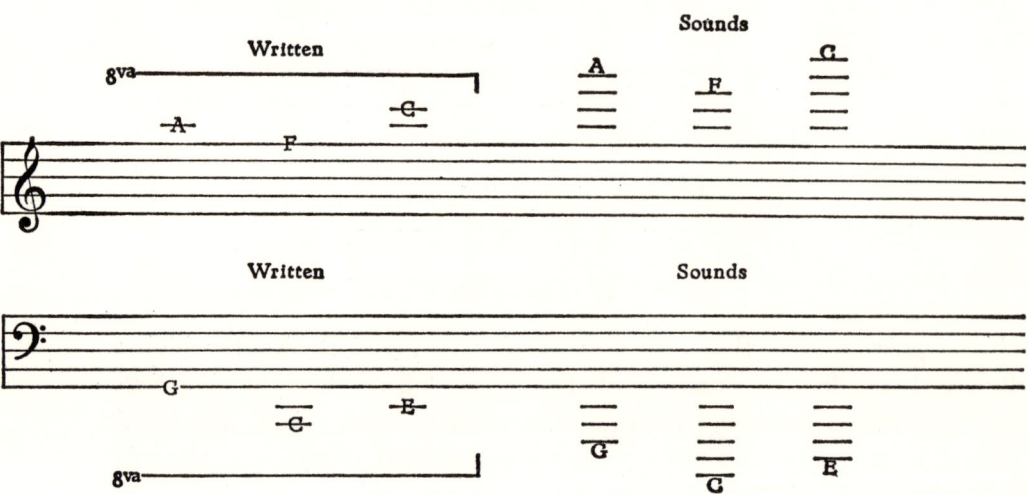

Today the treble and bass clefs are used for all vocal and keyboard (piano, organ, etc.) music. Only these clefs will be used in this book. For a third type of clef, the C clef, which is used for other instruments, see Appenddix II, page 235.

Memorize the names of the lines and spaces of the grand staff. Flash cards are an aid to such a study.

HISTORY OF THE STAFF

In the very early music of Western civilization there was no great need for exactness of pitch. As the chant of the Church, folksongs, and the tunes of entertainers of that period demonstrate, most early music consisted of a single vocal line. Such music, called *monophony* (from Greek *mono*, one + *phōnē*, sound), dominated the musical scene in the early Middle Ages. Because monophonic music is entirely melodic, the musician before the ninth century had little or no concern that the pitch of the same tone and the distance between two tones varied from time to time. However, from the ninth century on, interest gradually grew in a type of musical composition where two or more different pitches were produced at the same time. Such music is called *polyphony* (from Greek *polys*, many + *phōnē*, sound). This development created a demand for some kind of system which would regulate pitch and the relation of two tones with regard to pitch.

A popular treatise of the Middle Ages described an instrument with one string stretched over a soundbox with graduated markings. It was called a *monochord*. The graduated markings were indicated by letters of the alphabet. This is the source of our use of the letters A, B, C, D, E, F, and G. About a hundred years later an Italian Benedictine monk, Guido of Arezzo, explained a staff system where the sounds ". . . are so arranged that each sound, however often it may be repeated in a melody, is found always in its own row. And in order that you may better distinguish these rows, lines are drawn close together, and some rows of sounds occur on the lines themselves, others in the intervening . . . spaces. Then the sounds on one line or in one space all sound alike." *

Guido did not use as many lines as we use today. He is credited with a four-line staff with the F and C lines colored and identified by the letters F and C. Guido also used syllables for the tones of the scale. With some minor changes, his syllables have been standard for about the past 300 years: *do - re - mi - fa - sol - la - ti - do.*

* Guido of Arezzo, quoted in Oliver Strunk, *Source Readings in Music History*, New York, Norton, 1950, pp. 118–119.

CHAPTER 3

THE PIANO

Music is the art of organized tones. Because it deals with musical sounds, no musical composition achieves realization until it receives an artistic performance. Music on the printed page is dormant, and the performing artist must awaken it to fulfill the composer's vision. The performer's medium is an instrument, or his own voice (which is itself a kind of instrument).

Musical instruments are many and varied, but those instruments of the keyboard family offer the greatest possibilities for independent performance. Of the several common keyboard instruments—piano, organ, and accordion—the piano is the most practical.

The piano is a versatile instrument. It is excellent for solo work; it can serve as the accompanying medium for the voice or other instrument limited to a single melodic line; and it is "at home" in a small ensemble or in a large orchestra. The piano is so adaptable that a modest command of it can be useful in making music with others, to say nothing of the great amount of personal pleasure which comes from playing it alone.

For The History of the Piano, see the end of this chapter.

NAMES OF WHITE KEYS

The modern standard piano keyboard has 88 keys, 52 white and 36 black, ranging from an A of 26⅔ cycles per second to a C of 4,096 cycles per second (when middle C has 256 cycles per second). The names of the keys, like the names of the lines and spaces of the staff, come from the markings on the monochord (see History of the Staff in preceding chapter); therefore, the same letters of the alphabet are used: A, B, C, D, E, F, G. Only the white keys have their own letter names. Beginning with the lowest pitch, the white key A at the extreme left of the keyboard, these letters are used seven complete times. With a final A, B, and C added at the extreme right, the highest pitch is a white key, C. The left of the keyboard is called the bottom and the right is called the top. When we go to our left we go *down* the keyboard and when we go to the right we go *up* the keyboard.

Left side—lowest pitch *Right side—highest pitch*

Notice how the black keys are grouped in twos and threes. These groupings can help you memorize the names of the white keys. Two black keys are in the midst of the white keys C, D, and E; three black keys are in the midst of the white keys F, G, A, and B. Now we shall learn to identify the white keys.

Exercise for learning the white keys

Sit at the keyboard, a little to the right of middle C. (Middle C is the fourth C counting from left to right; it can be found readily by locating the C nearest to the keyhole or name plate.) Play all the C's on the keyboard. Then play all the E's, finding them just to the right of the group of two black keys. Next play all the D's—the white keys between the two black ones.

The F's are to the immediate left of the group of three black keys. Play all of them; then play all of the B's—the white keys to the immediate right of this group. In between are the G's and A's (G's, left of center and A's,

THE PIANO

right of center). Find and play all the G's and A's. Repeat with all the letter names. Practice until you can find quickly any white key on the piano.

NAMES OF BLACK KEYS—CHROMATIC SIGNS

The sharp

The black keys usually get their names from the white keys next to them. Each black key has at least two names although only one is used at a time. When considered in the direction of *left to right* (or up), the black key takes its name from the white key to its left and is called a *sharp*. A sharp is symbolized by the *chromatic* (from Greek *chrōmatikos,* suited for color) *sign* ♯. The first of the group of two black keys (the left one of the group), in relation to the white key to its left, is call C-sharp (C♯); the second of the group of two black keys, in relation to the white key to its left, is called D-sharp (D♯). In like manner, in the group of three black keys, the left is called F♯, the middle, G♯, and the right, A♯.

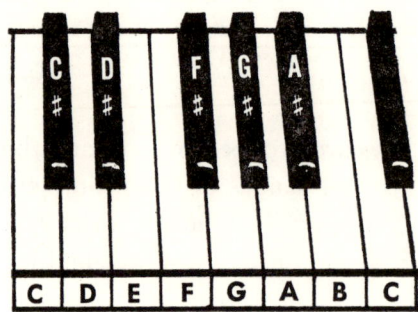

The flat

When considered in the direction of *right to left* (down), the black key takes its name from the white key to its right and is called a *flat*. A flat is symbolized by the chromatic sign ♭. The first of the group of two black keys, in relation to the white key to its right, is called D-flat (D♭); the second of the group of two black keys, in relation to the white key to its right, is called E-flat (E♭). In like manner, in the group of three black keys, the left is called G♭, the middle, A♭, and the right, B♭.

THE PIANO

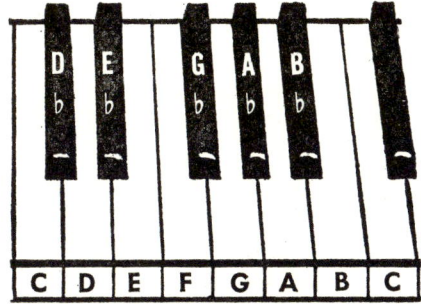

Exercise for learning the black keys

Again, sit at the keyboard. Always take a position a little to the right of middle C. Play all the C♯s on the keyboard. These are the black keys on the left in the groups of two. Call the keys by name as you play them. Now, play all the D♭s on the keyboard. These are the same black keys on the left in the groups of two. Notice that although these black keys have two names, C♯ and D♭, the pitches are identical in the respective octaves. In the same manner, play all the black keys on the right of the groups of two. These are named D♯ or E♭. As before, call the keys by name as you play them.

The black keys on the left in the groups of three are F♯ or G♭; those on the right are A♯ or B♭; while, those in the middle are G♯ or A♭. Find and play all these black keys. Call the keys by name as you play them. Repeat with all the names of all the black keys. Practice until you can find quickly any black key on the piano.

The octave

The octave has been mentioned frequently. In the last chapter it was represented by the next same-letter name on the staff: from one C to the next is an octave. Earlier, the octave was considered in terms of a pitch that has twice or half the frequencies of another: 128 frequencies produce a pitch that is the octave of 64 and 256 frequencies.

While striking the keys of the piano you must have noticed that all the keys with the same letter name produce a similar sound though the pitches may be higher or lower. This occurs because they are in octaves, that is, each pitch has twice or half the frequencies of the next pitch of the same name.

Thus, an octave defines (1) the distance from one letter name to the next same-letter name on the staff or keyboard, in either direction, and

(2) the relationship between the sounds or tones which such letter names represent.

Octave exercise

Stretch the thumb and little finger to reach from one key to the next of its kind, an octave. Skipping about the keyboard, play a great number of octaves. As you do, call them by name. This exercise should be done with each hand separately and then with both hands together, *on both white and black keys.*

The pedals

The piano has either two or three pedals. The one on the right is called the *damper pedal*. When it is depressed, it raises all the dampers of all the strings, leaving them free to vibrate. With all the strings of the instrument free to vibrate, resonance is so multiplied that there is an increase of loudness while the piano is played; therefore, this pedal has commonly been called by the erroneous name of *loud pedal*.

The pedal to the left is called the *soft pedal*, or *una corda pedal* (Italian *una corda*, one string). When this pedal is depressed, it moves the hammers in such a way as to effect a softer sound. In a grand piano, this pedal moves the entire action (keys, hammers, etc.) sideways so that the hammers can no longer make complete contact with all the strings producing each pitch. In most upright pianos, the soft pedal moves the bank of hammers closer to the strings with the result that the thrust becomes less forceful than when the hammers are in their normal position.

When there are three pedals, the middle one is called the *sostenuto pedal* (Italian, *sostenere*, to sustain). When it is depressed, it engages and keeps raised only those dampers associated with the keys which are being held down at that moment. When the pedal is released the dampers are returned to their normal position.

HISTORY OF THE PIANO

The harpsichord, spinet, and clavichord were in general use before the advent of the piano. In none of these instruments is the tone big because of the manner in which the sound is produced. In the harpsichord and spinet the sound is produced by a plucking of the strings with projections, called quills; in the clavichord, by a gentle touching of the strings by flat-ended metal pins, called tangents. At the beginning of the eighteenth century there arose in many countries an interest in creating a hammer action for keyboard instruments. Credit for the actual invention of an instrument using this action—that is, the piano—goes to Bartolomeo Cristofori, a harpsichord maker of Padua and Florence. In 1709 he made a mechanism which struck the strings with hammers instead of plucking them with quills. This development enabled the player to so control the sound that the dynamics could be varied from soft to loud. Since the Italian name for harpsichord is *gravicembalo*, Cristofori called his new instrument *gravicembalo col pian e forte*, "harpsichord with the soft and loud." Subsequently the instrument was called the *pianoforte*, and the name today, contracted, is simply *piano*.

One of Cristofori's pianos, made in 1720, is now in the Metropolitan Museum in New York City. It has 54 keys, ranging from the C below the bass staff to the F above the treble.

CHAPTER 4

PLAYING THE PIANO

The first consideration in learning to play the piano is proper posture at the keyboard. The development of a good technique depends upon a comfortable and relaxed position. Face the keyboard a little to the right of middle C. This will place the body equidistant from the ends of the keyboard. Sit high enough to bring the arms parallel with the floor and at a distance from the keyboard sufficient to permit the fingers to rest on the full part of the white keys. The middle fingers should about touch the end of the black keys. Until you learn to use the pedals, keep both feet flat on the floor. Do not cross the legs.

PLAYING THE PIANO

23

To get the feel of the keyboard, place your right hand on the first five notes of the middle-C octave. For either hand, the fingers are counted in this way: 1—thumb; 2—second or index finger; 3—third or middle finger; 4—fourth or ring finger; 5—little finger. Place the thumb (1) on middle C, the second (index) finger on D, the third on E, the fourth on F, and the fifth on G.

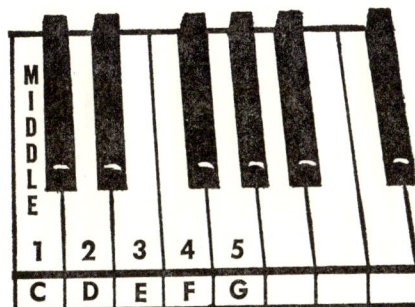

With the aid of the following chart, play the familiar melody adopted for the nursery rhyme, "Mary Had A Little Lamb." Play the marked keys using the fingering indicated. Before beginning to play, study the chart on the following page.

PLAYING THE PIANO

24

Mary Had A Little Lamb
Right Hand

To play the same melody with the *left* hand, place the fingers on the first five notes of the C octave below middle C. The little finger (5) should be placed on C and the thumb (1), on G, for although our hands are symmetrical, the fingering is reversed.

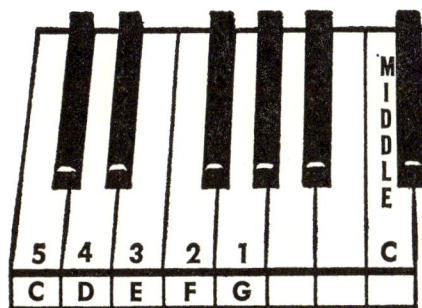

Notice that the progression of fingering for the left hand is in a direction opposite to that for the right hand. When the right hand plays the first three notes of "Mary Had A Little Lamb" the fingering is 3 - 2 - 1; for the left hand it is 3 - 4 - 5.

PLAYING THE PIANO

Mary Had A Little Lamb
Left Hand

Ma	3 E (MIDDLE C)	lit	4 D
ry	4 D	tle	4 D
had	5 C	lamb,	4 D
a	4 D	lit	3 E
lit	3 E	tle	1 G
tle	3 E	lamb,	1 G
lamb,	3 E		
Ma	3 E	its	3 E
ry	4 D	fleece	4 D
had	5 C	was	4 D
a	4 D	white	3 E
lit	3 E	as	4 D
tle	3 E	snow.	5 C
lamb,	3 E		

When you played "Mary Had A Little Lamb," you didn't have to move your hand during the entire piece because the melody lies within the first five notes of an octave. However, this is unusual—most melodies have a larger compass. As you learn to play other pieces you will find that the hand must be able to move about freely to exploit the many possibilities of the keyboard.

The next melody is the French favorite, "Frère Jacques." In playing this piece the hand will have to move away from its original position just a bit so that the desired keys will always lie comfortably under the hand. For this melody, the hand will assume three different positions.

First, let us consider playing the melody with the right hand. To begin the piece, the fingers should rest over the same five keys as in "Mary Had A Little Lamb."

Position I

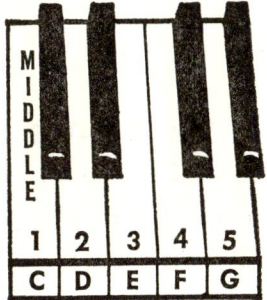

For the next position, the thumb remains over middle C while the four fingers shift up the keyboard (to the right), *one key each,* so that now the second, third, fourth, and fifth fingers are over the keys E, F, G and A.

Position II

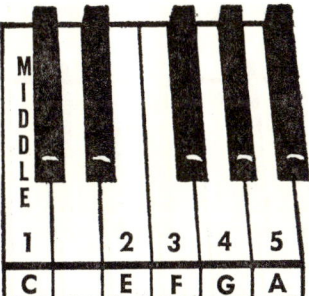

The third position embraces only two notes: middle C and the G below middle C. From the second position move the hand quickly down the keyboard (to the left) until the third finger rests on middle C. Stretch the thumb down to the G below middle C. Only these two fingers and keys are needed for the final tones of the melody.

Position III

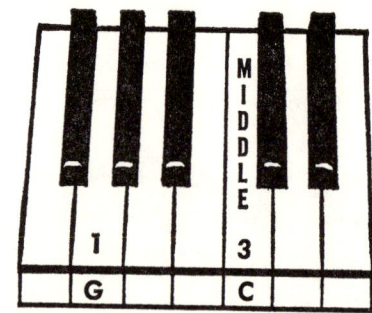

Practice placing your right hand over the keys in the three positions and continue until you can move the hand quickly and silently from one position to the other. When you master this you will be able to play the correct keys for "Frère Jacques."

POSITION I   Fingers   1 2 3 1——1 2 3 1——3 4 5——3 4 5
                Keys   C D E C——C D E C——E F G——E F G

POSITION II   Fingers   4 5 4 3 2 1——4 5 4 3 2 1
                Keys   G A G F E C——G A G F E C

POSITION III   Fingers   3 1 3——3 1 3
                Keys   C G C——C G C

In playing "Frère Jacques" with the left hand the same-named keys (an octave below) will be employed because the melody remains the same, but the fingering will change because of the difference in the two hands. At the start, the fingers rest over the same five keys used in playing "Mary Had A Little Lamb" (the first five keys of the C octave below middle C).

Position I

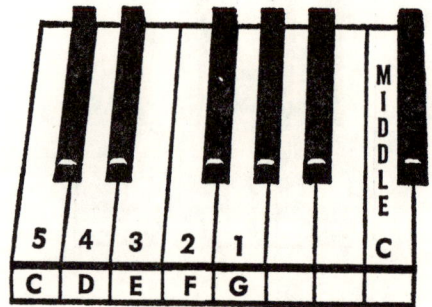

For the next group of keys the little finger remains over the C below middle C while the fourth, third, second fingers and thumb shift up the keyboard (to the right) over the keys E, F, G, and A.

Position II

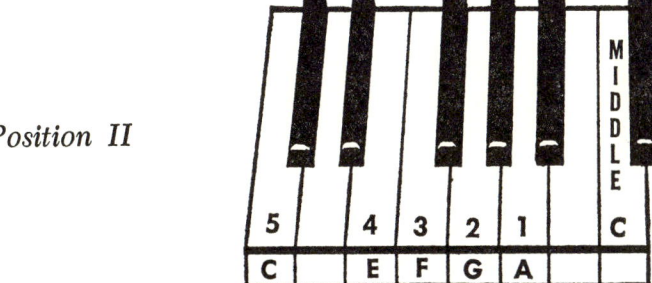

The third position calls for only two keys: the C below middle C and the G below that. From the second position move the hand quickly down the keyboard (to the left) until the second finger rests on the C just played by the little finger. Stretch the little finger down to the G below C.

Position III

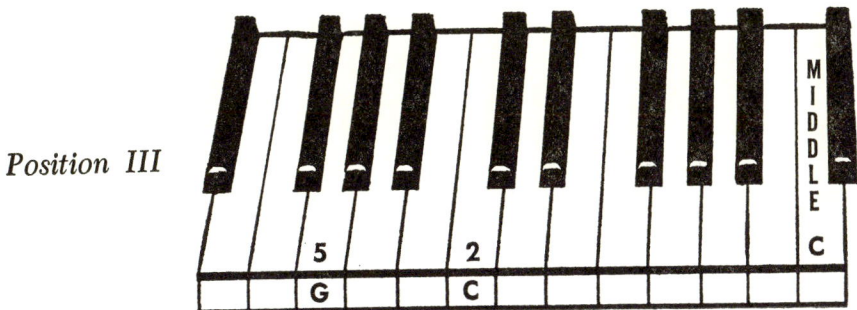

As with the right hand, practice placing the left hand over the keys in the three positions and continue until you can move the hand quickly and silently from one position to the other. Then play the indicated keys.

POSITION I   Fingers: 5 4 3 5——5 4 3 5——3 2 1——3 2 1
               Keys: C D E C——C D E C——E F G——E F G

POSITION II   Fingers: 2 1 2 3 4 5——2 1 2 3 4 5
               Keys: G A G F E C——G A G F E C

POSITION III Fingers: 2 5 2——2 5 2
               Keys: C G C——C G C

In playing "Three Blind Mice" the hand has four different positions. No more than simple shifts are involved in moving from the first position to the second, and from the second to the third. The piece ends with the hand in the original position. To insure smoothness in the change from the third to the fourth and last position, a technique is employed wherein fingers are changed on one note which serves as a pivot between the two sections.

Three Blind Mice—Right Hand

I
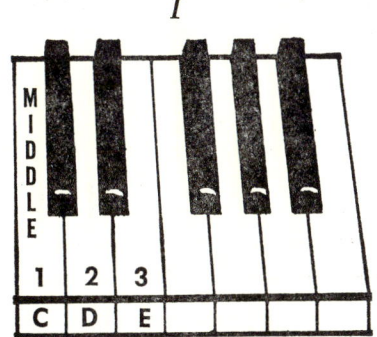

II
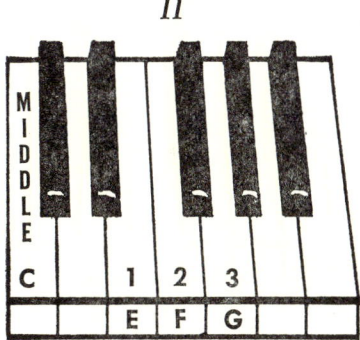

III
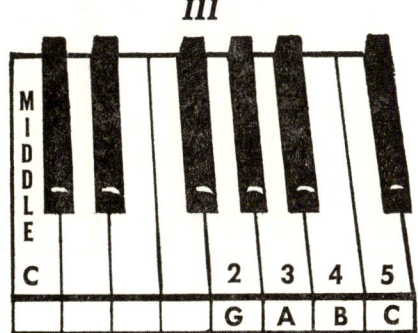

Pivot and IV
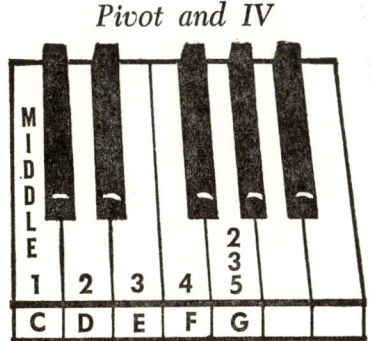

POSITION I	Fingers:	3 2 1——3 2 1
	Keys:	E D C——E D C

POSITION II	Fingers:	3 2 2 1——3 2 2 1
	Keys:	G F F E——G F F E

POSITION III	Fingers:	2 5 5 4 3 4 5 2 2——2 5 5 5 4 3 4
	Keys:	G C C B A B C G G——G C C C B A B
		5 2 2 2 5 5 5 4 3 4 5
		C G G G C C C B A B C

PIVOT	Fingers:	2 3 5
	Key:	G G G

POSITION IV	Fingers:	4 3 2 1
	Keys:	F E D C

PLAYING THE PIANO

Three Blind Mice—Left Hand

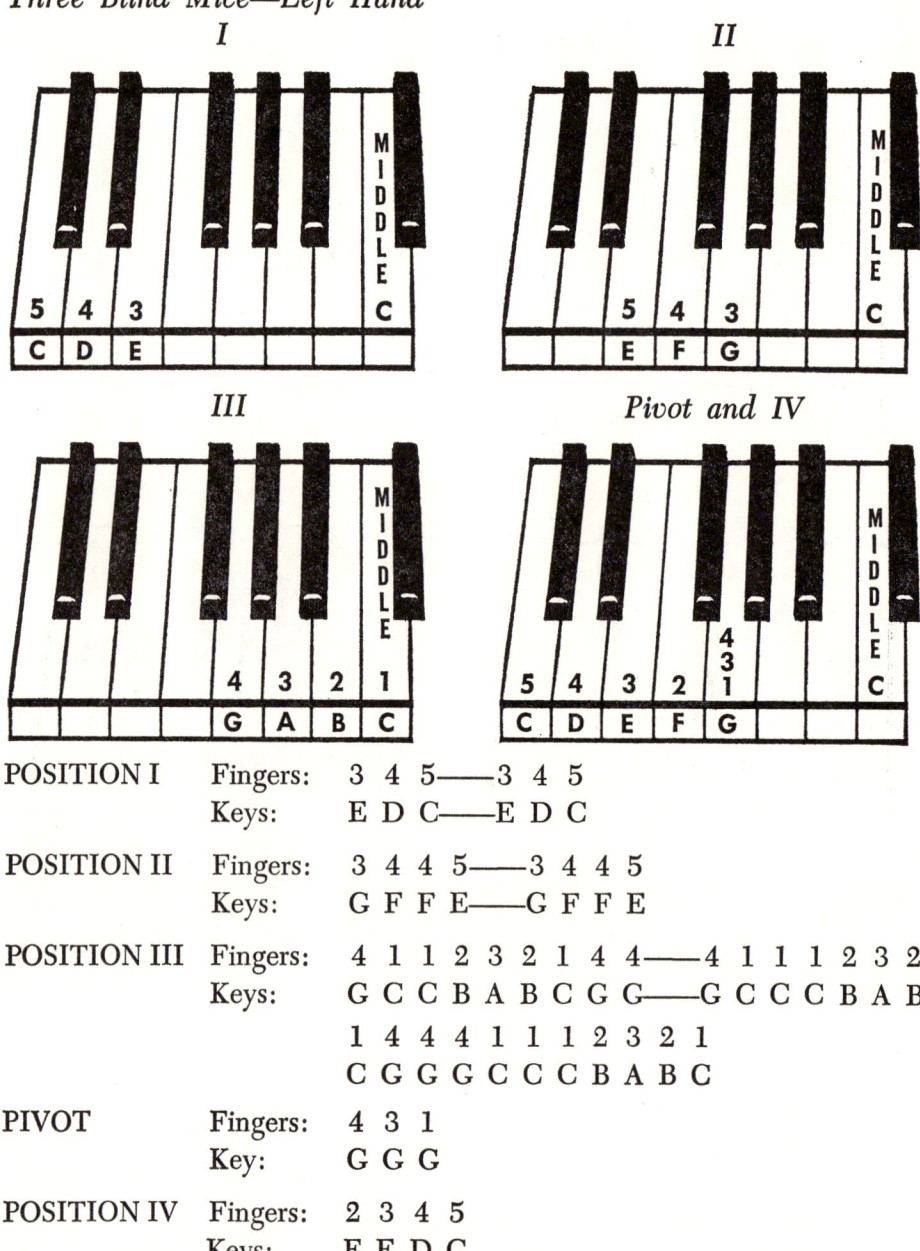

POSITION I	Fingers:	3 4 5——3 4 5
	Keys:	E D C——E D C
POSITION II	Fingers:	3 4 5——3 4 4 5
	Keys:	G F F E——G F F E
POSITION III	Fingers:	4 1 1 2 3 2 1 4 4——4 1 1 1 2 3 2
	Keys:	G C C B A B C G G——G C C C B A B
		1 4 4 4 1 1 1 2 3 2 1
		C G G G C C C B A B C
PIVOT	Fingers:	4 3 1
	Key:	G G G
POSITION IV	Fingers:	2 3 4 5
	Keys:	F E D C

In this chapter we have learned how to play the piano. Of course, the method used to locate the desired keys is complicated and bears no relation to the staff. But it is useful to demonstrate that the art of piano playing is within the capabilities of the average person. The student will find that progress will be rapid if he practices daily.

CHAPTER 5

THE STAFF AND THE KEYBOARD

Earlier we saw that, in music, we use the staff with an appropriate clef to locate an exact pitch. With what we have learned about the treble and bass staffs we can locate all pitches in the vocal range. Now, in the form of the grand staff, we shall relate these two staffs to the keyboard. By this means we can find on the piano the keys which correspond to the pitches represented by the lines and spaces of the staffs.

For the present it is sufficient to learn the relationship which exists between the grand staff and the four central C octaves on the keyboard. With the following chart before you, sit at the piano and at random call out a letter name and, as quickly as possible, strike the key which is identified with that letter name. Continue until you have played all the white keys in the four octaves. Speed is of the utmost importance in the mastery of this relationship. Finally, close your eyes, visualize a letter name on the staff, and strike the key which it represents. Do this repeatedly with the letter names of both staffs.

THE STAFF AND THE KEYBOARD

Five C's

THE STAFF AND THE KEYBOARD

WRITING A MELODY ON THE STAFF

If a group of people wanted to sing a song they would need a starting pitch that would place the song within the vocal range of the majority of the singers. In seeking such a starting pitch for "Mary Had A Little Lamb" they might find, through trial and error, that middle E is a comfortable one for the female voice, and its octave below for the male voice.

Since the function of the staff is to locate different pitches, we can write the syllables and words of this nursery tune on the proper lines and spaces. First, we must make a choice of staffs. We shall write the syllables and words of "Mary Had A Little Lamb" on the treble staff because it accommodates the range of women's voices. The men will unconsciously sing the song an octave lower. (Today, tenors read and sing from both the treble and bass staffs. When they sing from the treble staff, the sound they produce is actually an octave below the pitch indicated.)

Unlike the example in Chapter 2, where this song was written without regard to definite pitch, each syllable will now be identified with a specific pitch. Beginning with the syllable *Ma* on the E in the middle-C octave, here is how the words look printed on the treble staff.

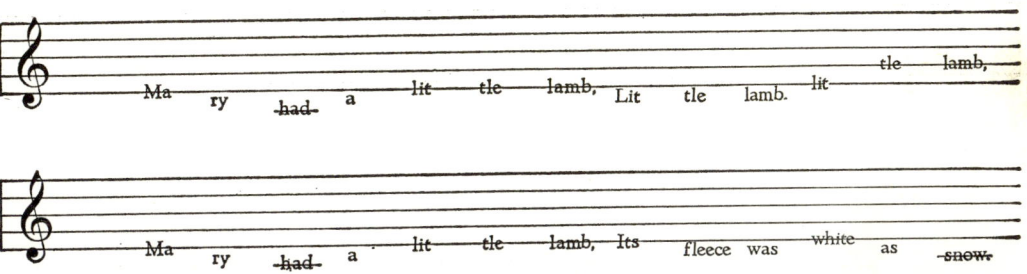

Because of its greater range, "Frère Jacques" uses more lines and spaces than "Mary Had A Little Lamb." Each line and space is a *degree* of the staff; therefore, the melody of "Frère Jacques" covers a distance of nine staff degrees.

THE STAFF AND THE KEYBOARD

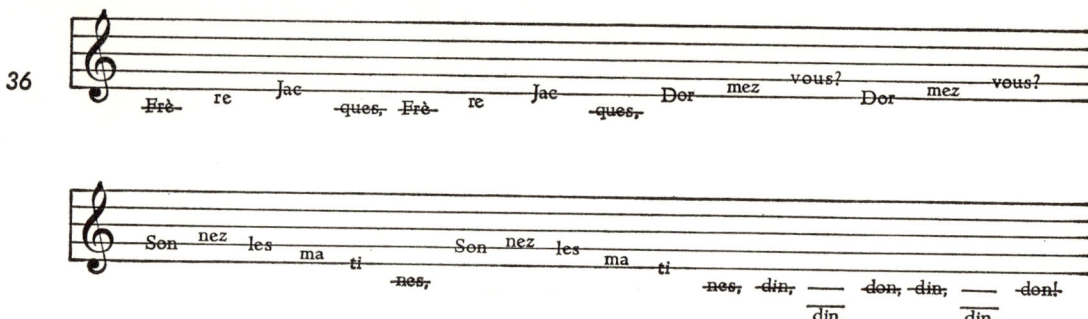

"Three Blind Mice," written in the same manner, encompasses eight staff degrees, or an octave.

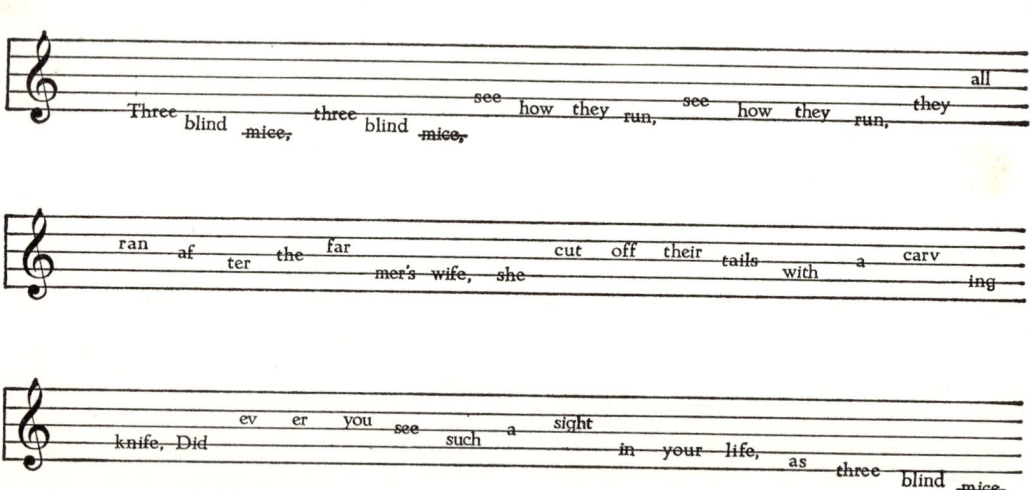

Use of letter names

It is obvious that the writing of words on the staff is far from the perfect solution to the proper notation of a song. Although this system has some advantages for a singer, it doesn't help an instrumentalist because it does not establish any relationship between the staff and an instrument. However, this relationship can be established readily by substituting for the words of the song the letter names of the lines and spaces. If, instead of reading "Ma-ry had," or "Three blind mice," we were to read "E, D, C" we would be reading letters which have an exact identification with positions or keys on an instrument. Thus, both singer and player are served and the melody can be either sung or played by anyone with or without a foreknowledge of the piece.

THE STAFF AND THE KEYBOARD

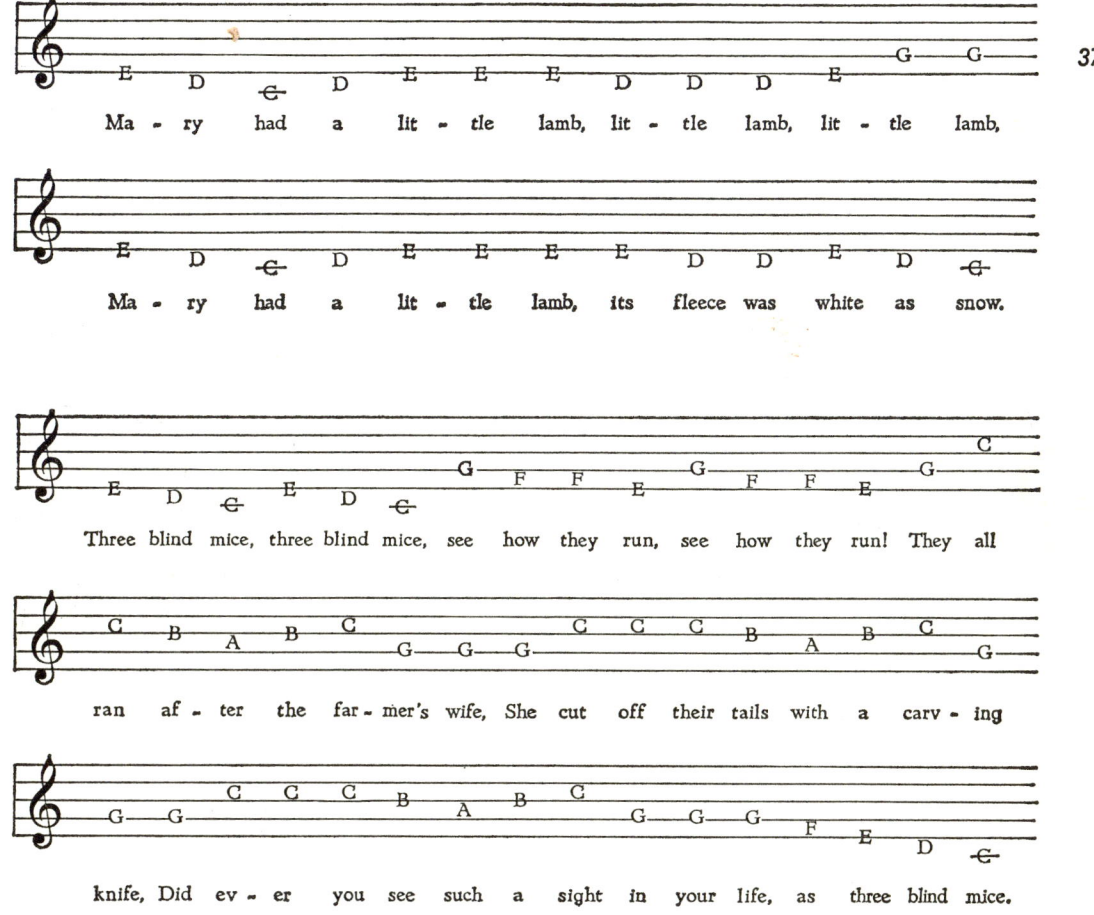

On music-manuscript paper, write "Frère Jacques" in like manner, substituting the letter names of the staff degrees for the syllables of the text.

THE STAFF AND THE KEYBOARD

Now we are prepared to relate the staff to the keyboard. Before proceeding, review the positions the hands assume in playing "Mary Had A Little Lamb," "Frère Jacques," and "Three Blind Mice" in Chapter 4.

In playing the following examples keep your eyes *on the staff* (not on the keyboard) and call *aloud* the letter names of the melody as you go from one to the other. Use the right hand first, then, the left hand. When you are able to play the piece easily with separate hands, place both hands on the keyboard and play them together.

THE STAFF AND THE KEYBOARD

Mary Had A Little Lamb

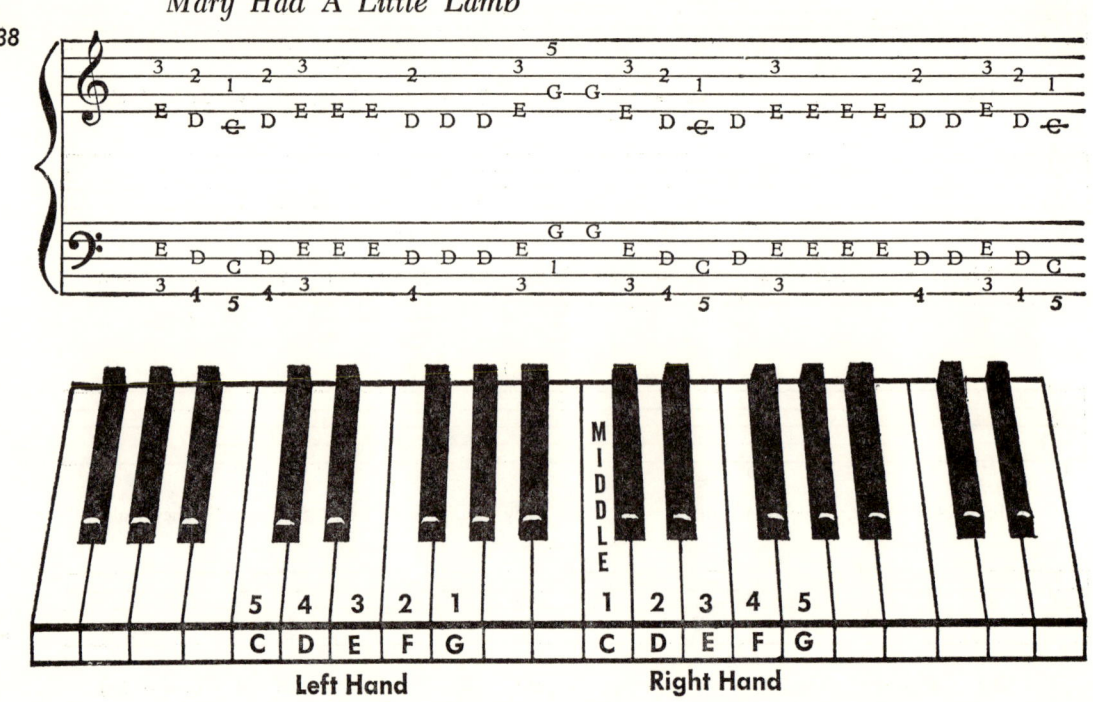

Frère Jacques

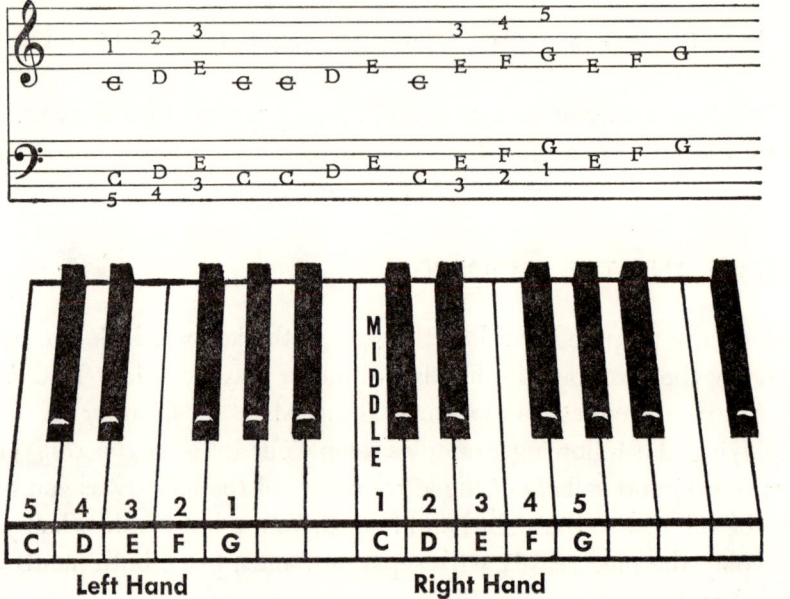

THE STAFF AND THE KEYBOARD

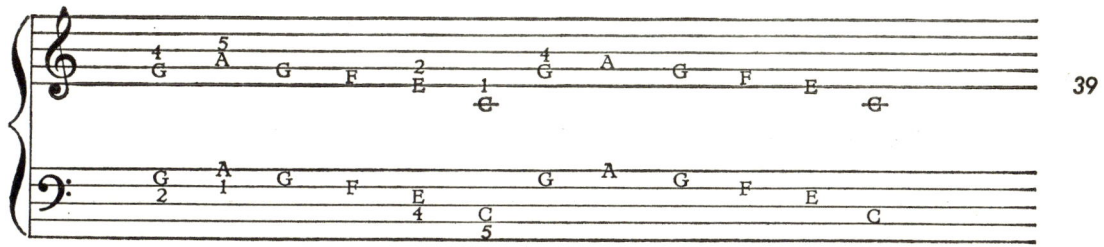

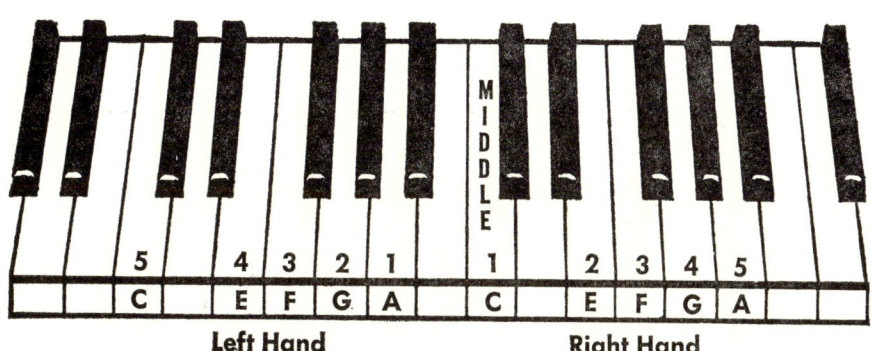

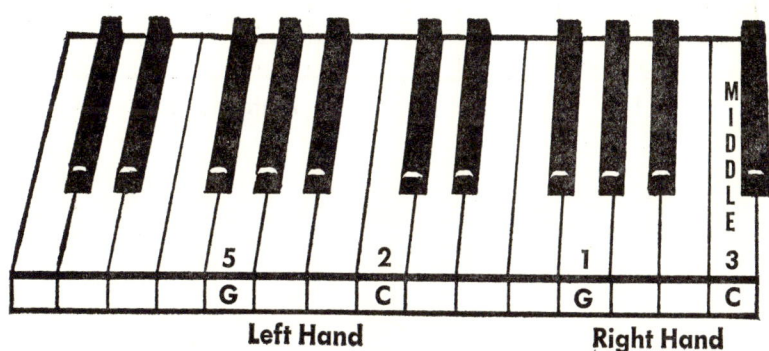

THE STAFF AND THE KEYBOARD

Three Blind Mice

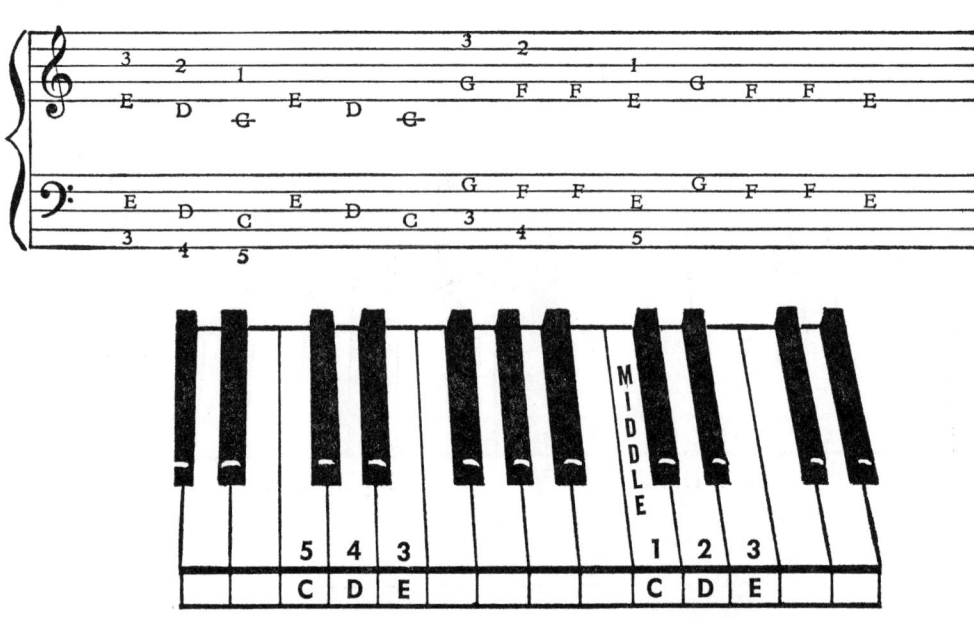

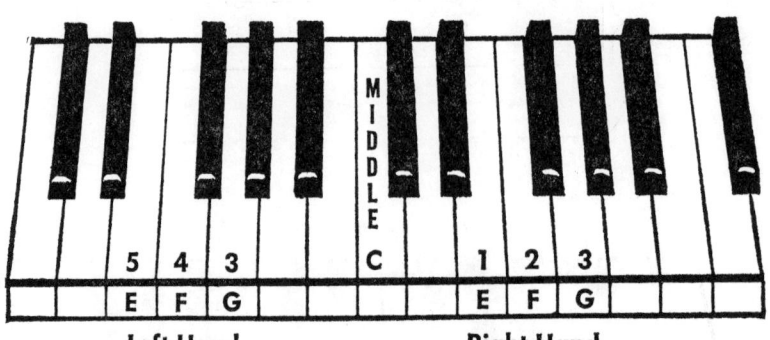

THE STAFF AND THE KEYBOARD

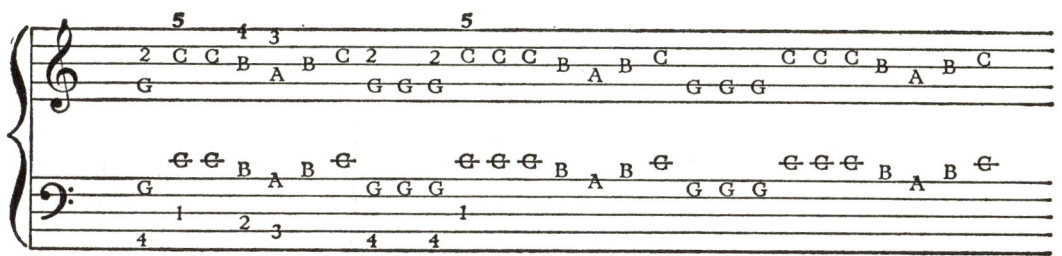

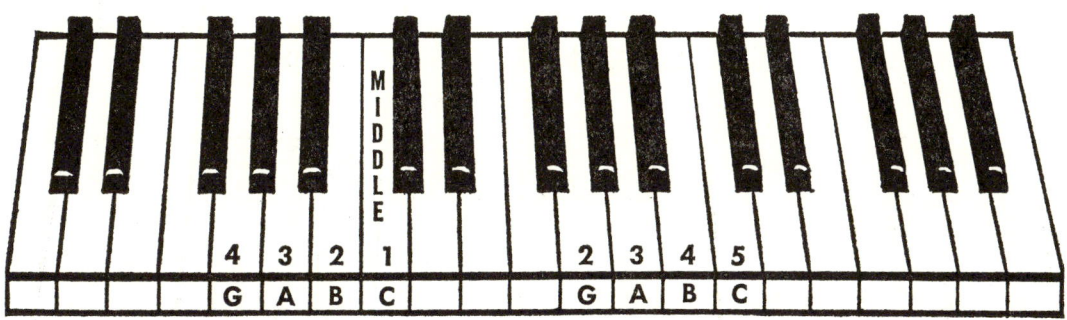

THE STAFF AND THE KEYBOARD

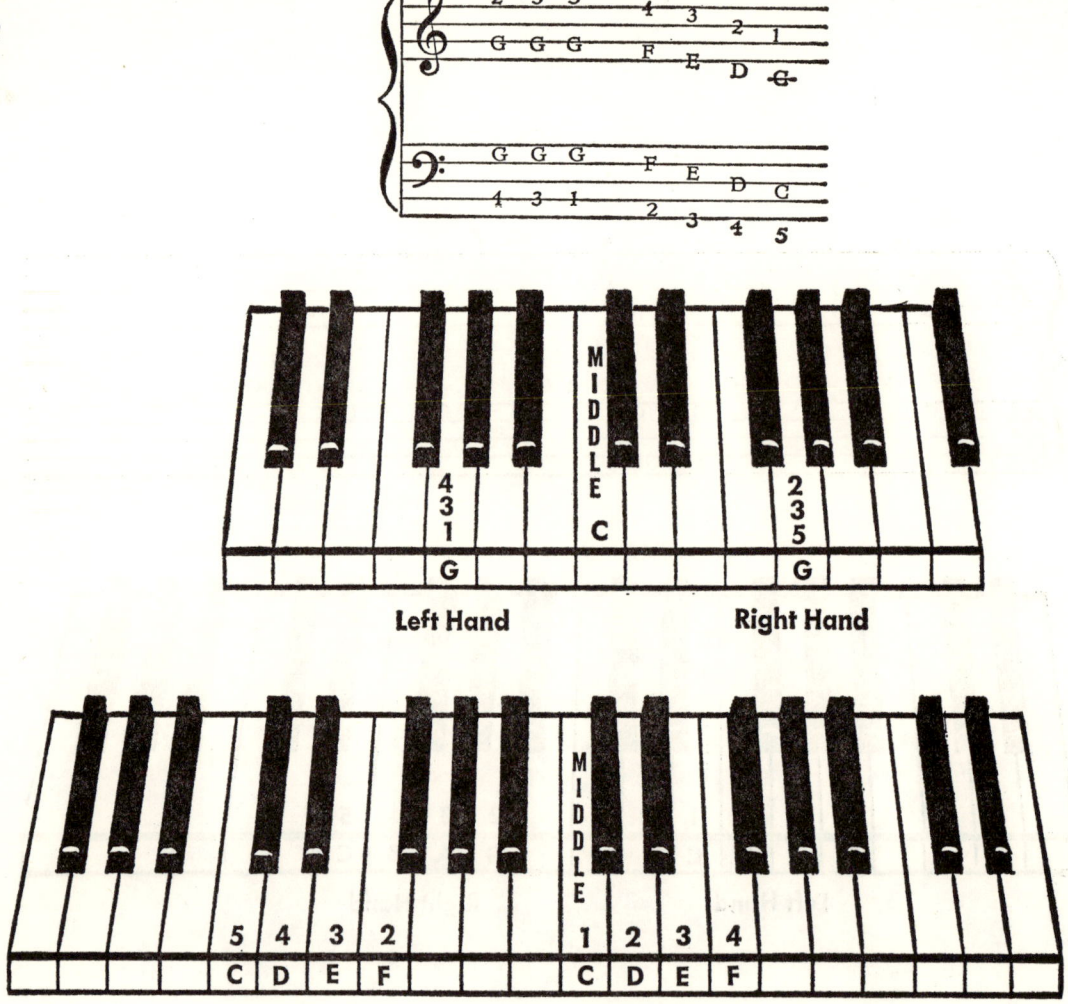

Up to this point we have learned about the keyboard and the staff and the relation of one to the other in terms of pitch. But we have not discussed another important element of music: duration of sound and silence. In preparation for the study of the symbols which represent duration of sound and silence, we shall discuss the element of music called *rhythm*.

CHAPTER 6

RHYTHM

Rhythm exists in all things; it is in the heartbeat of man, in the order of day and night. Rhythm is the life in all things animate and inanimate.

Like electricity, it has defied definition and when the subject is pursued one finds himself usually speaking about meter, accent, time, or anything else that has to do with the movement or flow of music. To be sure, the source of the word is the Greek *rhein*, "to flow," but the Greeks themselves could not work with this connotation and so employed the word *rhythmos* meaning "measured motion."

But if we cannot define rhythm we can observe it and characterize its many manifestations. We note a rhythmic quality in all of nature—the seasons of the year, the rise and fall of the tide, the break of waves upon the shore. Sometimes this rhythm is for anyone to see, to feel, to grasp, but other times it is so complex that we are unable to understand or to represent it.

For History of Rhythm, see the end of this chapter.

METRICAL PATTERNS IN POETRY

The rhythm of poetry is similar to the rhythm of music. An examination of the one can lead to an understanding of the other.

RHYTHM

In order to sense the flow and metrical design of poetry, let us consider some familiar verses which have melodies known to us from childhood. Recite the words to "Twinkle, Twinkle, Little Star."

```
TWIN - kle,  TWIN - kle,    LIT - tle  STAR,
HOW    I     WON - der WHAT   you  ARE!
UP     a -   BOVE   the WORLD  so  HIGH,
LIKE   a     DIA - mond  IN    the SKY.
```

In "Twinkle, Twinkle, Little Star" the pattern is STRONG-weak. In some verses, the pattern is the reverse: weak-STRONG.

```
O BEAU - ti - FUL   for  SPA - cious SKIES,
For   AM - ber   WAVES   of  GRAIN,
For   PUR - ple MOUN - tain MAJ - es - TIES
A - BOVE   the    FRUIT - ed   PLAIN.
A - MER - i - CA!   A - MER - i - CA!
God    SHED  His  GRACE  on  THEE,
And   CROWN thy  GOOD with BROTH-er-HOOD
From    SEA   to   SHIN - ing  SEA
```

In many verses a strong syllable is followed by two weak ones. For example:

```
SING your way HOME at the CLOSE of the DAY,
SING your way HOME, drive the SHAD - ows a - WAY.
SMILE ev - 'ry MILE, for wher - EV - er you ROAM
It will BRIGHT - en your ROAD,
It will LIGHT - en your LOAD,
If you SING your way HOME.
```

Any of the foregoing units (STRONG-weak, weak-STRONG, STRONG-weak-weak) may be compared to a wave with its peak representing the accented syllable and its trough the one or more unaccented syllables. Such a pattern is called a metrical foot (meter fr. Greek *metron*, measure; Latin *metrum*, measure). In poetry there are four important feet:

```
Trochee  ′ ⌣    STRONG - weak         ( BÉT - ter  )
Iamb     ⌣ ′    weak - STRONG         (  a - LÓNE  )
Dactyl   ′ ⌣ ⌣  STRONG - weak - weak  (MÓTH - er - ly)
Anapest  ⌣ ⌣ ′  weak - weak - STRONG  (af - ter - NOÓN)
```

There are two more common feet, the spondee (′ ′) and the pyrrhus (⌣ ⌣) but their metrical expression comes in combination with others. The possible combinations of various metrical feet are as many as the inventive genius of the poet can create.

Characteristic Greek prefixes identify the number of feet in a line of poetry: *mono*meter (1 foot), *di*meter (2 feet), *tri*meter (3 feet), *tetra*meter (4 feet), *penta*meter (5 feet), *hexa*meter (6 feet).

A metrical pattern is determined by the flow of the accents and the number of feet to the line. "Twinkle, twinkle, little star" is *trochaic tetrameter* because the rhythmic flow is STRONG-weak and there are four feet to the line, while, "O beautiful for spacious skies" is iambic tetrameter because the flow is weak-STRONG, though the number of feet is the same (four).

To feel the rhythmic pulsations in poetry, one should read aloud—conscious of the strong, accented syllables. Take care to keep the flow inherent in the lines. Do not hesitate or stop except as the meaning demands, for continuous motion is necessary to give proper expression to the thought. Since *this is equally true in musical performance,* you should maintain a continuous motion when you sing or play an instrument.

Exercises in scansion of verses

In addition to reading aloud it is well to scan the verses, that is, to go through them foot by foot, marking the metrical structure. Using the customary signs (′ ⌣) for the accented and unaccented syllables, scan the following:

>   Mary had a little lamb,
>   Its fleece was white as snow,
>   And ev'ry place that Mary went
>   The lamb was sure to go.
>
>   Oh, do you know the Muffin Man,
>   The Muffin Man, the Muffin Man;
>   Oh, do you know the Muffin Man
>   That lives in Drury Lane?

>   The north wind doth blow, and we shall have snow,
>   And what will poor robin do then? Poor thing!
>   He'll sit in a barn to keep himself warm,
>   And hide his head under his wing. Poor thing!

RHYTHM

METRICAL PATTERNS IN MUSIC

In scanning these verses you have worked with some metrical schemes in poetry. Presently we will see that the principle of strong and weak stresses is much the same in music. In the poem "Mary Had A Little Lamb," we noted a succession of STRONG-weak and weak-STRONG syllables. Recite the verse as the first two lines have been adapted for the song.

> Mary had a little lamb,
> Little lamb, little lamb,
> Mary had a little lamb,
> Its fleece was white as snow.

Notice that the accented syllables themselves vary in intensity—there are primary and secondary accents. This might be represented by placing a vertical line before each of the primary accents.

|MÁ - rў	HÁD	ă	|LÍT - tle	LÁMB,	
|LÍT - tle	LÁMB,		|LÍT - tle	LÁMB,	
|MÁ - rў	HÁD	ă	|LÍT - tle	LÁMB,	Its
|FLÉECE was	WHÍTE	as	|SNÓW.		

Recite the verse again. As you say the lines move your right hand down and up with the pulse of the meter. The downward movement should coincide with the primary accent and the upward movement with the secondary accent.

Now, *sing* the song. Sing smoothly and without stopping, moving your hand down and up with the regularity of a clock's pendulum. Do not stop the movement of the hand until you feel that the tune has run out completely.

As you sing the tune you will observe that although the scansion above is very like the rhythmical pattern of the melody there are some differences. Careful attention to the placement of the syllables will show that *MA* is held slightly longer than most of them, but *ry* is shorter. *Its* finds a place in the last group of the third line. The first three *LAMB*s and *SNOW* are sustained for a half-cycle of the down-and-up movement of the hand. We can get a graphic representation of this flow by spacing the syllables exactly as they occur in the music.

MÁ - ry HÁD a	LÍT - tle LAMB,
LÍT - tle LAMB,	LÍT - tle LAMB,
MÁ - ry HÁD a	LÍT - tle LAMB, Its
FLEÉCE was WHÍTE as	SNÓW.

Turn back to the verses, "Twinkle, Twinkle, Little Star" (p. 44), "The Muffin Man" (p. 45), "Frère Jacques" (p. 9), and "Three Blind Mice" (p. 10). Find the primary and secondary accents and mark them as you did with "Mary Had A Little Lamb" (p. 46). Then sing their melodies. Accompany the singing with a regular downward motion of the hand on the primary accent and an upward motion on the secondary accent. Do not falter in either the singing or in the regularity of the movement of the hand.

In the discussion of pitch we saw that the placement of the words of a song on the lines and spaces of the staff was less than adequate to relate the pitches of a melody to the keys or positions on an instrument. In the same way, the spacing and marking we have employed in this chapter can give only an approximation of the real flow of the music. However, instead of this inexact method, there is a system of notation that satisfies this need. It consists of *notes* and *rests*.

HISTORY OF RHYTHM

Primitive people usually accompanied their emotional responses to joy, sorrow, or pain with rhythmic motions. These were bodily movements: the stamping of feet, clapping of hands, or slapping parts of the body. They were crude and irregular but eventually became ordered by instinct because of the inherent rhythmic property of nature.

An artistic interest in rhythm was developed in early cultures. This is particularly noticeable in the measurable patterns of Greek poetry. Instrumental music played a very minor role because the ancients believed that important ideas could be expressed only through music which was vocal. Greek music was so closely allied with poetry that it was virtually dependent upon it. Plato emphasized that rhythm follows the words, not words the rhythm. In poetry, metrical design was considered from the viewpoint of duration, that is, the amount of time consumed in the pronunciation of a syllable. Syllables were thought of as either long or short, and this was the governing principle in elocution and song.

Until about the fourth century A.D., the principle of the long versus the short syllable was also the basis of Roman versification. But as a result of certain changes in the language, Latin versification developed a new rhythmic character where accentuation played the important role, and a new principle of strong and weak (qualitative) replaced the earlier one of long and short (quantitative).

Thus, for the past millennium and a half, metrical designs in poetry have been determined by accents. Up until the thirteenth century nearly all the recorded music of the Western world was vocal, and its metrical structure depended upon the laws of poetry. And, be it vocal or instrumental, music—to this day—often continues under the spell of poetry. This in spite of Dryden's dictum, "Poetry is articulate music."

CHAPTER 7

NOTES AND RESTS

The symbols used to show the duration of musical sounds and silences are called notes and rests.

Notes

Notes have the same mathematical relation to each other as do a whole and its divisions that follow the progression of halves, quarters, eighths, and so on. Indeed, we now call the symbol that represents the largest note value a *whole note*. This comparison might have justified the use of a perfect circle to symbolize the whole note. But, in written music today, an ellipse is favored over the circle because it provides a more distinctive figure on the staff.

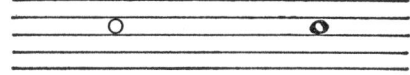

A *half note* represents a time value one-half that of a whole note. It consists of an *open head* and a *stem*. The stem may be drawn either up from the right side of the head or down from the left: 𝅗𝅥 or 𝅗𝅥.

The direction of a stem is determined by the location of the head on the staff. In a line of single notes, when the head is written on the *middle line* of the staff the stem may go up or down; when the head is *above* the middle

NOTES AND RESTS

line the stem usually goes *down;* when it is *below* the middle line the stem usually goes *up.**

A *quarter note* represents a time value one-fourth that of a whole note, or one-half that of a half note. It consists of a *solid head* and a *stem:* ♩ or ♩

An *eighth note* represents a time value half that of a quarter note. It consists of a *solid head,* a *stem,* and a *flag* (or *hook*): ♪ or ♪

Notice: The flag is always to the right of the stem regardless of whether the stem goes up or down. When two or more eighth notes are written they may have separate flags: ♪ ♪, or they may be connected by a *beam:* ♫

Sixteenth notes, representing half the value of eighth notes, have two flags or two beams: ♬ or ♬

Thirty-second notes, representing half the value of sixteenth notes, have three flags or three beams: ♬ or ♬

Sixty-fourth notes, representing half the value of thirty-second notes, have four flags or four beams: ♬ or ♬

One-hundred-twenty-eighth notes (rare), representing half the value of sixty-fourth notes, have five flags or five beams: ♬ or ♬

To repeat: Notes have the same relation to each other as comparable fractions have in mathematics. For example, two half notes equal one whole note as ½ + ½ = 1; or four eighth notes equal one half note as ⅛ + ⅛ + ⅛ + ⅛ = ½.

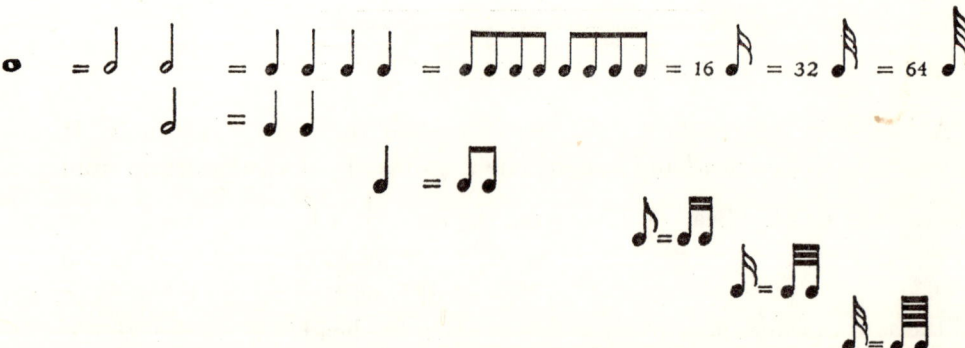

---

* For examples of the position of stems when two or more notes are played at the same time, see pages 147, 174, 216, and 217.

NOTES AND RESTS

A note on the staff represents the length of time a certain pitch is to be sustained. The features of a note determine its associated time value; the location of the note on the staff (thus, the staff itself) determines its pitch.

For History of Notation, see the end of this chapter.

Rests

As there are notes to represent durations of sound, there are other symbols to indicate durations of silence. They are called *rests*. Like notes, they have the same mathematical relation to each other as do a whole and its divisions that follow the progression of halves, quarters, eighths, and so on.

The *whole rest* and *half rest*, simple blocks, are usually written in the third space of the staff. To distinguish them, the whole rest is written *underneath and attached to the fourth line*, whereas the half rest is placed *above and attached to the third line*. The whole rest is customarily used to indicate an entire bar of silence regardless of the meter signature.

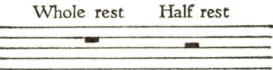

The *quarter rest*, usually set on the second line, has different forms, both printed and in manuscript.

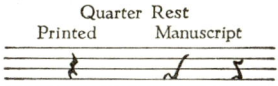

The *eighth rest, sixteenth rest, thirty-second rest, sixty-fourth rest* and the *one-hundred-twenty-eighth rest*, like their corresponding notes, have flags flying from a stem. But, contrary to the position of the flags of notes, the flags on *rests* all appear *to the left of the stem*. The top flag of the eighth and sixteenth rests is usually written in the third space; the top flag of the rests of smaller value is usually written in the fourth space.

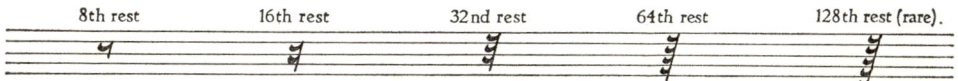

The tie and the dot

The duration of a note can be prolonged in two ways: by using a *tie* (⌣ or ⌢) to tie one note over to another of the same pitch or by placing a *dot* (•) to the *right* of the head. A tie adds to the time value of

NOTES AND RESTS

the first note the value of the succeeding note or notes that are joined together by the tie or ties.

A dot adds to the note one-half its time value. A dotted whole note has the time value of three tied half notes; a dotted half note the value of three tied quarter notes; a dotted quarter, of three tied eighths, etc. In short, a dotted note receives the time value of three times the next smaller value.

A dotted whole note also has the time value of two tied dotted half notes; a dotted half note, also the value of two tied dotted quarter notes; a dotted quarter note also the value of two dotted eighth notes, etc.

Though used less frequently, a dot may follow a rest as well as a note. As with the note, the dot lengthens the rest by one-half its value.

Every phase of modern notation stems from the demands of polyphony (p. 15). We have already traced the development of the symbols that represent the location of different pitches (staff and clefs) and those that indicate the duration of sound and silence (notes and rests). The new music of the thirteenth century needed still another system to integrate its several moving parts. Composers began to fashion the rhythmic structure of a voice part after the similar patterns of repeated long and short syllables found in poetic meter. They provided music with a new feature: similar patterns of repeated accented and unaccented pulses, or *beats*. Thus, the application and development of a concept found in poetry culminated in the element of music we call *meter*.

NOTES AND RESTS

HISTORY OF NOTATION

Notes have their origin in the accentuation signs used in classical antiquity to indicate the kind of vocal inflection an actor, singer, or declaimer should employ to bring out the full meaning of the words. The figures, hooks, and signs, which look like accent marks in various languages, are akin to those we now use for representing features of prosody rather than being related to the musical symbols we call notes.

Up to the Middle Ages the chant of the Church was handed down orally. The preservation of these melodies depended entirely upon the memories of the monks. The desire of the Church to keep the chants from being altered, as they were passed on from one singer to another, led to the use of marks called *neumes*. (The word neume comes from the medieval Latin *neuma*, a word of several meanings including that of a musical sign. Its origin, though uncertain, is probably Greek.)

In the first period of neume writing (the earliest extant manuscripts date from the late ninth century) the symbols were placed above the words of the text. While this system could not show exact degrees of highness or lowness it did indicate relative higher and lower pitches.

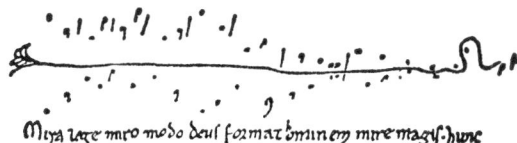

With the development of the staff in the late tenth century, the neumes were refined and placed on the lines and spaces. This kind of notation enabled the manuscript-writers to indicate with accuracy the relative pitches of the melodies. As with songs today, the text was written below the staff.

Neumes sufficed for Gregorian chant because its inherent rhythmic organization is determined by the text. Neumes have no exact time values, but neither do the tones of the chant; the music is not measured. Because these tones have no definite time value, Gregorian chant is also called Plainsong, a name used to distinguish it from measured music, which came later.

Neumatic notation worked well for the representation of the chant—direction and fairly exact pitch could be shown. That was enough. But for later music it was not

NOTES AND RESTS

enough. A system had to be devised to show time values, that is, the length of time the tones were to be sustained. In spite of its limitations, neumatic notation has served an important purpose. Without it, much of the chant would have been lost. Neumes are still used in the official publications of the Catholic Church for the notation of these melodies because Gregorian chant, flowing as it does with the natural accents of the words, has always remained unmeasured.

We noted earlier (page 15) that, from the ninth century on, the rise of polyphony created a demand for a system (the staff) that could define different degrees of pitch. The subsequent development of polyphonic music brought about further refinements of notation. Notes with exact time values were needed for the orderly movement of two or more simultaneous melodic lines. Thus, from the twelfth century on, a series of ingenious systems of notation evolved. By the seventeenth century, notation became more or less stabilized. Of course, some changes have taken place since then but they have been minor. Anyone able to read modern notation would have no great difficulty reading manuscripts or printed music of the seventeenth century.

CHAPTER 8

METER

Patterns of poetic meter can be compared with those of music. This can be illustrated by replacing with notes the signs used in the scansion of poetry. Let us refer to the verses on page 46 and substitute notes for the accent marks above the syllables. Although any note value may be chosen for the substitution, as will be shown later, we will use the eighth note here.

METER

56

Recite each line separately and indicate the accents with down-and-up motions of the arm. Notice that the flow of the verses can be represented with the notes of music. There is an even flow of the syllables preceding the word LAMB. Because the syllables *Ma - ry had a lit - tle* move at the same pace it is appropriate to assign to each a note of the same time value. This is also true of the syllables that precede the word SNOW: *Its fleece was white as*. However, the words LAMB in the first two lines and SNOW in the last cannot be equated with the other syllables. Since more time is given to them, eighth notes are too short to suffice for the full length of these syllables. It is obvious that notes of greater value must be used. The eighth notes must be replaced with quarter notes, because the words LAMB and SNOW are held twice as long as the shorter syllables.

♪	♪	♪	♪		♪	♪	♩
MA	ry	HAD	a		LIT	tle	LAMB,

♪	♪	♩		♪	♪	♩
LIT	tle	LAMB,		LIT	tle	LAMB,

♪	♪	♪	♪		♪	♪	♪	♪
MA	ry	HAD	a		LIT	tle	LAMB,	Its

♪	♪	♪	♪		♩	𝄽
FLEECE	was	WHITE	as		SNOW.	

As an experiment, write a half note over the word SNOW. As you recite the last line, sustain the word SNOW for the entire down-and-up motion of the arm. Isn't it a bit too long? Here the rest is as important as the note.

Now let us consider the flow of the *melody* of the song rather than the words. Refer to page 47. Sing the song instead of reciting the verses. In singing the melody, the tone for *Ma* is held longer than it is in recitation. The duration of this note is equivalent to an eighth note plus one-half its value; therefore, a dotted eighth (♪.). The tone for *ry* is shorter by half the value of an eighth note; therefore, a sixteenth note (♬).

Measure and bar line

Between the vertical lines drawn to indicate the primary accents in "Mary Had A Little Lamb" there is a uniform number of four eighth notes *or their mathematical equivalent*. Such a group of notes containing a primary, or strong, accent is called a *measure*. It may be compared to a foot in poetry. The grouping of the beats within the measure determines the *meter*.

The vertical line placed before the primary accent is called a *bar*, or *bar line:* | . Since the sixteenth century, the bar line has functioned in two ways: (1) to point out the note with the strongest accent and (2) to serve as a means of orientation when music is written for more than one voice or instrument. The distance between two bar lines is also called a *bar* and commonly, though not always correctly, a *measure*. The distinction between *bar* and *measure* is discussed on pages 59–60.

In written music, *the bar line is never drawn at the beginning of a staff before the first note*—not even when the first note comes on the primary beat. However, it is always drawn at the end of a line, provided that the bar is a complete one.

The end of a section, movement, or an entire piece is marked by a *double bar*. It consists of two vertical lines drawn close together: ‖ . Sometimes, the second vertical line is heavier than the first: ‖ . Although practice is not consistent, generally the equal-line double bar is used to indicate changes within a movement, or the end of a section; the heavier-second-line double bar indicates the end of a movement, or piece.

Time or meter signature

As you sing "Mary Had A Little Lamb" and keep time with your hand you will notice that the equivalent of two eighth notes fits into each of the down-and-up motions. In the notation of this melody, the pulse, or beat, is identified with a quarter-note value. Here, the quarter note is the unit—it receives one beat and there are two beats to the measure. Such an organization of note values is called two-quarter meter. It may be represented as $\frac{2}{\text{♩}}$ but is more commonly shown as $\frac{2}{4}$. This $\frac{2}{4}$ *is not a mathematical fraction*. It is, rather, an arrangement of numbers wherein the upper digit indicates that there are two beats to the measure while the lower one identifies the quarter note as the unit beat. These numbers, called a *time signature,* or *meter signature* (Medieval Latin *signatura,* fr. Latin *signare, signatum,* a

METER

sign), are placed on the staff, after the clef, at the very beginning of a piece. Unlike the clef, the time signature is not repeated at the beginning of each staff line but stays in effect as long as the meter remains the same. If a change in meter occurs, the time signature is changed to indicate the new meter. This is done by drawing a double bar and writing the new signature.

Rhythmic representation of a melody

In Chapter 5 we saw that a melody could be represented on the staff without regard to its rhythmic features. Now, we can show the rhythmic elements in a melody (accent, duration, measure, and meter) to the exclusion of its pitches. The rhythmic representation of "Mary Had A Little Lamb" is the following:

A rhythmic representation of a melody can be made using any note value as the unit. In the example above, a quarter note is used as the unit of measure; therefore, a 4 appears as the lower digit in the meter signature. However, any note value can be used as the unit without changing the number of pulses in the measure. Substitute a half note as the unit value and, on this basis, change every note in the song. With the new rhythmic representation before you, sing the song. Has the number of beats changed? Does the basic pulsation remain the same? Is there any difference in the primary and secondary accents? What is the time signature now? Substitute an eighth note as the unit. Does the pulsation remain the same? Is there any difference in the accents? What is the time signature now?

From these exercises you can see that a change in the note value of the unit beat does not alter the number of beats in the measure. In "Mary Had A

Little Lamb" there are two beats in each measure regardless of the unit beat, be it an eighth, quarter, or half-note. We may conclude that meter is determined by the number of beats in a measure, not by the unit beat. Therefore, the upper digit of the time signature tells the meter. For *common time* (C) and *alla breve* (¢) see page 67.

Music that has two beats to the measure is said to be in *duple* meter. When there are three beats, it is called *triple* meter; four beats *quadruple* meter; five, *quintuple* (rare); six, *sextuple;* and so on.

For History of Time Signatures, see the end of this chapter.

Measure vs. bar

In the chapter on rhythm, the reader was directed to scan the verses of "The Muffin Man" (page 45). Now, let us replace the accent signs with note values. Like "Mary Had A Little Lamb," "The Muffin Man" is in duple meter—the strong accent comes on the first of every two beats. But note, "The Muffin Man" does not begin with the primary accent. The verse and melody begin before the first strong accent, which comes on the word *do*. Such an anticipation is called an *anacrusis* (fr. Greek *anakrousis*, fr. *anakrouein,* to push up or back). In prosody, it is the one or two unaccented syllables prefixed to a verse which properly begins with an accented syllable. In music, the term (more commonly called an *upbeat*) is given to an initial note or notes occurring on or after an *unaccented* beat.

The following is a rhythmic representation of the song, "The Muffin Man" (p. 45).

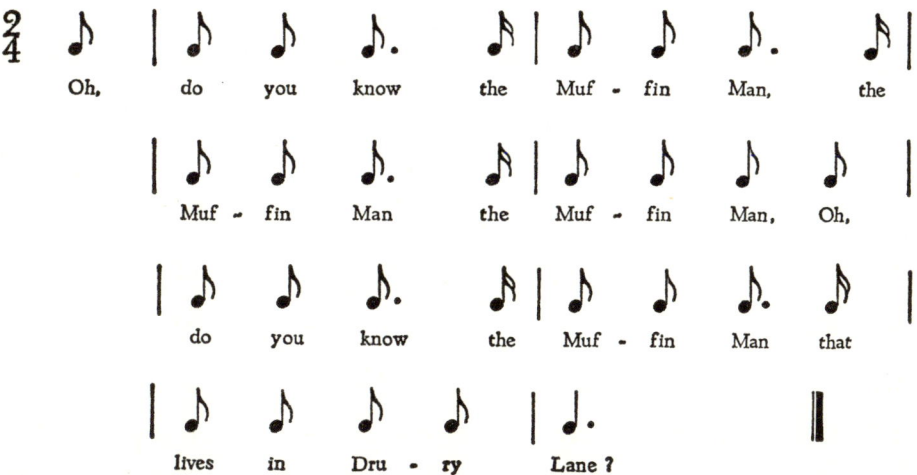

METER

The melody of this song, like many other melodies, begins with an upbeat, or anacrusis. When a piece of music does not begin with the primary accent the measure is not identical with the bar. Here, the measure begins *half after two*:

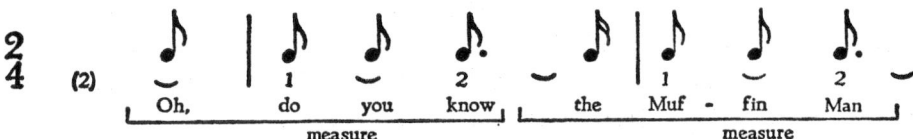

The piece continues in this manner to the end where the last *measures* are:

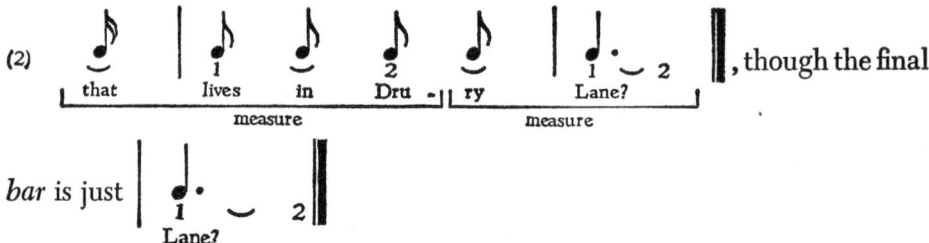

Thus, the measure and the bar are not always the same. Measures and bars are identical only when the music begins on a primary accent, as in "Mary Had A Little Lamb." *However, it has become common practice to speak of a measure as that distance between two bar lines.*

Rhythmic patterns of pieces in triple and quadruple meter

Sing the melody of the song "America." Using a quarter note as the **unit**, place the time signature ($\frac{3}{4}$) at the beginning of the stanza given here and write the proper note values above the syllables. Draw a single bar before every primary accent (except when it occurs at the beginning of a line) and at the end of *every line* if the last bar in that line is complete.

MY	coun - try,	'TIS	of	thee,
SWEET	land of	LIB -	er	- ty,
OF	thee I	SING.		
LAND	where my	FA -	thers	died!
LAND	of the	PIL -	grims'	pride!
FROM	ev' - ry	MOUN -	tain	side,
LET	free - dom	RING!		

METER

"Frère Jacques" is in quadruple meter. Like "The Muffin Man," it begins with an anacrusis—its measure is 3 - 4 - 1 - 2. Write the rhythmic notation of this piece, using a quarter-note as the unit note value.

Frè -	re	Jac -	ques,	Frè -	re	Jac -	ques,	dor -	mez
vous?			dor -	mez		vous?		Son-nez	les ma-
ti -	nes,	son-nez	les ma-	ti -	nes,		din,		din,
don.		din,	din,	don.					

Syncopation

"Old Folks At Home" is also in quadruple meter—the time signature is $\frac{4}{4}$. With the words before you, sing the song before writing the rhythmic notation.

𝅗𝅥	♪ ♪	♪ ♪	𝅘𝅥	𝅘𝅥	♪ 𝅘𝅥.
'WAY	down up - on	the	SWA -	nee	Riv - er
FAR,	far	a -	WAY,		
THERE'S	where my	heart is	TURN -	ing	ev - er,
THERE'S where the	old	folks	STAY.		
ALL	up and	down the	WHOLE	cre -	a - tion
SAD -	ly	I	ROAM,		
STILL	long- ing	for the	OLD	plan -	ta - tion
AND for the	old	folks at	HOME.		
ALL the	world	is	SAD	and	drear - y
EV - 'ry	where	I	ROAM,		
OH,	broth-ers,	how my	HEART	grows	wea - ry,
FAR from the	old	folks at	HOME.		

In singing the melody you must have observed the irregularity of the rhythm on the words *Riv-er* (line 1) and *ev-er* (line 3), the syllables *a-tion* (line 5) and *ta-tion* (line 7), and the word *wea-ry* (line 9). Although the first of these double syllables falls *on* the third beat of the measure, the

METER

second comes *before* the fourth beat—it anticipates it, making an artificial accent. Such an interruption of the natural flow is called *syncopation* (fr. Greek *synkopē*, a cutting up). Syncopation occurs when one or more regular beats are negated by one or more irregular-beat accents. This "offbeat" irregularity characterizes jazz music; it was the jazz musician who added "offbeat" to American slang.

To find another example of syncopation write out the rhythmic pattern of "Good Night Ladies." Use a $\frac{4}{4}$ meter signature.

GOOD	night,	la - dies!	GOOD	night	la - dies!
GOOD	night,	la - dies!	We're GOING to	leave you	now.
MER - ri- ly	we	roll a - long,	ROLL a -	long,	roll a - long,
MER - ri- ly	we	roll a - long,	O'ER	the	deep blue sea.

Here, we might compare the meter of the refrain, "Merrily we roll along" with that of "Mary had a little lamb." The former is in $\frac{4}{4}$ meter while the latter is in $\frac{2}{4}$ meter. From this it is evident that the metrical design of a verse may receive more than one treatment in music. Because of this flexibility, the same poem is often set to music by several composers with entirely different, though satisfactory, results.

Simple and compound meters

There are two fundamental meters—that of twos, called *duple*, and that of threes, called *triple*. These are the basic *simple* meters. However, *quadruple* meter (the meter of fours) is so common that it, too, is considered a simple meter. These three, then, duple, triple, and quadruple, are the simple meters.

Simple meters (where the beats are grouped in twos, threes, and fours) do not always play a solo role in music. Often they are combined in such a way as to form a more extended and complex design. For example, two meters of three may be combined to form a meter of six. In this case, the first group of beats (1 - 2 - 3) functions as the leader of the second group of beats (4 - 5 - 6). The first beat is marked by a strong, primary accent while the fourth beat has a weaker, secondary accent. Combinations of simple meters, producing five or more beats and containing two or more principal accents within the measure, form what is called *compound meters*. The regular compound meters have six, nine, or twelve beats.

The songs we have examined are in duple, triple, or quadruple meter—the simple meters. Now, let us examine one in compound meter. Sing "Jack Horner" and notate its rhythmic design. (This tune appears on page 199.)

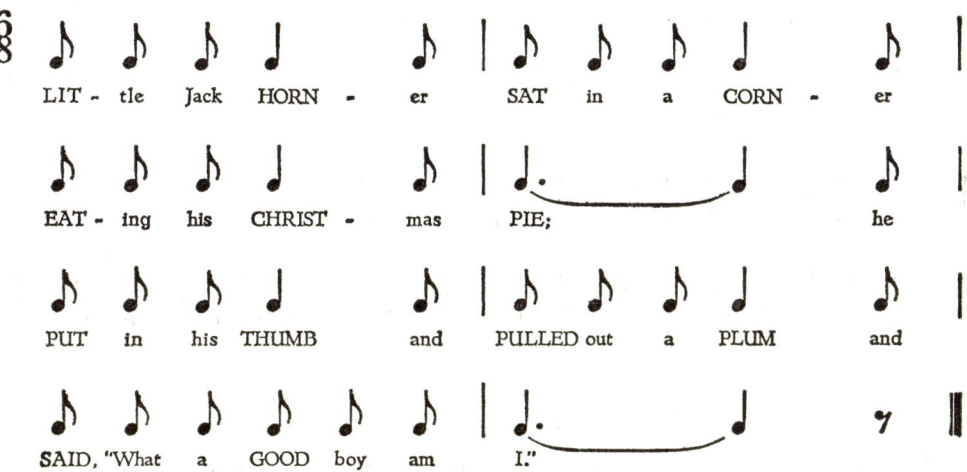

Like "America," this piece contains groups of three pulsations. But there is a difference. In "Jack Horner," the accents alternate between a strong, primary accent and a weaker, secondary one. This is an example of compound meter. It is a combination of two simple meters—in this case, two triple meters. Here, there are six beats to the measure with a strong accent on the first beat and a lesser one on the fourth beat. This is called *sextuple* meter.

In compound meters each beat may be felt independently if the music moves slowly, but when the rate of speed is moderate or fast the beat is usually felt only at the larger divisions. "Jack Horner" is such a case. The music moves too quickly for one to feel a pulsation on each note; rather, the notes are grouped so that the weak beats are lost in the over-all pattern. There is the feeling of two beats to the measure: the first, on beat *one*, primary; the other, on beat *four*, secondary.

Sample patterns in simple and regular compound meters

With a quarter or eighth note as the unit of time, the following are sample patterns in the simple and the usual compound meters. Observe that the sum of the note and rest values in each measure, or bar, is equal to the value represented by the meter signature.

METER

Simple Meters

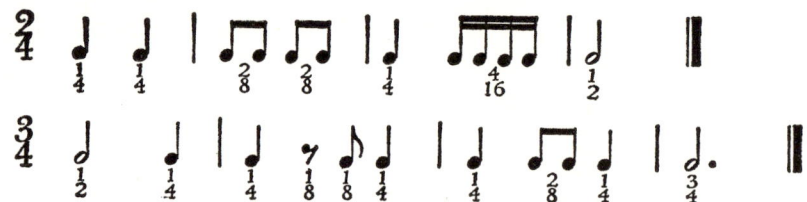

Write the mathematical values under the notes and groups of notes in the remaining examples.

Compound Meters

Irregular compound meters, such as *five, seven, eleven,* etc., are made by combining other meters. For example:

2 + 3

3 + 2

Metrical groups within the measure

In our system of notation each note or rest is equal to two of the next lower denomination. However, within the measure there are metrical groups designed to accommodate time values which do not fall into the ratio of 2 : 1. The most common of these is the *triplet*. In a triplet, notes and rests assume a value worth one-third of the next longer kind. They are grouped together and performed in the same amount of time that is normally given to two notes or rests of the same value.

A triplet is designated by the number 3 written alone, or outside or inside a bracket ⌐─┐ or slur * ⌢ . Triplets may be formed by notes of any kind ♫ ♪♪♪ or by notes and rests together ♪ 𝄾 ♪ ♫ 𝄾. Even a group of two notes or rests, one twice the value of the other, may be read as a triplet provided it is marked distinctively ♩ ♪ 𝄾 ♩ .

The function of the triplet can be demonstrated by singing the chorus of "Dixie" (pp. 202–203). As you sing, observe the rhythmic pattern.

The first three sixteenth notes (on the words, "Then I") receive no more time than any two sixteenth notes or any one eighth note in the piece. Such is a triplet. A triplet occurs again on the upbeat to the fifth bar (on the word, "in").

Any irregular metrical group may be made equal to a note or group of notes. It is done by binding the notes together with a beam, slur, or bracket and adding the appropriate numeral. Such an abnormal group has either more or less notes in it than mathematically fit a music time value. For example, a five-note group occupying the time value of a quarter note

---

* The *slur* and the *tie* (p. 51) are identical in appearance but they serve a different purpose. A slur binds together notes of different pitches or irregular metrical groups; a tie binds together notes of the same pitch in order to prolong the value of the first note.

METER

cannot be written simply as eighth, sixteenth, or thirty-second notes because neither 5/8, nor 5/16, nor 5/32 equal 1/4. But one of these groups must be used because our system does not provide for others. The group selected is that one which has a mathematical value as near as possible to that of the note whose value is to be filled by the group. In this example, the five-note group would be written as five sixteenth notes because of the three, 5/16 is the value closest to 1/4.

On the other hand, if a group of five notes were written to occupy the time value of a half note, the eighth would be the value given to the group because, of the various possibilities, 5/8 is the value closest to 1/2. This is the principle that governs the writing of irregular metrical groups.

The most common irregular metrical groups are the *duplet (doublet), triplet, quadruplet (quadrolet), quintuplet (quintolet),* and *sextuplet (sextolet).*

With one exception, the irregular metrical groups have one or more additional notes "squeezed in" to occupy a time value that normally accommodates fewer notes of the same kind. The exception is the duplet. The duplet employs two notes to occupy the time value of three—for example ♩♩ = ♩♩♩. The same duplet might also be written ♩♩ = ♩♩♩ because the mathematical value 2/2 is as close to 3/4 as is the value 2/4. This alternate notation is possible only with the duplet.

Sample irregular metrical groups and how they may be written

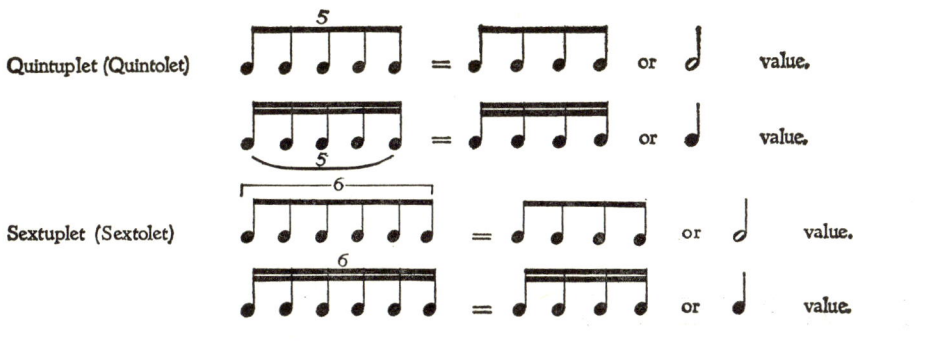

HISTORY OF TIME SIGNATURES

The time signature goes back to the fourteenth century. Then, time was considered as either *perfect* (in threes—triple meter) or *imperfect* (in twos—duple meter). The indications were either the number 3, or a full circle (O) for perfect time and the number 2, or a broken circle (C) for imperfect time. Medieval thought saw a relationship between perfection, the unbroken circle, the number three, and the Holy Trinity (three divine persons in one being). Thus, for the most part, the serious composer concerned himself with music in triple meter.

In the fifteenth and sixteenth centuries there was a shift toward duple meter. In Italy, even as early as the fourteenth century, duple meter rose above the stigma of "imperfect" time until it found greater favor among composers than the old "perfect" or triple time. By the seventeenth century, however, quadruple was the most usual or *common* time and the broken circle (C) was used to express this meter. It is still in use today but let it be remembered that the symbol, C, is not the letter C, nor does it stand for the word "common." Instead, it stands for $\frac{4}{4}$ meter, which is called *common time*.

One more symbol from these early days which is also now in use as a time signature is the crossed half circle (¢). This sign is called *alla breve* (Italian, *according to the breve*), a term which dates from the Renaissance. Then, it meant that one *breve* (□), or double whole note, filled a measure. The sign now indicates that the modern half note (♩) is the unit of the inherent beat and that there are two beats to the measure. The figure ¢ means the same thing as the time signature $\frac{2}{2}$.

CHAPTER 9

WRITTEN MUSIC AND THE KEYBOARD

When you played "Mary Had A Little Lamb," "Frère Jacques," and "Three Blind Mice" as illustrated on pages 38–42, the problem was one of relating the pitches of the song to the keyboard. This was solved by indicating on the staff the letter names of the pitches and associating them with the appropriate keys on the piano. Such a procedure is excellent to find correct pitches but it is inadequate to represent a melodic line properly because a melody contains the element of rhythm as well as pitch. A system is needed to show the rhythmic features. Thus by using notes instead of letter names, the melody can be presented accurately, for *the combination of staff and notes shows both pitch and rhythm.*

In place of letter names which we previously wrote on the staff we will now employ notes for "Mary Had A Little Lamb."

HINTS FOR PRACTICE

Counting

The time signature is $\frac{2}{4}$. To repeat: $\frac{2}{4}$ indicates that there are two beats to the measure and that the quarter note receives one beat.

As you play the piece count aloud ONE - two, ONE - two, etc. Keep a steady beat; avoid any hesitation as you play. A continuous "flow" must be maintained to bring out the true character of the music. The first note, a dotted eighth note, has the time value of three sixteenth notes, or 3/4 of a beat. Hold this note long enough that the next one will have to come quickly, just before the second beat. Always conscious of the note values, count ONE - two, ONE - two, etc. You will find the notes falling nicely into place. Some may suggest that you count ONE - and, TWO - and; ONE - and, TWO - and, etc., in order to be absolutely accurate with the time values. But where mathematical perfection is secured by this method, there is the danger of losing the "flow" which gives life to the music.

Tempo

By being unflagging in your beat from the beginning to the end you will succeed in keeping throughout the same *tempo* (Italian, rate of speed). The wise student will begin slowly or moderately and maintain the same pace. Do not fall into the trap of playing the easier parts quickly. If you do, you will have to slow down when a more difficult place occurs and this unevenness will destroy the shape of the music. Hamlet's speech to the Players (Act III, Scene 2) applies equally well to performers of music, especially the admonition, ". . . but use all gently; for in the very torrent, tempest, and (as I may say) whirlwind of your passion, you must acquire and beget a temperance that may give it smoothness."

Fingering

Arabic numerals above or below the notes indicate fingering. It is important to retain the same fingering every time you play the piece. Fingers trained to play the same notes respond easily. Continual changes in the fingering lead to confusion.

WRITTEN MUSIC AND THE KEYBOARD

With your *eyes on the staff*, with your *fingers resting on the proper keys,* and with a *steady count of slow or moderate tempo,* play

Mary Had A Little Lamb

After you have learned to play this piece with the right hand, play it with the left hand, observing all previous instructions and the different fingering.

When you have mastered the piece with separate hands play both hands together.

"Frère Jacques" has a different time signature. Here the meter is $\frac{4}{4}$, indicating that there are four beats to the measure and each quarter-note receives one beat. This piece does not begin on ONE but on *three*, because

WRITTEN MUSIC AND THE KEYBOARD

the primary accent does not occur until the third note. To ensure a steady beat you might start counting ONE - two - three - four and begin to play as you say *three*. This piece really has no special counting problems. Be careful of the fingering for each hand. First play the right hand alone; then the left hand alone; finally, both hands together.

Frère Jacques

WRITTEN MUSIC AND THE KEYBOARD

"Three Blind Mice" has a time signature of $\frac{6}{8}$. This indicates six beats to the measure with the eighth note receiving one beat. The first two notes are dotted quarter notes, each of which is equivalent to the time value of three eighth notes. Thus, each dotted quarter note receives three beats. The first note will be played as you say ONE and sustained through beats two and three. The second note will be played as you say *four* and sustained through beats five and six. The second bar of the piece contains a dotted quarter note tied to a quarter note. This note will be sustained for five beats. The last beat in this bar is an eighth rest denoting one beat of silence. The finger must be lifted from the key as you say *six*. During this beat of silence prepare to play the next note, which is sounded as you say ONE.

Three Blind Mice

After having mastered this piece with the right hand, do so with the left hand alone,

and then with both hands together.

The three melodies you have learned to play can be managed by either hand without too many adjustments. "Mary Had A Little Lamb" lies directly under the five fingers. "Frère Jacques" and "Three Blind Mice" need but moderate shifting of the hand to permit the melody to flow smoothly and easily.

A MELODY PLAYED BY TWO HANDS

Fingering is not always as easy as it is for the first three melodies in this book. The proper fingering and position of the hand can become a problem for the beginner. Many times you might like to play a melody which has come to your attention. For example, "List To The Bells" may appear in a song book in the following manner:

WRITTEN MUSIC AND THE KEYBOARD

74

List To The Bells

To play this piece you need not wait until you have complete independence of hands at the keyboard. The technical difficulties of a melody might be shared by both hands so that what is awkward for one hand alone may become fairly easy when the melodic line is divided between both right and left hands. Melodies often lie within the eight notes of an octave. Place the hands so that the fingers of the left hand (5 - 4 - 3 - 2) are above the four lowest notes and the fingers of the right hand (2 - 3 - 4 - 5) are above the four highest notes.

The following examples of this approach to playing tunes should give the beginner an immediate tool. After you have acquired a facility in playing these melodies, experiment in like manner with others you may know.

Notes with *stems up* are to be played by the *right hand;* those with *stems down* are to be played by the *left hand*.

WRITTEN MUSIC AND THE KEYBOARD

List To The Bells

Sometimes it may be convenient to play the two middle notes with the thumbs. In the next examples, notes with two stems (one up and one down) may be played with either the second finger of one hand or the thumb of the other. The student should be encouraged to try both ways.

Row, Row, Row Your Boat

Traditional

WRITTEN MUSIC AND THE KEYBOARD

In vocal music, notes have separate stems when the notes match separate syllables. When two or more notes are sung to one syllable the notes are bound by a slur (see p. 65). This is demonstrated in the following examples.

Hickory Dickory Dock

Traditional

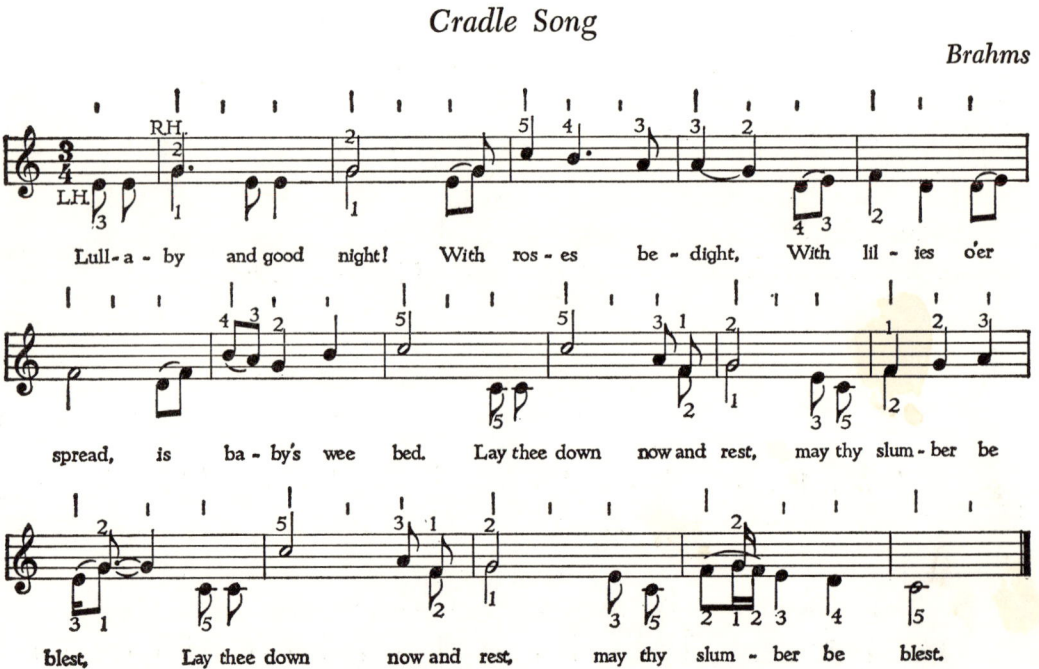

Cradle Song

Brahms

Note: In the twelfth bar, on the word "blest," there is an example of both the *slur* and the *tie*. The first two notes are slurred (smoothly connected); the second and third notes are tied.

CHAPTER 10

ROLE OF RIGHT AND LEFT HANDS IN KEYBOARD MUSIC

In the last chapter we learned to play several melodies with the right and left hands. The ability to play a melody on the piano is rewarding both practically and aesthetically. However, the piano (like other keyboard instruments) is not limited to the sounding of one tone at a time—it can sound many simultaneously.

In order to give fuller musical expression to the melodies you have learned and will learn to play, consideration will be given to ways of highlighting the rhythm and *harmony* (the agreement of united sounds) inherent in a melody. In keyboard music the melody is, for the most part, played by the right hand while the left hand is engaged, more often, in supplying the rhythmic and harmonic elements. Let us explore these possibilities.

In the following arrangement of "Mary Had A Little Lamb" you will play the melody with the right hand just as you have done before. The left hand, however, will play a very few different notes but enough to underline the implied harmonies and to punctuate the most important beat in the music: the most strongly accented beat of the measure, ONE.

Study the piece before attempting to play it on the piano. Which are the

ROLE OF RIGHT AND LEFT HANDS IN KEYBOARD MUSIC

new notes written on the bass staff? On which beat do they occur? What is the fingering for the left hand? Get a mental image of what both hands will perform before starting to play. Hold your hands up before you and move the fingers as they would be moved in playing the piano. When you feel that you know what your hands should do, play the piece *slowly; with both hands together.*

In the arrangement you have just played there was a greater degree of musical completeness than when you played the melody alone. True, not a great deal was added, but that which was added gave a warmth to the piece by stressing its rhythmic flow and by outlining its basic harmonic characteristics. Here, there was not more than a skeleton of the harmony and a punctuation of the beat, but these gave a fuller meaning to the melody than when it stood alone.

The next setting of "Mary Had A Little Lamb" has been designed to give an even richer harmonic quality to the piece. This has been accomplished

ROLE OF RIGHT AND LEFT HANDS IN KEYBOARD MUSIC

by writing for the left hand several notes to be played at the same time. When several tones are sounded together they form a *chord* and in the following example we have a chordal accompaniment.

Look carefully at the part for the left hand. Place your fingers, as indicated, over the notes of the first chord, C – E – G. Notice that this chord is repeated in most of the bars, but there is a change in the third and seventh bars. Silently move your fingers to this new position so that the correct fingers will rest on B – F – G. Change back to the original position and do this over and over again until it can be done smoothly and quickly.

Now, hold your hands up before you and move the fingers as they would be moved in playing this piece.

When you are ready to play, place both hands in position on the keyboard. Before striking the keys count aloud several times with a steady tempo: ONE - two, ONE - two, etc. At all times be conscious of a *constant, unwavering beat*.

Mary Had A Little Lamb II

From the point of view of rhythm, the accompaniment in the first two arrangements of "Mary Had A Little Lamb" does no more than stress the primary accent. The piece remains fairly static. The rhythmic flow can be enhanced, however, by a simple rearrangement of the notes of the accompaniment in the second example. Instead of playing all the notes at the same time as *solid chords* they may be played separately as *broken chords*, creating a motion which not only accentuates the brightness of the dotted figures in the right hand but gives an atmosphere of gayety and charm to the entire composition.

ROLE OF RIGHT AND LEFT HANDS IN KEYBOARD MUSIC

Before the invention of the piano, composers of keyboard music were almost required to use broken chords—for good reason: the harpsichord had neither volume nor resonance comparable to that of the piano. A broken chord accompaniment kept the harmonies alive. Such a figure is called an *Alberti Bass* after the composer Domenico Alberti, 1710–1740. It is useful in pieces written for the piano, especially when a melody calls for clean articulation so that its character will not be blurred by an injudicious use of the damper pedal.

Practice procedure is identical with that suggested for the first two arrangements of this piece.

Mary Had A Little Lamb III

"Frère Jacques" was presented in Chapter 4 to show that from time to time we must change the position of the hand in order to exploit fully the possibilities of the keyboard and to play smoothly a musical line. In the following arrangement nothing has been changed in the right hand. However, the skip of an octave has been introduced in the left hand. This necessitates the stretching of the hand in order to achieve a *legato* (Italian, connected) effect from one octave to the other. A certain melodic line has also been given to the left hand so that an independence of hands may be developed. By nature one hand wants to act with the other but a command of the piano requires complete independence of each hand.

Note: The measure in this piece is three - four - ONE - two. Count aloud and keep the beat steady throughout.

ROLE OF RIGHT AND LEFT HANDS IN KEYBOARD MUSIC

Frère Jacques I

In the sections on history in Chapters 2 and 7, we noted that the early development of the staff and the later standardization of a system of time values derived, to a large extent, from the needs of polyphony. "Frère Jacques" is a piece of polyphonic music. But it is a special kind of polyphony. You know that this song has melody and rhythm because you have sung and played it, but have you been aware of its harmonic structure? Whoever composed "Frère Jacques" constructed it in such a way that chordal harmony results when four persons sing the song if each begins at a specific, different time. In this song each fresh beginning, or entrance, should occur when the first singer has reached first the word *dormez,* then *sonnez,* and finally *din.* Ask three other persons to join you in singing this song and notice the beautiful result. The four singers should continue singing the song round and round as long as the leader repeats it from the beginning. In fact, this kind of song is called a *round.* It is a special kind of imitative music designed to be sung, but it can be played as well. Playing music of this sort will help you to develop the independence of hands so necessary to keyboard performance.

The following example is a two-part version of the normally four-part round.

ROLE OF RIGHT AND LEFT HANDS IN KEYBOARD MUSIC

Frère Jacques II

"Three Blind Mice" is also a four-part round. Team up with three other people to sing it as such. Experiment to find the proper places for the different entrances.

Here it is presented in three arrangements for piano. The first has a simple part for the left hand. In playing this piece count: ONE - two, ONE - two; ONE for the primary and *two* for the secondary accent. When there are six beats to a measure, as in this piece, a secondary accent comes on the fourth beat. Count slowly at first and increase the speed slightly until you can play the piece at a tempo consistent with the character of the song.

ROLE OF RIGHT AND LEFT HANDS IN KEYBOARD MUSIC

Three Blind Mice I

In the second arrangement of "Three Blind Mice" the left hand has more movement: the ONE - two pulsation is continuous. From bar eleven to the end, chords have been substituted for single notes. In the last three bars, the right hand has, for the first time, more than one note to play at a time.

Adhere to the fingering indicated. Be careful to use the same fingering at all times. Fingers are inclined to seek the keys they have been taught to play. If you use the same fingering every time you play a piece you will obtain perfect performances; if you change the fingering every time you play a piece you will experience confusion and disappointment.

As suggested on pages 77 and 78, study the music carefully and silently. When you are ready to play, place both hands in position on the keyboard and count aloud several times with a steady tempo before striking the keys. At all times be aware of a *constant, unwavering beat*.

ROLE OF RIGHT AND LEFT HANDS IN KEYBOARD MUSIC

Three Blind Mice II

In the final arrangement of "Three Blind Mice" the right hand has a richer part to play while the left hand has broken chords in a steady eighth-note pattern. As before, count aloud with only two beats to the measure.

ROLE OF RIGHT AND LEFT HANDS IN KEYBOARD MUSIC

Three Blind Mice III

CHAPTER 11

TRANSPOSITION

In all three arrangements of "Mary Had A Little Lamb" (pages 78, 79, and 80) the melody began on the E above middle C. In singing this song someone might prefer to have the whole piece lie a little bit higher, while someone else might find it more singable in a somewhat lower register. Such a change can be obtained by starting on either a higher or a lower tone and singing or playing all the notes in the piece at the same relative distance above or below the same notes in the original setting. The process of shifting every note of a musical composition to a relatively higher or lower pitch is called *transposition*.

In order to transpose we must understand how distances between tones are measured. The distance from one piano key to its nearest neighbor is called a *half step*, or *semitone*. This is true whether the adjoining keys are both white, or one white and one black. For example, the key closest to C on its left is a *white key*, B, though the nearest key to the right of C is a *black key* which may be called either C-sharp (C♯) or D-flat (D♭). B, then, is a half step or semitone *below* C; whereas C♯ or D♭ is a half step or semitone *above* C. A tone is a *whole step* or *whole tone* higher or lower than another when the distance between them is equal to two adjacent half steps: C to D, E to F♯, G♯ to A♯, D♭ to E♭, etc. By the same token, D to C,

TRANSPOSITION

F♯ to E, B♭ to A♭ are whole steps, though in the opposite direction. Thus, distances are measured by the number of half steps between one key and another. E is three half steps or a step and a half below G; B♭ is three half steps or a step and a half above G; A is two whole steps above F, and so forth.

Suppose you wanted to play "Mary Had A Little Lamb" a whole tone higher than written. Turn back to page 78. In playing this arrangement the right hand rested above the keys C - D - E - F - G, while the left hand poised with the second finger over the C an octave below middle C and the little finger above the G below.

Original Position

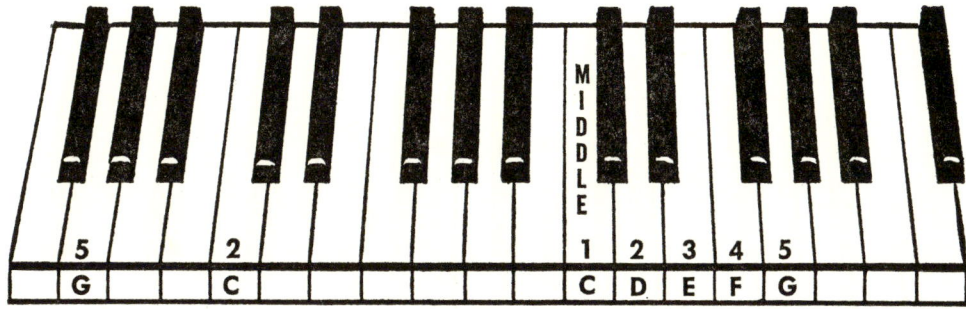

To transpose this piece a whole tone higher one need only shift the hands up the keyboard to a point where the fingers will lie on the keys one whole step above the original.

Transposed Position Up One Whole Step

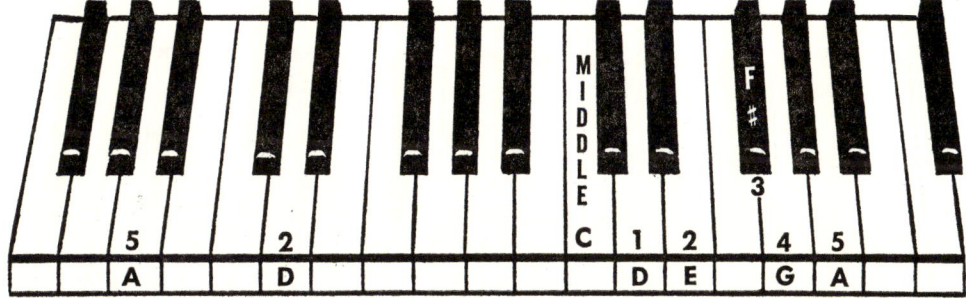

Up to now there has been no occasion to employ black keys in playing the given pieces, but the transposition of "Mary Had A Little Lamb" up one whole step brings the third finger of the right hand over the first black

TRANSPOSITION

key in the group of threes, F♯. With your hands in this new position, **look at the original arrangement** on page 78 and *play the piece transposed.*

Note: There is no difference in the movement of the melody (right hand) and the accompaniment (left hand). The meter and rhythm have not been changed—transposition does not involve changes in note values. Only the pitch is affected, but even in this respect the melodic *pattern remains the same* because the degree of change in pitch is constant throughout.

Practice, alternating between the original and transposed positions, until you can play the piece comfortably and with assurance in these two versions.

To play the piece still another step higher, place your hands over the keys which are two whole steps above the original ones. Play as before, starting with the third finger of the right hand and the second finger of the left hand.

Transposed Position Up Two Whole Steps

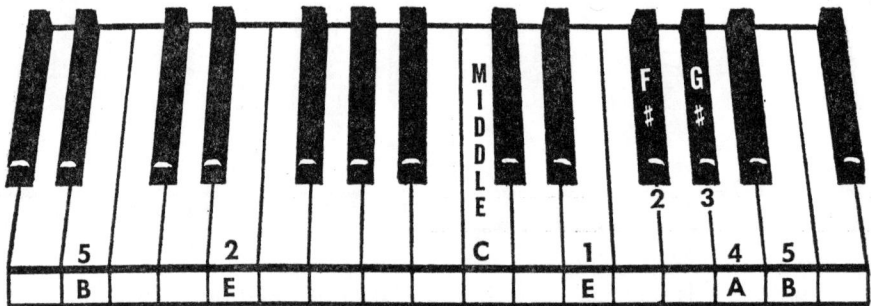

To transpose the piece downward, move the hands to the left. "Mary Had A Little Lamb" may be transposed down one step and a half by playing the keys indicated in the following illustration.

Transposed Position Down One Step And A Half

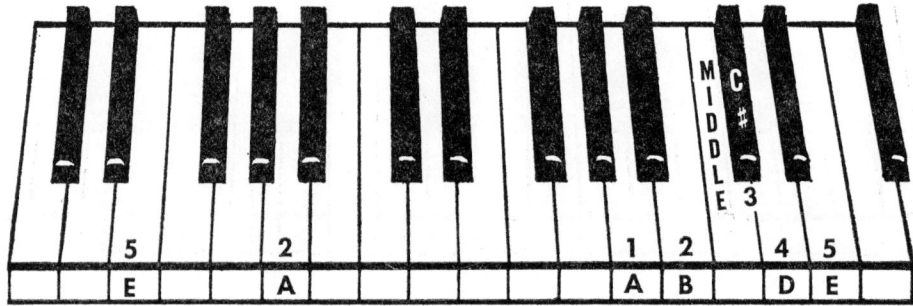

After you have mastered these transpositions, try the following folk song. Transpose it up and down.

"Haenschen-Klein"

German Folk Song

Haen - schen - Klein ging al - lein in die wei - te Welt hin - ein,
Lit - tle Jack, stock and pack, ran a - way on Sat - ur - day,

Stock und Hut steht ihm gut, er ist wohl - ge - muth.
Spir - its high as the sky, he was bright and gay.

A - ber Mut - ter wein - et sehr, hat ja nun kein Haen - schen mehr.
But his moth - er, left a - lone, cried for Jack - ie to come home,

Da be - sinnt sich das Kind, kommt nach Haus ge schwind.
Sun - day, Jack did come back, nev - er more to roam.

Now turn to the second and third arrangements of "Mary Had A Little Lamb" (pages 79 and 80). Play these arrangements transposed up and down.

Apply the same left-hand parts (solid and broken chords) to "Haenschen-Klein." After you have adapted the two left-hand versions to "Haenschen-Klein," transpose the piece up and down the way you have done with "Mary Had A Little Lamb."

The arrangements of "Frère Jacques" and "Three Blind Mice" offer additional easy material for exercises in transposition. Experiment with other pieces of your own choosing.

The next chapter, Chapter 12, is historical. Although the student is encouraged to read it and play the melodies at the end of the chapter, the course of study will not be impaired by moving ahead to Chapter 13, The Major Scale.

* Little Jack went alone into the wide world. Stick and hat become him well; he is in good spirits. But mother cries very much—she no longer has little Jack. The child reconsiders; he comes home quickly.

CHAPTER 12

ORIGINS OF OUR SCALES

Greek Modes

From earliest times, Greek music was characterized by singing—melody being its most important element. Their melodies moved within the framework of one or two groups of four successive tones called *tetrachords* (fr. Greek *tetrachordos,* four-stringed). These tetrachords formed the basis for their seven scales or *modes* (Latin *modus,* "form") as they are commonly called. The names given to these modes refer to supposed characteristics of ancient Greek tribes and districts. *Dorian* (Sparta and the Peloponnesus) was strong and brave; *Phrygian* (North Western Asia Minor), spirited and gay; *Lydian* (South Western Asia Minor) was soft, sweet, and effeminate. The remaining four modes were related to these: *Hypodorian,* majestic; *Hypophrygian,* active; *Hypolydian,* voluptuous; *Mixolydian,* sorrowful.

The study of Greek thinking about the philosophical and scientific aspects of their modes is fascinating but our modes, or scales as we more commonly call them, do not derive from the Greek. Rather, their historical background is found in the Church or Ecclesiastical modes.

Church Modes

The *Church* or *Ecclesiastical* modes stem from the earlier Eastern and Mediterranean melodies and are based on their modal principles. An organization of these melodies, in or about the time of Saint Gregory I (Gregory the Great, reigning Pope from the year 590 to 604), form what is now called *Gregorian chant,* or *plainsong* (see page 53). The Church identifies these modes only by Roman numerals. Modes I, III, V, and

ORIGINS OF OUR SCALES

VII are called *authentic* (from Greek *authentes,* someone who acts himself and not through others) because the "keynote" of each is the first degree of the mode; II, IV, VI, and VIII are called *plagal* (from Greek *plagios,* sidewise) because in these modes the "keynote" is in the middle of the series.

From the tenth century on, some monks (the only educated musicians of the times) began to adopt the Greek names for the ecclesiastical modes, but, because of a misinterpretation of early writings, they did not apply them to the same modes as the Greeks had. Nevertheless, the names given in that period remain to this day. The authentic modes were called: I, Dorian; III, Phrygian; V, Lydian; and VII, Mixolydian. The plagal modes have their names from the corresponding authentic modes because the "keynote" is the same in each pair. They were called: II, Hypodorian; IV, Hypophrygian; VI, Hypolydian; and VIII, Hypomixolydian. The prefix *hypo* (Greek, below) indicates that the first pitch of the plagal mode is four steps lower than the first pitch of its related authentic mode.

In the following examples the "keynote" is indicated by the half note.

Church Modes

By the sixteenth century the eight Church modes were losing ground to two other modes which we now know as the *major* ° and *minor* † scales. In an attempt to give

° See chapter 13, and further discussion in chapter 15.
† See chapter 14, and further discussion in chapter 15.

ORIGINS OF OUR SCALES

status to these more popular modes, a twelve-mode system was introduced. The four additional modes were called: IX, *Aeolian* ‡ (now called minor) together with its plagal form X, *Hypoaeolian;* and, XI, *Ionian* ‡ (now called major) together with its plagal form XII, *Hypoionian.*

Four Additional Church Modes

Pentatonic Scale

A mode of very great antiquity that is found in almost every part of the world is the five-tone mode or *Pentatonic Scale.* Its pitches can be noted easily by playing, in any order, the five black keys of the piano, or the white keys C–D–E–G–A, F–G–A–C–D, or G–A–B–D–E.

To a large extent the folk music of western civilization falls into the patterns of the pentatonic and the six authentic modes. Art music, too, gives evidence of composer's conscious efforts within these modes.

The following beautiful melodies are representative of some of the modes described. Because they can be identified with the white keys of the piano it is easy to play them and to study their characteristics. Listen to the subtle difference in each of them. To facilitate performance, divide the notes between the right and left hands. Use the *right* hand to play the notes with *stems up;* the *left* hand to play the notes with *stems down.* (The neumes of the chant have been replaced with modern notation.)

Lux Aeterna

[May eternal light shine upon them, O Lord: With Thy saints forever; because Thou art merciful. *Trans. by Konrad Gries.*]

‡ Aeolian and Ionian, names from the Greek modes, refer to the Greek tribes that settled in Aeolia and Ionia in Asia Minor.

ORIGINS OF OUR SCALES

[That day of wrath, that day (of dread)
Will lay the world in ashes (gray),
As David with the Sybil said. *Trans. by Konrad Gries*]

ORIGINS OF OUR SCALES

The Drunken Sailor

Dorian Mode — *Sea Chanty*

Mister Frog

Pentatonic scale — *Appalachian Folk Song*

ORIGINS OF OUR SCALES

95

Chorale: O Haupt Voll Blut Und Wunden
(O Sacred Head, Now Wounded)

Phrygian Mode J. S. Bach

English Version by James W. Alexander

* ⁀ Fermata and † :|| Repeat Sign explained on page 155.

CHAPTER 13

THE MAJOR SCALE

Most of the music of Western civilization is characterized by a series of seven steps (half and whole), rising from one tone to its octave. Of Greek origin, such a series is called a *diatonic* scale, from the words *scala* (Italian, stairs) and *diatonikos* (Greek, from *dia* and *tonos*, meaning through all the steps of the scale or mode). Music in our culture is dominated by two kinds of diatonic scale: *Major,* the subject of this chapter, and *Minor,* the subject of Chapter 14.

In playing "Mary Had A Little Lamb," "Frère Jacques," and "Three Blind Mice" in the original and transposed positions, you must have noticed that, regardless of the register (high or low), there is in each of these pieces one tone above all others which sounds tranquil and reposed, without tension or excitement driving the piece forward. Although it occurs in other places as well, this tone is invariably the last one in each of these melodies.

Let us examine "Three Blind Mice." Beginning on E, play the melody. You will hear that the C possesses a quality of repose and completeness which is not to be found in any of the other tones. The reason does not lie in any special quality that C might have in itself but, rather, in the context in which it is found: the whole-step half-step relationship in the eight different pitches ranging from middle C to its octave above. These may be extracted from the melody and arranged in a stepwise progression to form a scale.

THE MAJOR SCALE

Melodic Tones

Scale of Melody

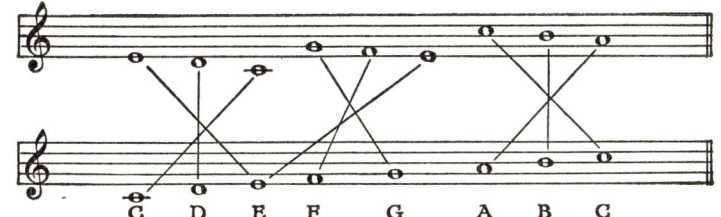

Starting on middle C, play this scale upward. Listen to the quality each tone has as it is related to the others. Certainly C gives the feeling of finality, or complete repose. Play the scale again, but this time stop on B. Notice the dynamic quality of the seventh degree coming as it does after C - D - E - F - G and A. Begin with the high C and play the scale downward as far as the fourth degree, F; as far as the second, D. When you stopped on the fourth degree, F, did you notice the drive toward the third, E, a tone of less tension? After resting on the second degree, D, didn't you feel the need to progress to the first, C?

With the first degree or step of the scale (and of course with the eighth which is its octave) one has the feeling of having arrived "home" after a tonal adventure marked by greater and lesser tensions. The affinity of different tones for one in particular is called *tonality* or *key*.*

That tone which is the point of departure and return is known as the *tonal center, keynote,* or *tonic* (Greek *tonikos,* pertaining to tension and thus to tone). It gives its name to the key. For example, a piece whose keynote, or tonic, is C is said to be in the key of C; if the tonic is G, the piece is in the key of G. In Chapters 9 and 10, "Mary Had a Little Lamb," "Frère Jacques," and "Three Blind Mice" are written in the key of C and, in each, the tonic is C.

Names of the scale degrees

Each of the seven different degrees of the diatonic scale is represented by a Roman numeral and has a name descriptive of its character or position in the scale.

The first degree of the scale is indicated by the Roman numeral I. It is called the *Tonic*. It is the most important tone in the scale because it is the keynote or tonal center; that is, all the other tones have an affinity for it. The next tone of importance in the diatonic scale is the fifth degree. It is

---

* *Key* is a word of several meanings. It refers to (1) the affinity of different tones for one in particular; (2) the front end of levers by which keyboard instruments are played; and (3) the levers on wind instruments such as the clarinet and trumpet by which the sound-holes are opened and closed.

THE MAJOR SCALE

called the *Dominant*, V. The Dominant is the first tone other than the Tonic which appears in the series of partials (see p. 7). The dynamic character of the Dominant is felt in its drive toward the Tonic.

The second degree is called the *Supertonic*, II, because it comes after and is above the Tonic. The fourth degree is called the *Subdominant*, IV, because it comes before and is below the Dominant.*

The third degree gets its name from its position between the Tonic and the Dominant: numerically, this degree is midway between 1 and 5, therefore, it is called the Mediant, III.

The sixth degree gets its name from its position between the Subdominant and the upper Tonic (the Tonic at the top of the "stairs"): numerically, it is midway between 4 and 8; therefore, the sixth degree is called the *Submediant*, VI. The seventh degree is called the *Leading Tone*, VII. Its strong, dynamic quality leads the progression to the *Tonic*, VIII (I), the tone of final repose.

There is no difficulty in learning the names of the scale degrees if one remembers that I is the Tonic and V is the Dominant. All the other degrees take their names from their relation to these.

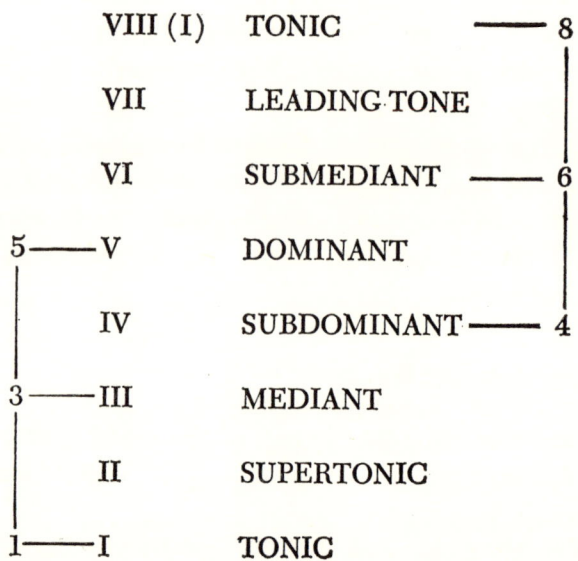

Major scale pattern

The major scale has a distinctive pattern of whole and half-steps which marks the progression from a tonic to its octave. This pattern never varies; the major scale always has the same quality of sound. Let us examine the

---

* Some theorists hold that the fourth degree is called the Subdominant because it is as far below the Tonic as the Dominant is above it.

THE MAJOR SCALE

stepwise progression in the scale which was extracted from the melody "Three Blind Mice" (page 97).

Pitch	C	D	E	F	G	A	B	C
Degree	1	2	3	4	5	6	7	8
Distance in steps	whole	whole	half	whole	whole	whole	half	

This is a major scale. A *major scale* is one which has a whole step between every degree except between 3 and 4, and 7 and 8, where there are half steps. (The major scale has the same pattern of whole and half steps as the Ionian mode, illustrated on page 92.)

The scale derived from "Three Blind Mice" when that piece begins on E is called the C Major scale. The melody is said to be in the key of C major because C is the tonal center. Play the C major scale again: start with the left hand (5 - 4 - 3 - 2) and finish with the right hand (2 - 3 - 4 - 5). This demonstrates that the major scale consists of two tetrachords (two groups of four successive tones) of identical pattern:

```
  1       2       3      4    5       6       7       8
WHOLE   WHOLE   HALF   whole  WHOLE   WHOLE   HALF
```

The *kind of sound* that is associated with the major scale is always the same, whether the scale is played on the piano, violin, or any other instrument; whether it lies in a high or low register; or whatever different tonal center it may have. Furthermore, each degree has its own quality of rest or activity in relation to its tonal center: the tonic is restful, the leading tone active, and so forth. In the key of C, C is a rest tone while B is an active tone. This is valid so long as C is the tonal center.

Now that we have sampled one major scale, let us learn to form all of the other major scales. A major scale may be constructed by beginning with any key on the piano and following the major scale pattern of whole and half steps through to its octave. By applying the pattern to each white and black key *as a new tonic*, we can construct twelve different major scales. Start with a C and play a major scale. Then start with C♯ and, using the same pattern, play its major scale. Proceed *chromatically*, that is, by semitones, through the rest of the twelve white and black keys that lie between C and its octave, C, and play the remaining major scales.

THE MAJOR SCALE

The written scale

When major scales are represented on the staff, certain signs are used to indicate the raising or lowering of a tone or tones necessary to the completion of the pattern of whole and half steps. Thus, proper notation can identify the white and black keys needed to produce the sound of the desired scale.

The C Major Scale can be represented on the staff without any special sign because the lines and spaces of the staff, like the C Major Scale itself, match the white keys of a keyboard instrument. This can be seen in the following illustration:

C *Major Scale on the staff*

C *Major Scale on the piano*

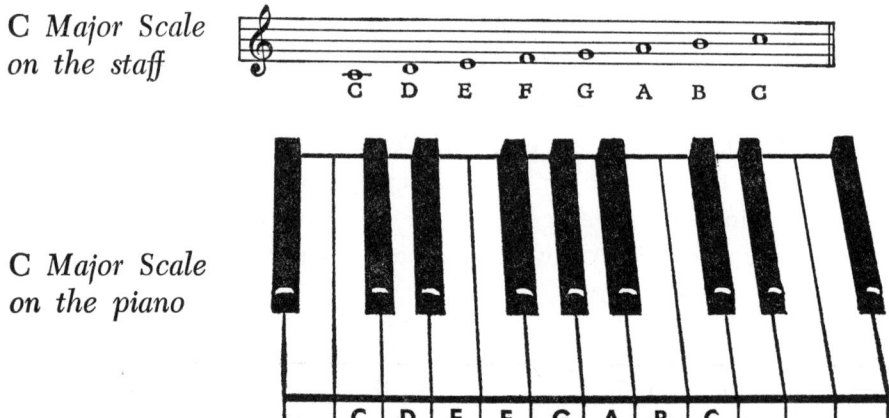

This is not true of the other major scales. For these, sharps and flats (pp. 18–19) are used in written music to show the change from a *natural* or white-key location of a letter name to a different key location and variation of the same letter name.

Use of the sharp

In writing the G major scale we use the following staff lines and spaces:

These lines and spaces indicate the following white keys:

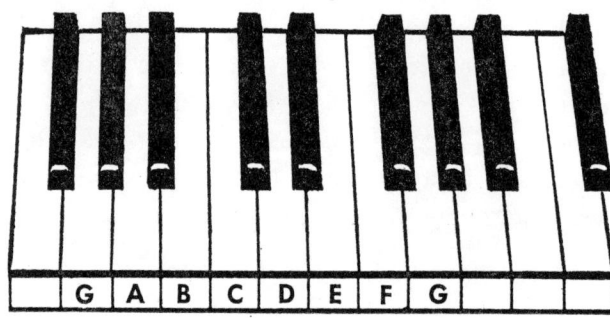

THE MAJOR SCALE

Play what has been written above and compare the sound of this scale with the sound you recognize as a major scale. The ear is dissatisfied with the sound of the progression E - F - G. The white key E is the sixth degree of the G major scale. The major scale pattern calls for the seventh degree to be a whole step higher than the sixth degree. F follows E in the alphabet, so the letter name F *must be used* for the seventh degree. However, since the white key F is only a semitone higher than E, it does not satisfy the major scale pattern. Therefore, the black key to the right of F must take the place of the white key F. In this case the black key takes its name from the white key F and is called *F-sharp*, or *F♯*. This is shown in written music by placing the chromatic sign, ♯, *before the note* on the F line of the staff.

G Major Scale on the staff

G Major Scale on the piano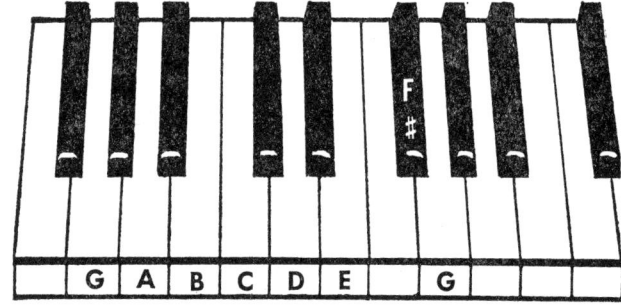

Use of the flat

Some major scales call for another kind of chromatic alteration. In writing the F major scale we use the following staff lines and spaces:

THE MAJOR SCALE

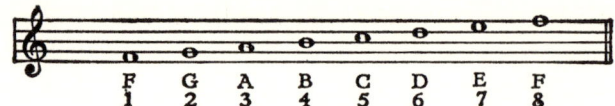

These lines and spaces indicate the following white keys:

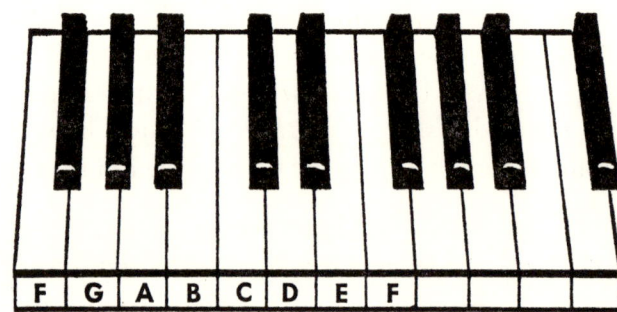

Play what has been written above and compare the sound of this scale with the sound you recognize as a major scale. In this instance, the progression A - B - C does not satisfy. The white key A is the third degree of the F major scale. The major scale pattern requires that the fourth degree be but a semitone higher than the third degree. B follows A in the alphabet, so the letter name B *must be used* for the fourth degree. However, since the white key B is a whole tone higher than A, it does not satisfy the major scale pattern. Therefore, the black key to the left of B must take the place of the white key B. In this case the black key takes its name from the white key B. Remember: In correct musical *spelling*, letter names are used but once in a scale; they cannot be repeated. In this scale the letter A has been used for the third degree; therefore, the fourth degree cannot be called by the letter name A; the black key cannot be called A-sharp. The letter name for the fourth degree of a scale beginning on F must be B and in the F major scale the black key representing the fourth degree takes its name from B and is called *B-flat*, or B♭. This is shown in written music by placing the chromatic sign ♭ *before the note* on the B line of the staff.

THE MAJOR SCALE

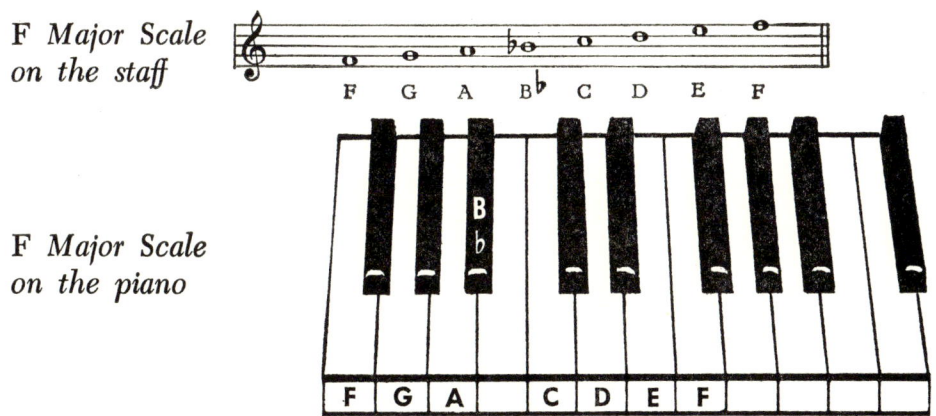

F *Major Scale on the staff*

F *Major Scale on the piano*

To sum up: the sharp sign ♯ is placed before a note to indicate that the tone represented by the letter name is to be *raised* a half step; the flat sign ♭ is placed before a note to indicate that the tone represented by the letter name is to be *lowered* a half step. In writing chromatic signs, the sign must be placed on the line or space to which it refers. It is not sufficient to have only the note on the proper staff degree—the chromatic sign must be properly located, too.

Right   *Wrong*

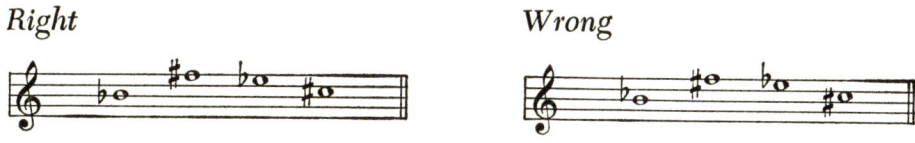

Accidentals

Chromatic signs are also called *accidentals* (from Latin *accidens,* something that happens to, and therefore changes, something else). Strictly speaking, the term *chromatic* refers to tones not in the regular diatonic scale; the term *accidental* refers to the occasional use of such signs in the course of a composition.

For the History of Accidentals, see the end of this chapter.

An accidental raises or lowers the pitch of a note but it does not destroy the letter-name identity of that note. For example, a ♯ before B raises the pitch a half step from B to B-sharp. Certainly, the pitch of B-sharp is the same as that of the white key C-natural, because C-natural is only a half step above B-natural, but the sharp refers to B, and its altered pitch has identity with the letter name B and not with the letter name C. Because the white keys B and C, and E and F are not separated by black keys they may have additional names: B may be B-natural or C-flat; C may be C-natural or

THE MAJOR SCALE

B-sharp; E may be E-natural or F-flat, and F may be F-natural or E-sharp.

Single chromatic alterations as they appear on the staff and are located on the keyboard:

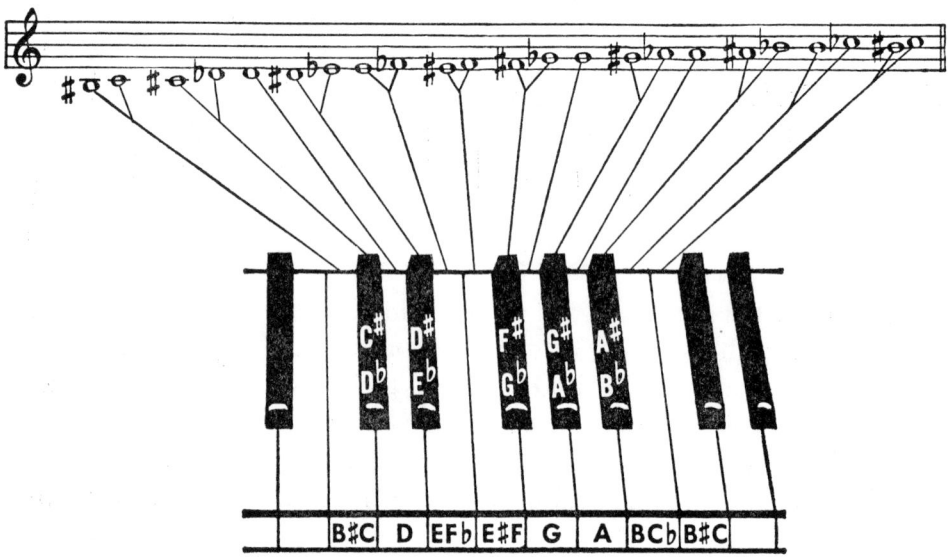

An accidental affects the pitch of a note through the entire bar unless it is counteracted by another kind of accidental. However, the bar line cancels all accidentals that appear within the bar before it. In order to continue a temporary alteration of pitch, an accidental must be repeated in each succeeding bar, unless the note affected is tied over from one bar to the next.

In addition to the sharp and flat, there are three more chromatic signs or accidentals: the *natural,* the *double sharp,* and the *double flat.*

The natural

The symbol ♮, called a *natural* or *natural sign,* is used to cancel any previous chromatic alteration.

The double sharp and double flat

The *double sharp* (𝄪) and *double flat* (♭♭) came into common usage about the time of the composition of "The Well-Tempered Clavier" [a collection of preludes and fugues in all the major and minor keys] by Johann

THE MAJOR SCALE

Sebastian Bach (Vol. I, 1722; Vol. II, 1742). The double-sharp sign is used to indicate that a tone is to be raised two half steps, or one whole step. Likewise, the double-flat sign is used to indicate that a tone is to be lowered two half steps, or one whole step. (A use of the double sharp is shown on p. 125; the double flat is rarely used.)

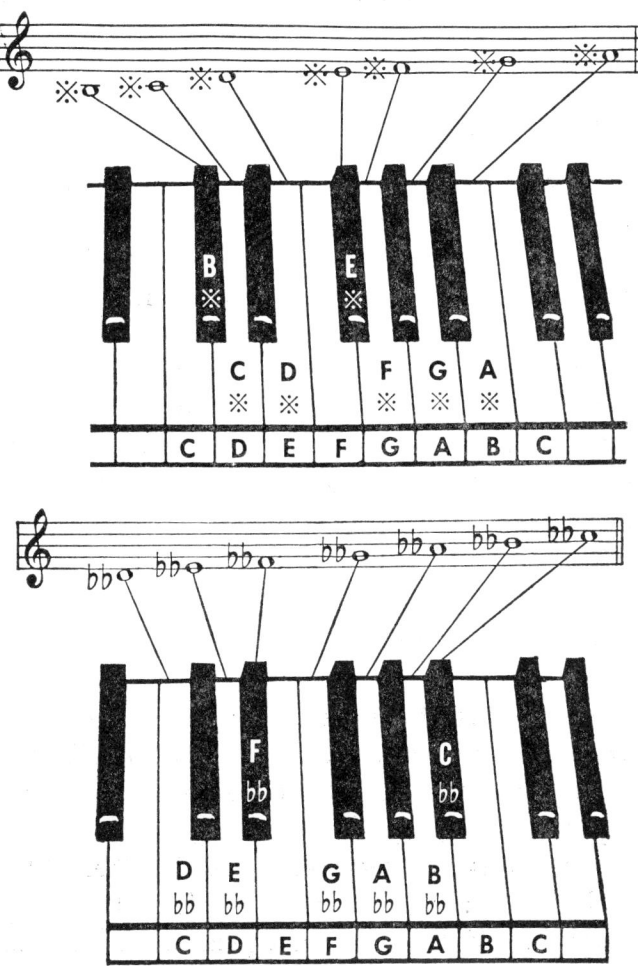

Within a bar, to indicate a natural note after a double flat or double sharp, simply write a ♮ before the note. To indicate a flatted note *after* a double flat write ♮♭ before the note; to indicate a sharped note after a double sharp write ♮♯ before the note.

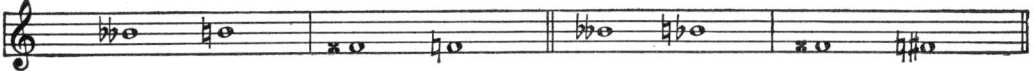

THE MAJOR SCALE

In our discussion of the piano (Chapter 3) we stated that the white keys have names of their own and that the black keys usually get their names from the white keys next to them. Now we see that even the white keys may have second names: B♯ has the same pitch as C♮; F♭ has the same pitch as E♮, and so forth. Furthermore, the double sharp and double flat create additional names for both white and black keys. For example, C♮ has the same pitch as D♭♭ and B♯; C♯ has the same pitch as D♭ and B𝄪.

Enharmonic change

The reader may ask why we write F𝄪 when it sounds the same as G♮. The answer lies in the requirements of correct musical *spelling*. To illustrate: One of the chords we can build on E♭ contains three notes: E♭–G–B♭. However, if (because of the context in which it is found) the same-sounding chord were built on D♯, the notes would be correctly spelled: D♯–F𝄪–A♯. Such a change in notation which affects the spelling but does not affect the pitch of a note or group of notes is called *enharmonic change*.

As an exercise in the principle of enharmonic change, give other names for the twelve half steps which lie within an octave: C, C♯, D, D♯, E, F, F♯, G, G♯, A, A♯, and B.

PLAYING THE MAJOR SCALES

Scales, in whole or in part, form the substance of many songs and much piano music. It is important, then, for the student not only to understand the principle of the major scale, but also to be able to play the different ones on the piano.

The following chart shows the major scale with 15 different tonics or keynotes. They are listed with suggested fingerings for both the right and left hands. The student should be able to recognize all of them, but he must master a few. A command of nine major scales: C, G, D, A, E, F, B♭, E♭, and A♭ is enough to meet the demands of most songs and simple piano pieces.

Note: In practicing scales use the same fingering every time. Finger memory, a result of exact repetition, is an important aid in learning to play scales smoothly and quickly.

THE MAJOR SCALE

Major Scales
with suggested fingerings

107

THE MAJOR SCALE

Summary of suggested fingerings for major scales

C and Sharp Scales

Right Hand

C, G, D, A, E, and B major scales
    4th finger on 7th step

F♯ and C♯ major scales
    4th finger on A♯

Left Hand

C, G, D, A, and E major scales
    4th finger on 2nd step

B, F♯, and C♯ major scales
    4th finger on F♯

Flat Scales

Right Hand

All flat scales
    4th finger on B♭

Left Hand

F major scale
    4th finger on 2nd step

B♭, E♭, A♭, and D♭ major scales
    4th finger on 4th step

G♭ and C♭ major scales
    4th finger on G♭

The major scales have been presented on the treble staff. On music-manuscript paper, write all the major scales on the bass staff.

ORDER OF SHARPS AND FLATS

Major scales

In major scales having sharps, the fifth degree (Dominant) of one scale is the same as the first degree (Tonic) of the scale having one additional sharp. For example, the Dominant (V) of the C major scale is G; G is the Tonic (I) of the scale having one sharp. V of the G major scale is D; D is I of the scale having two sharps.

The keys of major scales having sharps progress in a series of *ascending fifths*. Play the following series on the piano.

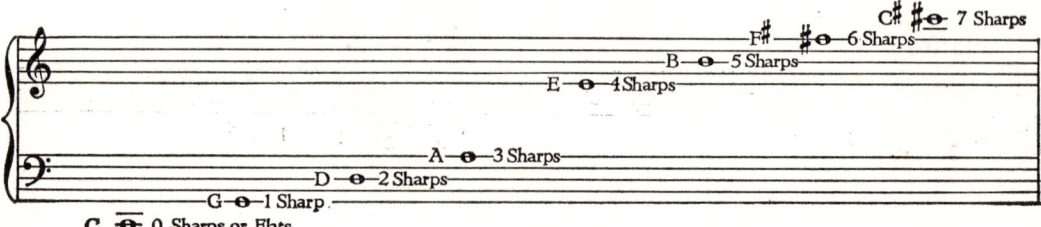

THE MAJOR SCALE

In major scales having flats, the fourth degree (Subdominant) of one scale is the same as the first degree (Tonic) of the scale having one additional flat. For example, the Subdominant (IV) of the C major scale is F; F is the Tonic (I) of the scale having one flat. IV of the F major scale is B♭; B♭ is I of the scale having two flats.

But notice: the *fourth step up* the scale is the same as the *fifth step down*. Therefore, keys of major scales having flats progress in a series of *descending fifths*. Play the following series on the piano.

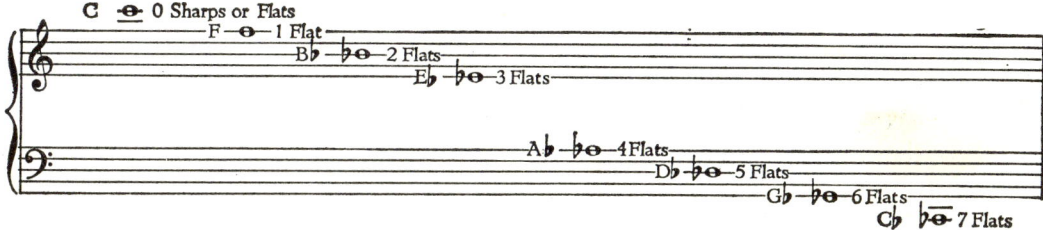

Circle of fifths
(Major scales)

A standard method of charting the order of sharps and flats is one which employs the locations of the hours on a clock. The progression of sharps

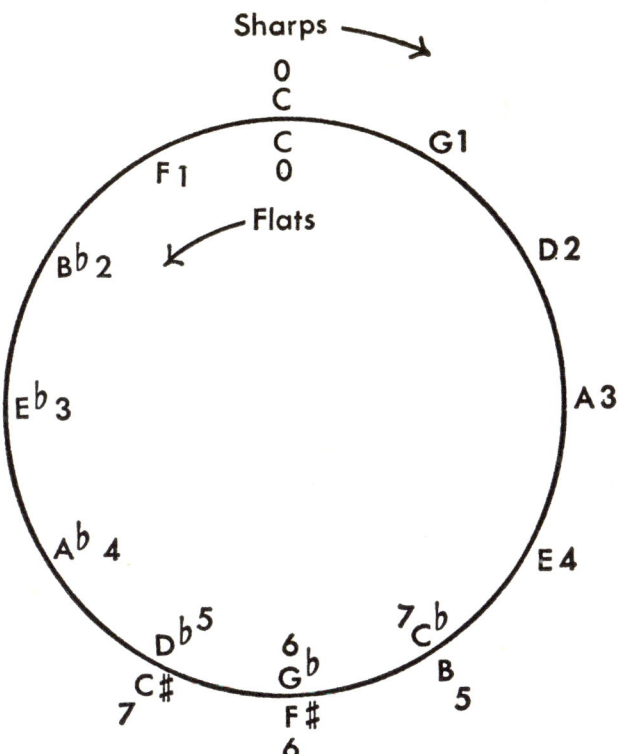

THE MAJOR SCALE

(1 to 7) is shown in a series that proceeds clockwise on the dial; the progression of flats (1 to 7) is shown by a series that proceeds counterclockwise. Observe: In three instances, the flat scale and the sharp scale, at 5, 6, and 7, are identical in sound—only the spelling differs. B major (at 5) sounds the same as C♭ major; F♯ major (at 6) the same as G♭ major; and, C♯ major (at 7) the same as D♭ major.

Key signatures

In the major-scale chart (page 107), each sharp or flat was placed before the note it affected. As the number of sharps and flats increase the readability of music is lessened because of the great number of accidentals that must stand before the notes. The separate writing of accidentals in a composition whose tonality calls for many sharps or flats becomes tedious for the composer and an annoyance to the performer. This can be avoided when a piece remains, in general, within the same tonality. The accidentals are simply grouped at the beginning of the staff to the right of the clef. This is called a *key signature*. So long as the key signature remains the same, it is repeated after the clef *at the beginning of every staff line*.

The order of sharps or flats in a key signature is determined by the order in which the sharps or flats occur in the major scales.

The key of G major has but one sharp: F♯; therefore, F♯ is the first and only sharp written for the key signature of G major. The key of D major has two sharps: F♯ and C♯; therefore, in the key signature for D major, F♯ is written first and C♯ is written second. In the key of A major, the key signature is written as follows: F♯, first; C♯, second; and G♯, third. In this manner, the order of writing sharps in the signature continues through the seven sharp keys.

The key of F major has but one flat: B♭; therefore, B♭ is the first and only flat written for the key signature of F major. The key of B♭ major has two flats: B♭ and E♭; therefore, in the key signature for B♭ major, B♭ is written first and E♭ is written second. In the key of E♭ major, the key signature is written as follows: B♭, first; E♭, second; and A♭, third. In this manner, the order of writing flats in the signature continues through the seven flat keys.

THE MAJOR SCALE

Major Key Signatures

111

THE MAJOR SCALE

HINTS

The key signature, itself, offers a clue to the major key it represents. The keynote of a major key with sharps is one half step above the last sharp in the signature. For example, the last sharp in the signature of two sharps is C♯—the keynote is D; the last sharp in the signature of four sharps is D♯—the keynote is E. (Illustrated on p. 111.)

The keynote of a major key with two or more flats is the same as the *next-to-last flat* in the signature. For example, the next-to-last flat in the signature of two flats is B♭—the keynote is B♭; the next-to-last flat in the signature of four flats is A♭—the keynote is A♭. (Illustrated on p. 111.)

An arithmetical oddity occurs when we add the number of sharps and flats that are in the two keys with the same letter name. The total is always 7.

The key of C major has neither sharps nor flats; therefore, its key signature is one of no sharps or flats. If the number of accidentals in this signature is paired with those of C♯ major (seven sharps) the combination is $0 + 7 = 7$; if paired with those of C♭ major (seven flats) the combination is the same $0 + 7 = 7$. Each of the other pairs of keys with the same letter name also have a number of sharps and flats which adds up to 7 accidentals.

PAIRED KEYS		PAIRED SHARPS AND FLATS		TOTAL ACCIDENTALS
G	G♭	1	6	7
D	D♭	2	5	7
A	A♭	3	4	7
E	E♭	4	3	7
B	B♭	5	2	7
F♯	F	6	1	7

The major-minor system plays a very important part in the music of our heritage. An understanding of the various aspects of the major scale is essential to the study of the minor scale (next chapter) and that branch of music theory which deals with intervals (Chapter 15) and harmony (Chapters 16 ff.).

HISTORY OF ACCIDENTALS

Chromatic signs were introduced about the year 1000 A.D., after letter notation was in use. The first of these signs was the flat. In two of the Church modes, Dorian (same as the white-key scale beginning on D) and Lydian (same as the white-key scale beginning on F) the B was often changed to B♭ to give a "softer" sound. Later, to distinguish between the flatted B which became common to these modes and the natural B which was characteristic of the others, the tone B♭ was given a letter name all its own, the round B (b), called *b rotundum,* while B-natural was shown by the square B ♮, called *B quadratum.* Thus, B♭ was added to the tones available for melodic composition. Since then the round b has become our flat sign, ♭; the square B our natural sign, ♮.

The sharp sign (♯) came later and derives from the square B. Called *B cancellatum,* it was a latticed figure ✶, used to indicate that the tone B-flat was to be raised to B-natural. Subsequently it was used to direct the raised alteration of other tones. The Saint Andrew's cross ✗ also was adopted as a sharp sign and in the course of time it assumed various forms: ※ ✕.

CHAPTER 14

MINOR SCALES

As the major scale is identified with the Ionian mode, so the minor scale has identity with the Aeolian mode (Chapter 12). The important difference between the major and minor scale is the size of the step between 2 and 3. In the major scale the distance is a whole step; in the minor scale, a half step. However, unlike the major scale, which has but one pattern of whole and half steps marking the progression from a tonic to its octave, the minor scale has no completely exclusive pattern. Several kinds of minor scale (each with its own pattern) have found a place in modern usage: *natural* or *pure minor*, *harmonic minor,* and *melodic minor*. Generally speaking, since the Baroque Era (c. 1600–1750) few compositions have been written in only the natural, harmonic, or melodic minor. In practice, composers have employed a mixture of all three forms, altering certain degrees according to their function. Nevertheless, these three forms are considered here for the purpose of showing their characteristics and providing specific keyboard association.

Natural minor scale

The natural minor scale is so called because, like the major scale, its pattern demands no accidentals other than those in the key signature. The pat-

MINOR SCALES

terns of the other two minor scales require chromatic alterations in addition to those expressed by the key signature.

The natural minor scale, the same as the Aeolian mode, is most simply represented by the progression of the eight white keys beginning with A. Starting on the A below middle C, play this scale upward.

A Natural Minor Scale on the staff

A Natural Minor Scale on the piano

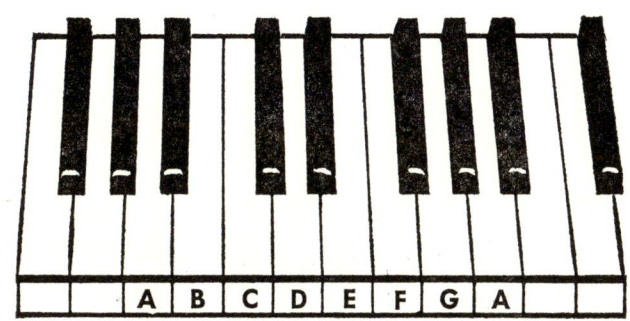

Notice the pattern of whole and half steps that attends this scale.

Pitch	A	B	C	D	E	F	G	A
Degree	1	2	3	4	5	6	7	8
Distance in steps		Whole	Half	Whole	Whole	Half	Whole	Whole

Here, the semitones, or half steps, occur between 2 - 3 and 5 - 6 instead of between 3 - 4 and 7 - 8, as in the major scale. The critical difference between the minor and the major scales lies in the half step coming between 2 - 3 instead of between 3 - 4. Play the first tone of the A minor scale, A; then the third tone, C. Play the two tones together. Now play the first tone of the A major scale, A; now the third tone, C♯. Play these two together. Notice the difference in the sound of A–C and A–C♯. Here is the important difference between major and minor: in all major scales the distance between the first and third degrees is two whole steps; in *all minor scales* the distance between the first and third degrees is only one whole step and one half step.

Relative major and minor

Note in the following example the relation that exists between the C major and the A minor scales: they both have the same key signature—no sharps

MINOR SCALES

or flats. Observe, too, that A (the keynote, or tonic, of this minor scale) is the sixth degree (VI, Submediant) of the C major scale. The sixth tone up a major scale is, of course, the same as the third tone *down*.

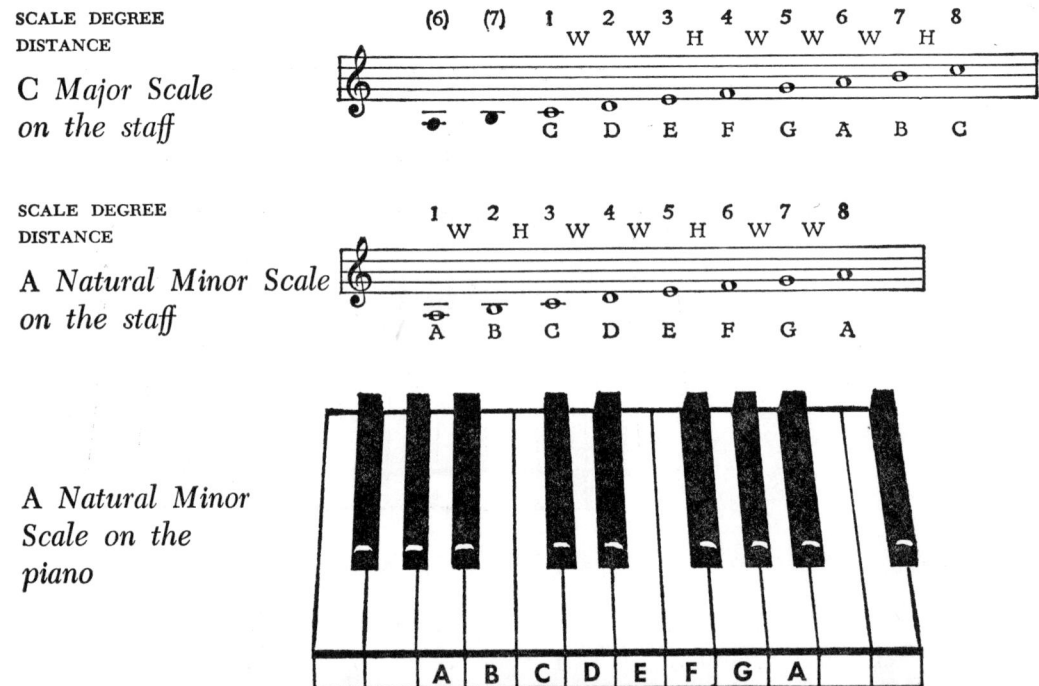

When major and minor scales and keys have the same key signature they are said to be related—C major is the *relative major* of A minor, while A minor is the *relative minor* of C major.

The key of G major has one sharp: F♯. The sixth degree (VI) of G major is E. G major is the relative major of E minor, while E minor is the relative minor of G major.

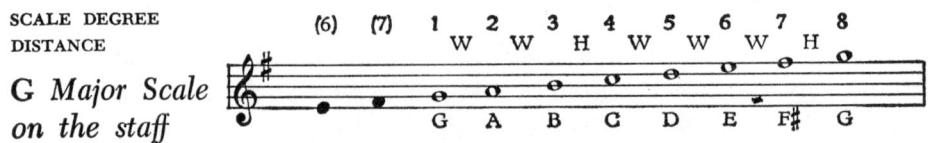

MINOR SCALES

SCALE DEGREE DISTANCE

E Natural Minor Scale on the staff

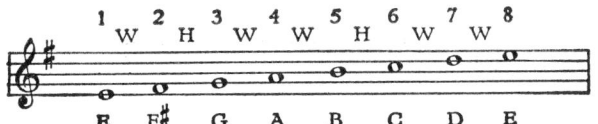

E Natural Minor Scale on the piano

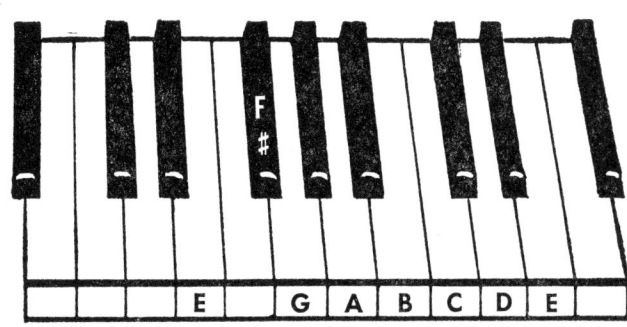

The key of F major has one flat: B♭. The sixth degree (VI) of F major is D. F major is the relative major of D minor, while D minor is the relative minor of F major.

SCALE DEGREE DISTANCE

F Major Scale on the staff

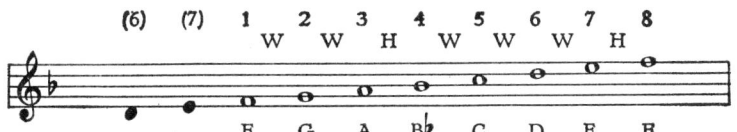

SCALE DEGREE DISTANCE

D Natural Minor Scale on the staff

D Natural Minor Scale on the piano

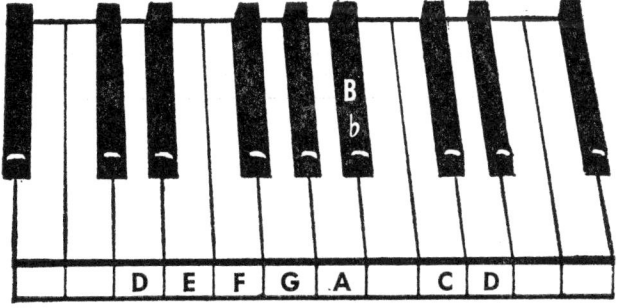

MINOR SCALES

ORDER OF SHARPS AND FLATS

Minor scales

The minor scales nave the same order of sharps and flats as the major scales. In minor scales having sharps, the fifth degree (V) of one scale is the same as the first degree (I) of the scale having one additional sharp. For example, V of A minor is E; E is I of the minor scale having one sharp. V of E minor is B; B is the I of the minor scale having two sharps.

The keys of minor scales having sharps progress in a series of *ascending fifths*. Play the following series on the piano.

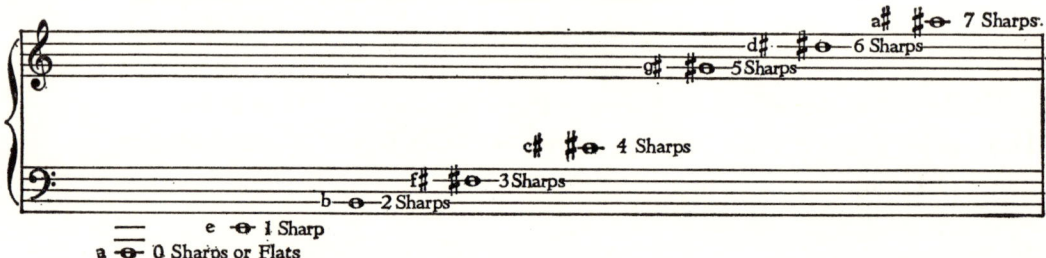

In minor scales having flats, the fourth degree (IV) of one scale is the same as the first degree (I) of the scale having one additional flat. For example, IV of A minor is D; D is I of the minor scale having one flat. IV of the D minor scale is G; G is I of the minor scale having two flats.

But, again, notice: the *fourth step up* the scale is the same as the *fifth step down*. Therefore, the keys of minor scales having flats progress in a series of *descending fifths*. Play the following series on the piano.

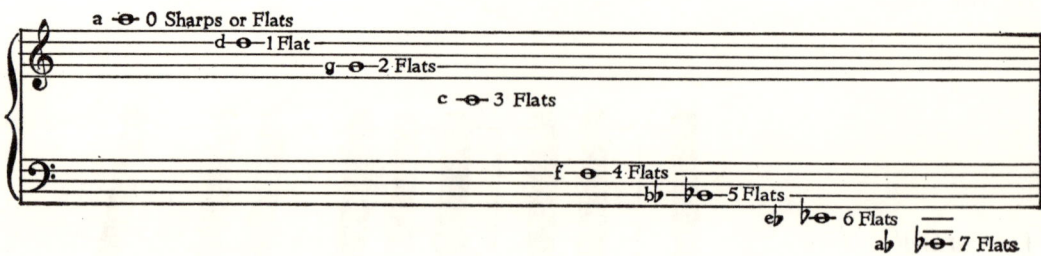

MINOR SCALES

Circle of fifths
Major and minor scales

Because the order of sharps and flats is the same for both the major and minor scales we may take the illustration on page 109 and add to the keytones of the major scales their relative minors. (*Capital* letters indicate major; *small* letters, minor.)

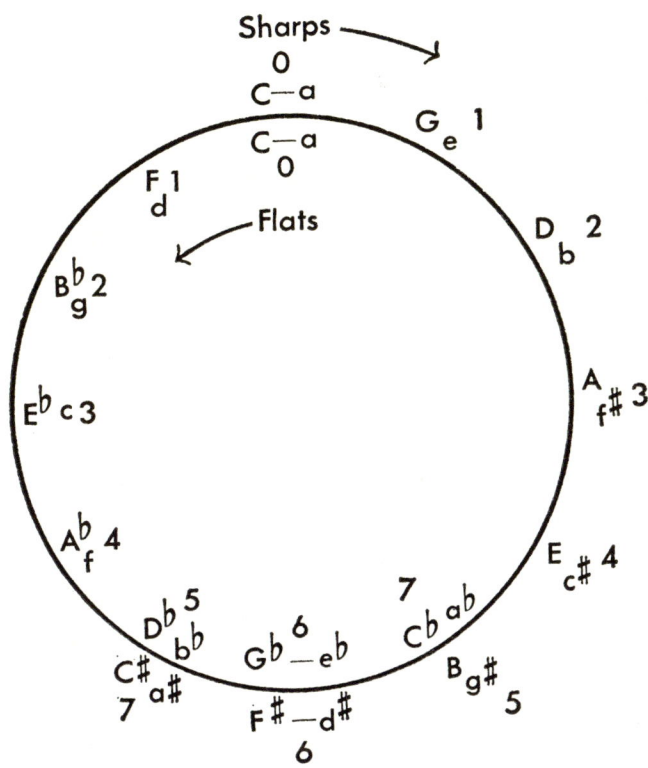

MINOR SCALES

Minor Key Signatures

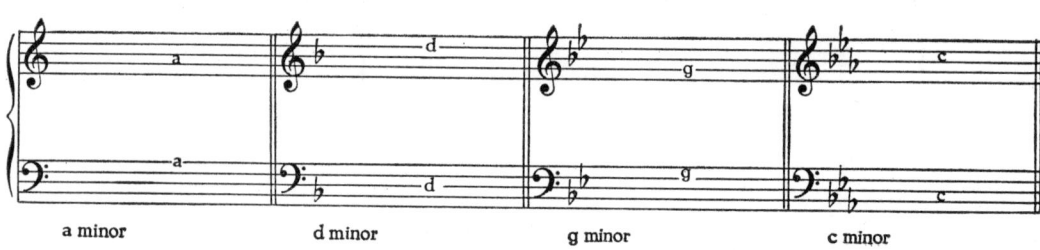

MINOR SCALES

PLAYING THE NATURAL MINOR SCALES

The following chart shows the major and their related natural **minor** scales with 15 different tonics or keynotes. Traditionally, the major tonic is indicated by a capital letter; the minor, by a small letter. The natural minor scales have suggested fingerings for both the right and left hands. The student should be able to recognize all of them, but he must master a few. Learn to play those through four sharps and four flats.

Note: It is important to use the same fingering every time a scale is practiced.

In these and the next charts, the minor scales are presented on the bass staff. This is done so as to give the student additional practice in reading the lines and spaces of the bass staff. On music-manuscript paper, write all the natural minor scales on the treble staff.

MINOR SCALES

122 *The Major and Relative Natural Minor Scales
with suggested fingerings*

The Sharp Scales

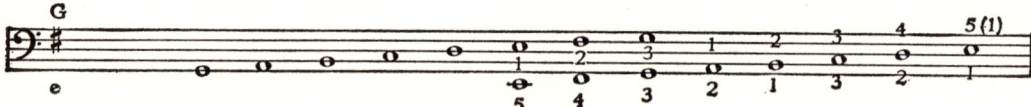

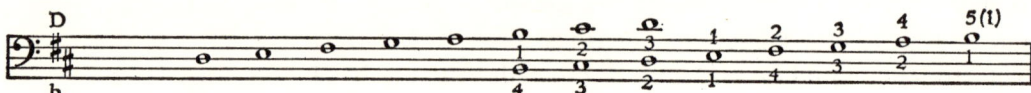

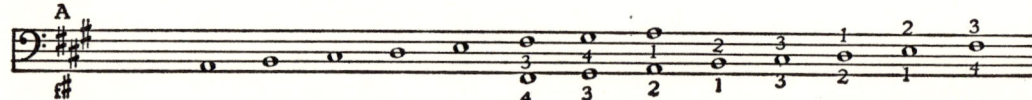

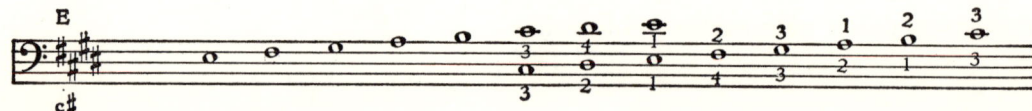

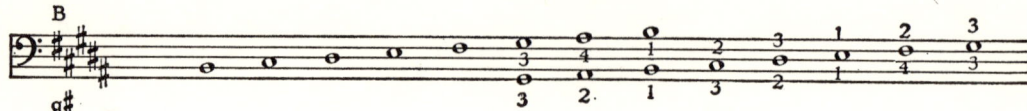

MINOR SCALES

The Flat Scales

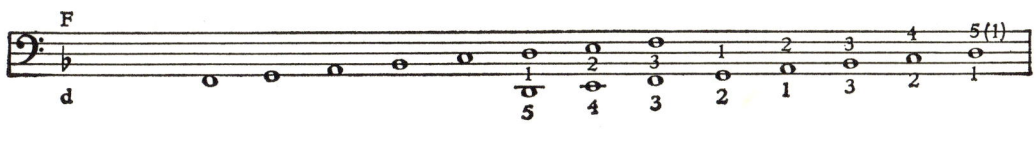
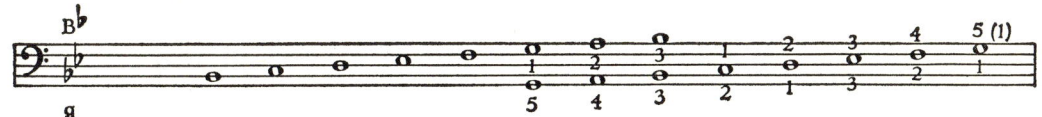

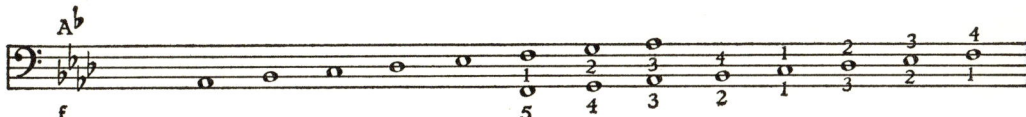
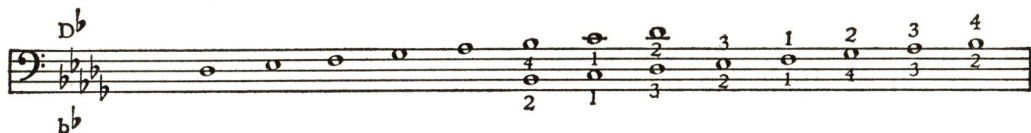
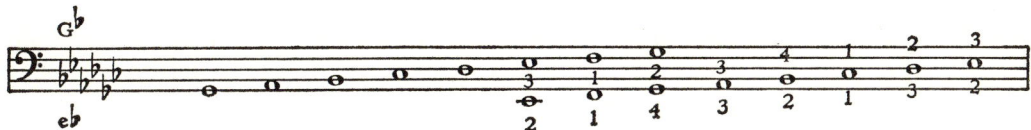

MINOR SCALES

Summary of suggested fingerings for natural minor scales

a and Sharp Scales

Right Hand

a, e, and b
    4th finger on 7th step
f♯, c♯, and g♯
    4th finger on 2nd step
d♯ and a♯
    4th finger on A♯

Left Hand

a and e
    4th finger on 2nd step
b, f♯, c♯, g♯, d♯, and a♯
    4th finger on F♯

Flat Scales

Right Hand

d, g, and c
    4th finger on 7th step
f, b♭, e♭, and a♭
    4th finger on B♭

Left Hand

d, g, c, and f
    4th finger on 2nd step
b♭, e♭, and a♭
    4th finger on G♭

VARIATIONS OF THE A MINOR SCALE

Harmonic minor scale

For History of the Harmonic Minor Scale, see the end of this chapter.

The *harmonic minor* is a term given to that variation of the minor scale in which the seventh degree is raised a half step so that the distance between 7 and 8 is only a half step. It is like the natural minor scale with this one exception, the raised seventh. The raised seventh is an identifying characteristic of the harmonic minor scale.

MINOR SCALES

a *Natural Minor Scale on the staff*

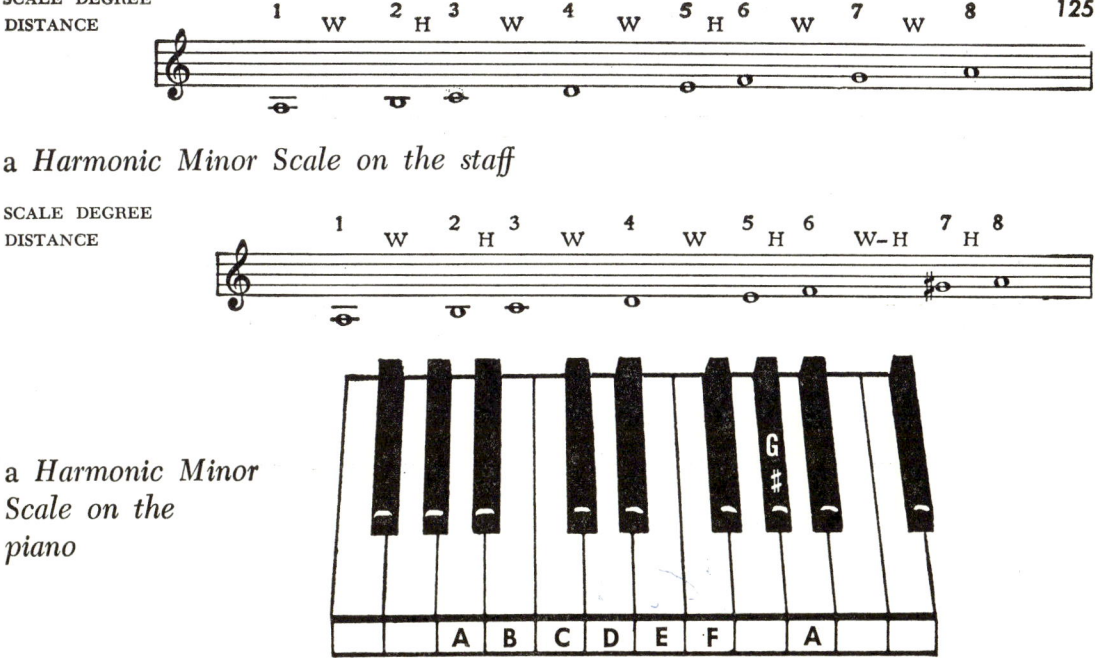

a *Harmonic Minor Scale on the staff*

a *Harmonic Minor Scale on the piano*

As in the natural minor scale, the key signature of the harmonic minor scale is the same as its relative major, and its tonic (I) is the same as the sixth degree (VI) of its relative major scale.

PLAYING THE HARMONIC MINOR SCALES

The following chart shows the major and their related harmonic minor scales with 15 different tonics or keynotes. As before, the major keynote is indicated by a capital letter; the minor, by a small letter. The harmonic minor scales have suggested fingerings for both the right and left hands. Learn to recognize all the harmonic minor scales; learn to play those through four sharps and four flats. On music-manuscript paper rewrite all the harmonic minor scales on the treble staff.

Note: In the g♯, d♯, and a♯ natural minor scales the seventh tone occurs already sharped by the key signature. The harmonic minor demands that the seventh tone be raised an additional half step. On page 105 we explained that the *double sharp* sign ✕ is used to indicate that a tone is to be raised two half steps, or one whole step. It is this sign which is placed before the seventh degrees in the g♯, d♯, and a♯ harmonic minor scales.

MINOR SCALES

The Major and Relative Harmonic Minor Scales with suggested fingerings

The Sharp Scales

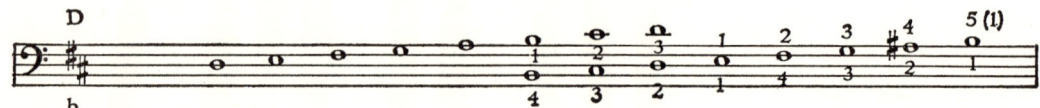
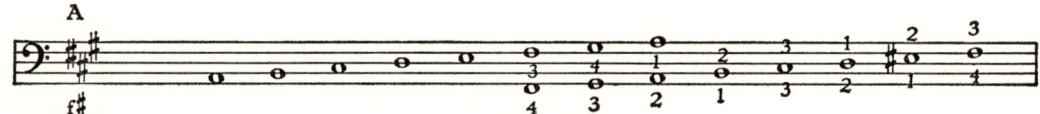
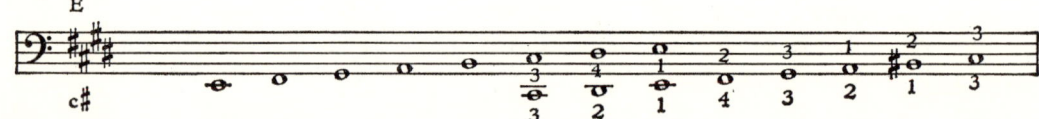

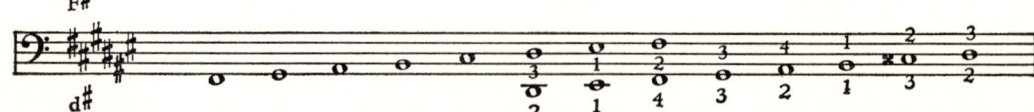

MINOR SCALES

The Flat Scales

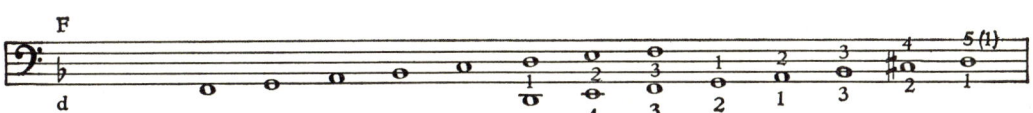
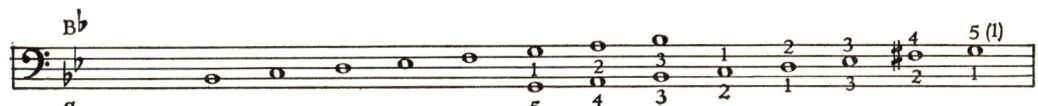

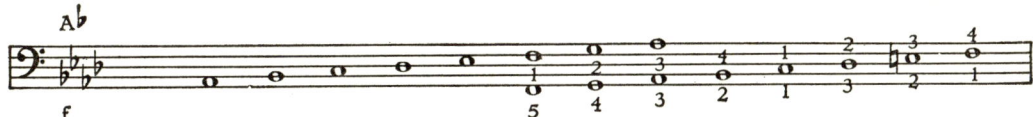

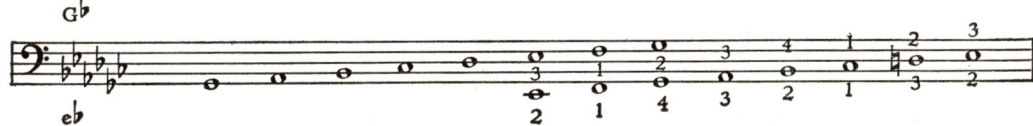

MINOR SCALES

Summary of suggested fingerings for harmonic minor scales

a *and Sharp Scales*	*Flat Scales*

Right Hand

a, e, and b
    4th finger on 7th step
f♯, c♯, and g♯
    4th finger on 2nd step
d♯ and a♯
    4th finger on A♯

Left Hand

a and e
    4th finger on 2nd step
b, f♯, c♯, and d♯
    4th finger on F♯
g♯ 4th finger on C♯
a♯ thumb on white keys

Right Hand

d, g, and c
    4th finger on 7th step
f, b♭, e♭, and a♭
    4th finger on B♭

Left Hand

d, g, c, and f
    4th finger on 2nd step
b♭ thumb on white keys
e♭ 4th finger on G♭
a♭ 4th finger on D♭

Melodic minor scale

For History of the Melodic Minor scale, see the end of this chapter.

Examine the harmonic minor scale; you will notice that the distance between the sixth and seventh degrees is a step and a half. This is larger than the distance between any other two degrees. Play the *a* harmonic minor scale on the piano.

MINOR SCALES

a *Harmonic Minor Scale on the staff*

a *Harmonic Minor Scale on the piano*

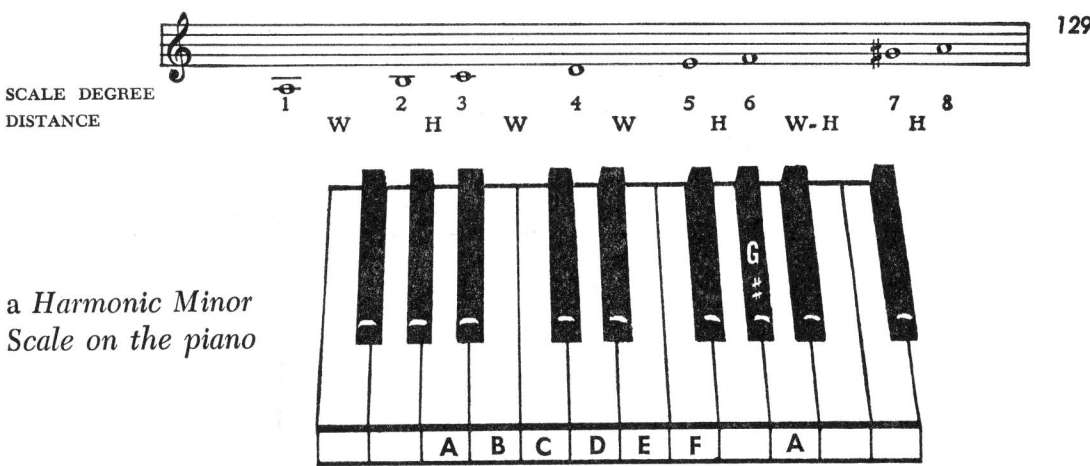

Sing the *a* harmonic minor scale. You may find it a bit difficult to sing the step and a half: F–G♯. In the seventeenth century, it was not only a vocal problem—it was harsh to the ear. To avoid this large skip, composers wrote melodies in which the sixth degree as well as the seventh degree of the natural minor scale was raised a half step *when the melodic line ascended*. With both degrees raised a half step the ascending minor scale became a progression of whole and half steps, with a smooth, dynamic drive to the upper tonic. Play the *ascending* scale on the piano; then sing it.

a *Melodic Minor Scale on the staff* (Ascending)

a *Melodic Minor Scale on the piano* (Ascending)

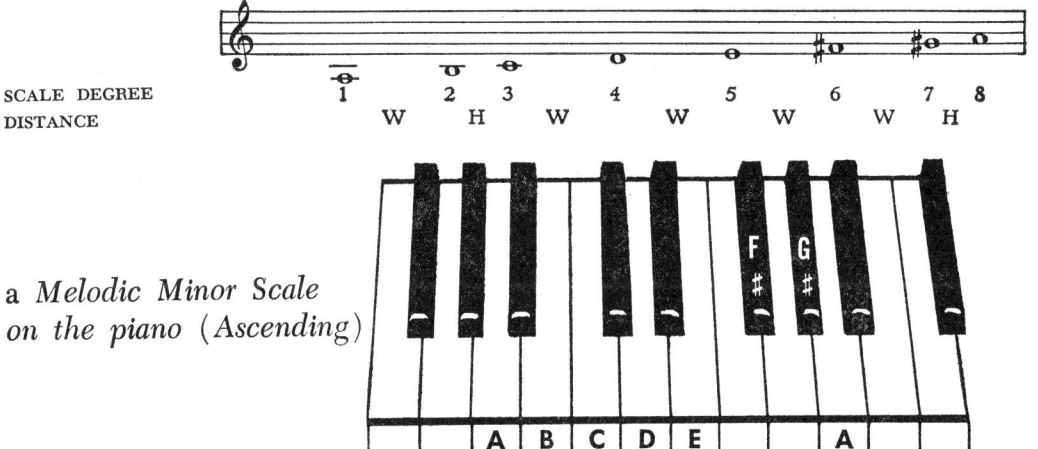

To provide a smooth *descending* melodic line which, at the same time, preserves the minor character of the scale, composers lowered both the sixth and seventh degrees to their *natural* (as in the natural minor scale) position.

MINOR SCALES

a *Melodic Minor Scale on the staff* (Descending)

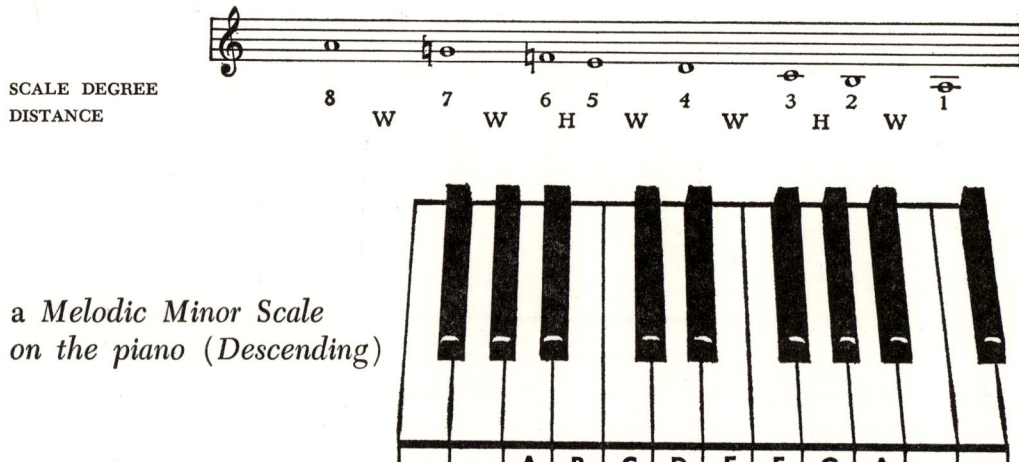

a *Melodic Minor Scale on the piano* (Descending)

PLAYING THE MELODIC MINOR SCALES

The following chart shows the major and their related melodic minor scales with 15 different tonics or keynotes. Again, the major keynote is indicated by a capital letter; the minor, by a small letter. The melodic minor scales have suggested fingerings for both the right and left hands. In five cases, the fingering for the ascending scale differs from that of the descending scale. These scales are:

Right Hand—f♯ and c♯   Left Hand—g♯, a♯, and b♭

Learn to recognize all the melodic minor scales; learn to play those through four sharps and four flats. On music-manuscript paper, rewrite all the melodic minor scales on the bass staff.

MINOR SCALES

The Major and Relative Melodic Minor Scales
with suggested fingerings

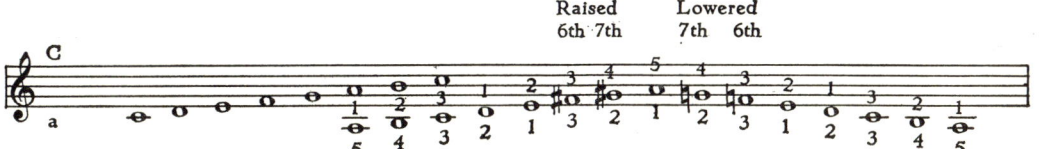

The Sharp Scales

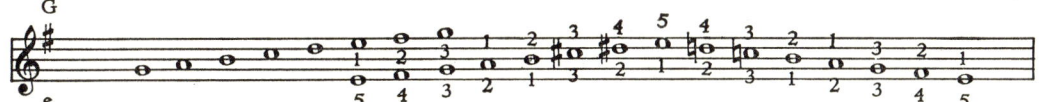

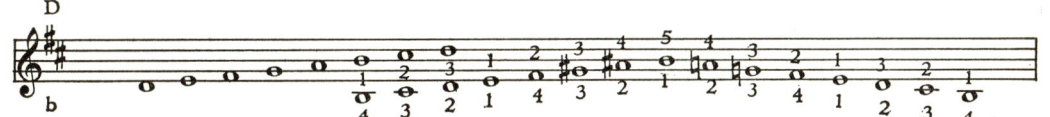

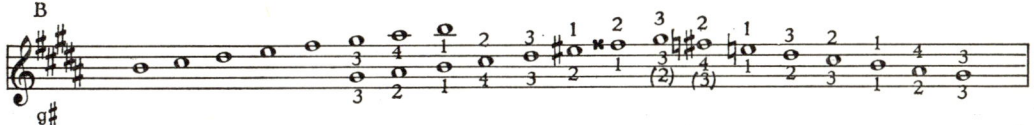

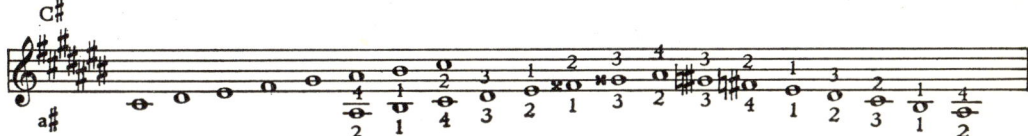

MINOR SCALES

The Flat Scales

MINOR SCALES

Parallel major and minor

A major key and its relative minor have the same key signature; likewise, a minor key and its relative major have the same key signature. However, this is all they have in common. For example, *C* major and *a* minor have the same signature—no sharps or flats. The similarity ends here. In every instance the scale degrees are different. The tonic (I) of *C* is *C*; the tonic (I) of *a* is *a*. The dominant (V) of *C* is *G*; the dominant (V) of *a* is *E*. The subdominant (IV) of *C* is *F*; the subdominant (IV) of *a* is *D*. No scale degrees are the same; neither are the harmonies they imply.

On the other hand, major and minor keys and scales with common tonics are closely related. For example, though *C* major and *c* minor have different key signatures, they have many scale degrees in common. The I, IV, and V of *C* major are the same as the I, IV, and V of *c* minor. Some other degrees are exactly the same; all have the same letter name. For this reason, keys and scales with the same keynote are called *parallel major and minor.*

MINOR SCALES

The key signature of a parallel *minor* may be obtained by *altering* the signature of its parallel *major* to the extent of *three* accidentals—basically, subtracting sharps and/or adding flats. The formula is implicit in the following chart.

GIVEN MAJOR		TO OBTAIN	PARALLEL MINOR		
Key	Signature		Signature		Key
C♯	7 sharps	decrease by 3 sharps	4 sharps		c♯
F♯	6 "	"	3 "		f♯
B	5 "	"	2 "		b
E	4 "	"	1 sharp		e
A	3 "	"	0 "		a
D	2 "	{ decrease by 2 sharps / increase by 1 flat }	1 flat		d
G	1 sharp	{ decrease by 1 sharp / increase by 2 flats }	2 flats		g
C	0 "	increase by 3 flats	3 "		c
F	1 flat	"	4 "		f
B♭	2 flats	"	5 "		b♭
E♭	3 "	"	6 "		e♭
A♭	4 "	"	7 "		a♭
D♭	5 "	"	8 "	(Includes 1 double flat)	d♭ = c♯ (4 sharps)
G♭	6 "	"	9 "	(Includes 2 double flats)	g♭ = f♯ (3 sharps)
C♭	7 "	"	10 "	(Includes 3 double flats)	c♭ = b (2 sharps)

The d♭, g♭, and c♭ minor scales are identical in sound with the c♯, f♯, and b minor scales. Because the last three have fewer accidentals in the signature, it is customary to make the enharmonic change when possible by writing music in the key of c♯ instead of d♭, f♯ instead of g♭, and b instead of c♭.

The key signature of a parallel *major* may be obtained by *altering* the signature of its parallel *minor* to the extent of *three* accidentals—basically, subtracting flats and/or adding sharps. The formula is implicit in the following chart.

MINOR SCALES

Key	GIVEN MINOR	Signature	TO OBTAIN	PARALLEL MAJOR Signature	Key
c♭	(Includes 3 double flats)	10 flats	decrease by 3 flats	7 flats	C♭
g♭	(Includes 2 double flats)	9 "	"	6 "	G♭
d♭	(Includes 1 double flat)	8 "	"	5 "	D♭
a♭		7 "	"	4 "	A♭
e♭		6 "	"	3 "	E♭
b♭		5 "	"	2 "	B♭
f		4 "	"	1 flat	F
c		3 "	"	0 "	C
g		2 "	{decrease by 2 flats / increase by 1 sharp}	1 sharp	G
d		1 flat	{decrease by 1 flat / increase by 2 sharps}	2 sharps	D
a		0 "	increase by 3 sharps	3 "	A
e		1 sharp	"	4 "	E
b		2 sharps	"	5 "	B
f♯		3 "	"	6 "	F♯
c♯		4 "	"	7 "	C♯

Summary

1. The tonic of a minor scale is the sixth degree of its relative major scale. It also may be considered as the pitch one and one-half steps below the tonic of its relative major. The sixth tone up a major scale is the same as the third tone down.
2. As with major scales, the fifth degree (V) of minor scales having sharps is the first degree (I) of the minor scale having one additional sharp. (Circle of fifths—clockwise.)
3. As with major scales, the fourth degree (IV) of minor scales having flats is the first degree (I) of the minor scale having one additional flat. The progression may be considered as the fifth step down the scale. (Circle of fifths—counterclockwise.)
4. The signature of relative major and minor keys is the same. As with major keys, an arithmetical oddity occurs when we add the number of sharps and flats that are in the two keys with the same letter name: the total is always 7.

The key of a minor has neither sharps nor flats in its signature. If the number of accidentals in this signature is paired with those of a♯ minor (seven sharps) the combination is $0 + 7 = 7$; if paired with those of a♭ minor (seven flats) the combination is the same: $0 + 7 = 7$. Each of the other pairs of keys with the same letter name also has a number of sharps and flats which adds up to 7 accidentals.

PAIRED MINOR KEYS		PAIRED SHARPS AND FLATS		TOTAL ACCIDENTALS
e	e♭	1	6	7
b	b♭	2	5	7
f♯	f	3	4	7
c♯	c	4	3	7
g♯	g	5	2	7
d♯	d	6	1	7

MISCELLANEOUS SCALES

The music of our time is, for the most part, derived from the major and minor modes. Therefore, the major and minor scales occupy a place of prominence in the study of this music. However, there are other scales which play an important part in our music, and the mathematical possibilities of additional ones are many.

Chromatic scale

The chromatic scale moves by half steps from one tone to its octave. It contains 12 different degrees. Because of the equal distance from one degree to the next, the chromatic scale does not have the significant individuality of the major and minor scales. The chromatic scale, or a segment of it, frequently acts as an embellishment to a melodic line. The use of chromaticism to express fervor dates back to the late Renaissance. However, the abundant use of chromatics as a device to portray deep emotion and to heighten descriptive passages is more characteristic of nineteenth-century romantic composers and their followers than those of any other time.

A chromatic alteration may be indicated by either a sharp or a flat. The choice depends upon the context in which it is found. Usually, sharps are employed in an ascending line while flats are used when the line descends.

MINOR SCALES

Ascending Chromatic Scale

Descending Chromatic Scale

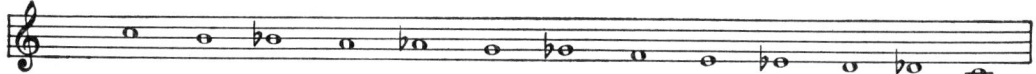

Whole-tone scale

The whole-tone scale moves by whole steps from one tone to its octave. It contains six different degrees. As in the chromatic scale, because of the equal distance from one degree to the next, the whole-tone scale does not have the significant individuality of the major and minor scales. The fluid melodic quality of the whole-tone scale made it useful in the hands of composers of the impressionist school.

Only two whole-tone scales can be written: one containing the white key C and the other containing the black key called either C♯ or D♭. A whole-tone scale beginning on any other tone will duplicate the pitches in either of these.

The two whole-tone scales written with sharps

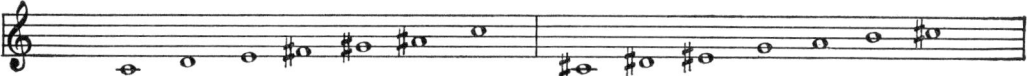

The two whole-tone scales written with flats

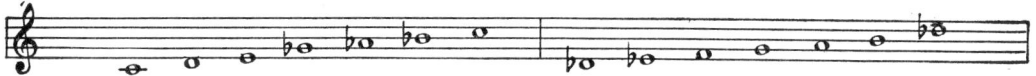

Other scales

Any succession of steps within an octave will produce a scale. If one considers that the division of the octave need not be limited to the half tones of our system, but may consist of quarter tones or even smaller steps as had the Greeks and Orientals, it is easy to imagine the multiple possibilities that exist in the realm of scales. Invent some of your own.

MINOR SCALES

HISTORY OF THE HARMONIC MINOR SCALE

The major and minor scales were foreshadowed in the thirteenth century when musicians, in performance, raised and lowered certain tones of a melody in order to make the melodic line more beautiful and easier to sing. B♭ and E♭ were the first flats to be introduced; F♯ and C♯, the first sharps. At that time, the rules of melodic progression which grew out of this practice of chromatic alterations were so well understood by the performers that composers seldom had to write the accidentals in their music. The performers, familiar with the theory of music, made the alterations themselves. By the sixteenth century the major and minor modes were established and within another hundred years the Church modes were practically abandoned by composers.

The seventeenth century witnessed the development of *homophony* (from Greek *homo*, single + *phōnē*, sound) wherein one melodic line is of chief interest and is supported by a chordal structure. The average songs, hymns, and most of the instrumental music of the nineteenth century are homophonic in nature. Within the framework of this chordal (harmonic) structure, the raised seventh became an important feature of music in the minor mode.

The history of Western music is marked by increases in levels of tension. A case in point is the raised seventh. In the natural minor scale (the Aeolian mode) the distance between the seventh and eighth degrees is a whole step. The progression of a whole step upward has much less dynamic quality, or tension, than the progression of a half step. This can be observed by playing the A natural minor scale. Listen to the movement from the seventh degree (G-natural) to the eighth degree (A). Play the scale again, but this time raise the seventh degree, that is, skip G-natural and play G-sharp in its place. In this context, G-sharp is more "active" than G-natural because the seventh degree is now drawn farther away from the sixth degree and closer to the eighth.

While the raised seventh offered some new melodic possibilities to composers of the seventeenth century, its chief function was harmonic in that, combined with other tones, it drove more successfully and conclusively toward the tone of resolution, the tonic. For this reason, the minor scale with the constantly raised seventh is called the *harmonic minor scale*.

HISTORY OF MELODIC MINOR SCALE

To repeat, in the seventeenth century the raised seventh became an important feature of music in the minor mode. It brought a new luster to the harmonic structure of music. To a much lesser degree it offered new melodic possibilities because the very process of bringing the seventh degree closer to the tonic created an awkward skip of a step and a half between the sixth and seventh degrees.

As its name implies, the melodic minor scale grew out of the action taken by composers to provide a smooth melodic line, ascending or descending.

CHAPTER 15

INTERVALS

A little treatise on harmony of the first century A.D. gives the following definition: "An interval is what is bounded by two notes differing as to height and depth." * The concept of intervals dates to the sixth century B.C., when the Greeks recognized the relationship of musical intervals to the arithmetical ratios of strings of different lengths but subject to the same physical conditions (material, tension, etc.). An understanding of the phenomenon of a compound sound (Chapter 1) is the first step in the study of intervals.

The size of an interval is determined by the number of staff degrees involved, reckoning from the lower to the higher pitch. This is unlike linear measurement, in which we begin with zero and proceed to the first unit. In measuring the size of an interval there is no zero. We consider the number of degrees making up the interval; the first degree is one. For example, C to E is the interval of a *third* because we count three degrees: C-D-E; likewise, E to C is a sixth (E-F-G-A-B-C).

Since intervals are not arithmetical fractions we never write ⅓ for a *third*, or ¼ for a *fourth,* and so on. There is no such meaning. What is involved is the number of scale degrees, *including* the extremes. However, a *second, third, fourth,* etc., may be indicated as a *2nd, 3rd, 4th,* etc.

* Quoted in Oliver Strunk, *Source Readings in Music History,* p. 35.

INTERVALS

140

Melodic and harmonic intervals

The difference in pitch between two tones sounded in sequence, one after the other, is called a *melodic interval;* when the two tones are sounded simultaneously it is called a *harmonic interval.*

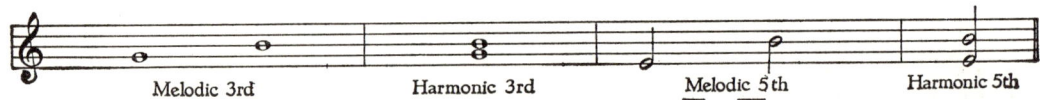

When two tones of the same pitch are sounded, the interval is called a *unison* (fr. Latin *unus*, one + *sonus*, a sound) or *prime* (fr. Latin *primus*, first). The interval of an eighth is called an *octave.* The two notes of harmonic intervals are usually written vertically, one above the other. The exceptions are the Unison and Second. Due to the smallness of the intervals and the nature of the staff their notes are written next to each other. A unison must be represented either by two notes or by one note with two stems (when the note value is less than a whole note). This indicates that two sounds of the same pitch form the interval.

Compound intervals

When an interval is greater than an octave it is said to be a compound interval. It may be described by either the larger number or by the number which describes its size as calculated within the octave. For example, D–F, a third; D–G, a fourth; D–A, a fifth.

INVERSION OF INTERVALS

The position of the tones of an interval may be exchanged. The bottom note may be moved up an octave (in the direction of the top note) or the top note may be moved down an octave (in the direction of the bottom note). Such an exchange of top and bottom positions is called an *inversion* and the interval is said to be *inverted—inverted up* when the bottom note is placed an octave higher; *inverted down* when the top note is placed an octave lower.

With the inversion of intervals the number 9 may be used for reference. A unison inverts to an octave ($9 - 1 = 8$), a second inverts to a seventh ($9 - 2 = 7$), and so forth.

Inversion Upward (Bottom note up one octave)

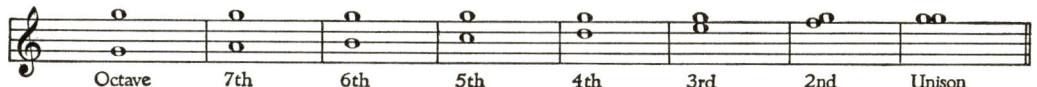

Inversion Downward (Top note down one octave)

CLASSIFICATION OF INTERVALS

Throughout the ages theorists have been trying to find a satisfactory terminology for classifying intervals. Among the terms are *consonant, dissonant; perfect, imperfect; major, minor, augmented,* and *diminished.*

An interval has always been regarded as a *consonance* (from the Latin *consonantia*, sounding together) or as a *dissonance* (from the Latin *dissonantia*, opposed to sounding together). The modern classification of intervals as to consonant and dissonant is treated after the discussion of *kinds of intervals.*

For History of Intervals, see the end of this chapter.

INTERVALS

KINDS OF INTERVALS

Intervals similarly numbered may differ in quality. For example, all thirds do not sound alike. Any quality of C (C♭, C♮, or C♯) in relation to any quality of E (E♭, E♮, or E♯) above C is a third because the letter names C and E bound three staff degrees: C-D-E. But C–E♭ does not sound the same as C–E, nor does C♯–E♭, nor C–E♯. Obviously, an interval has diverse qualities.

The three basic kinds of intervals are: *perfect, major* (also called *large*), and *minor* (also called *small*). Chromatic alterations of these account for two other qualities: *augmented* and *diminished*.

The perfect intervals are the *unison* or *prime, fourth, fifth* and *octave*. To test the quality of an interval examine it in its relation to the major scale. First, consider the lower tone as the tonic of a major scale; then, invert the interval and consider the new lower tone as the tonic of a major scale. If each tone of the interval occurs in the major scale of the other, the interval is, in present usage, a perfect interval.

For example, in the unison C and in the octave C each tone of these intervals is common to the same major scale, C major. Since the tones of a unison and an octave definitely occur in the major scales of each other, the unison and octave are perfect intervals.

Unison (C Major)   Inversions (C Major)   Octave (C Major)   Inversions (C Major)

Consider the interval of the fourth C–F. F occurs in the C major scale and C occurs in the F major scale. The fourth is a perfect interval.

Fourth (C Major)   Inversions (F Major)

The interval of the fifth C–G is similar. G occurs in the C major scale while C occurs in the G major scale. The fifth is a perfect interval.

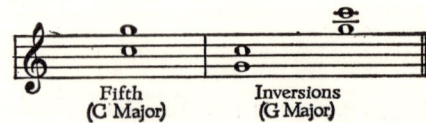

Fifth (C Major)   Inversions (G Major)

Thus, the unison, fourth, fifth, and octave are the perfect intervals.

The basic intervals of the second, third, sixth, and seventh are either *major* (*large*) or *minor* (*small*). They are major intervals when the top tone is in the major scale whose keynote is the lower tone. For example, C–D is a major second because D occurs in the C major scale. Its inversion, D–C, however, is not a major interval because C-natural does not occur in the D major scale—it falls short by a half step of the C-sharp which is the seventh degree of the D major scale. Such an interval is called a minor interval. *A minor interval is a half step smaller than a major interval.*

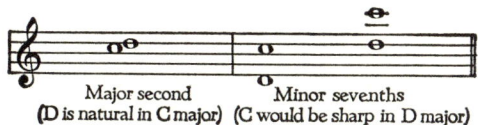

Major second Minor sevenths
(D is natural in C major) (C would be sharp in D major)

Note: The second does not qualify as a perfect interval because each tone of the interval does not occur in the major scale of the other.

Thirds, sixths, and sevenths are judged in the same way.

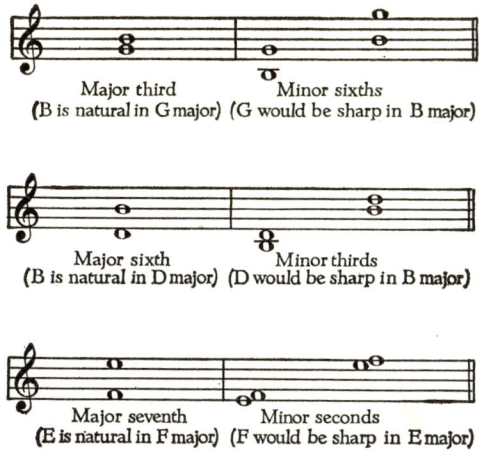

Major third Minor sixths
(B is natural in G major) (G would be sharp in B major)

Major sixth Minor thirds
(B is natural in D major) (D would be sharp in B major)

Major seventh Minor seconds
(E is natural in F major) (F would be sharp in E major)

The third, sixth, and seventh—like the second—cannot be considered perfect intervals because the tones of each interval are not in the respective major scale of each other. Finally, all major intervals invert to minor intervals.

INTERVALS

Conversely, a minor interval inverts to a major interval. For example, E–F is a minor second because the top tone F is a half step less than F♯ which occurs in the E major scale. Its inversion, F–E, however, is a major interval because the top tone E does occur in the F major scale.

Minor second   Major seventh
(F would be sharp in E major)   (E is natural in F major)

The same is true of minor thirds, sixths, and sevenths. They, too, invert to major intervals.

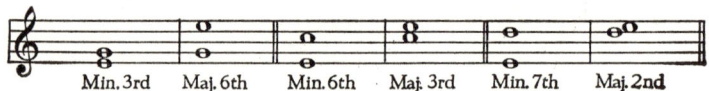

Min. 3rd   Maj. 6th   Min. 6th   Maj. 3rd   Min. 7th   Maj. 2nd

CONSONANCES AND DISSONANCES

In classifying intervals we stated that an interval has always been regarded as a consonance (a blending of two tones) or a dissonance (a refusal of two tones to blend). The consonances are: the perfect unison, fifth, and octave; the major and minor thirds and sixths. The perfect fourth may be classified as either a consonance or a dissonance depending on the context in which it is found. All other intervals are considered dissonances. They include the major and minor second and seventh and all other intervals formed by altering chromatically the perfect, major, and minor intervals.

INTERVALS ALTERED CHROMATICALLY

Perfect and major intervals can be made a half step larger to form *augmented* intervals. This is effected through chromatic alteration, either by raising the top tone a half step or by lowering the bottom tone a half step.

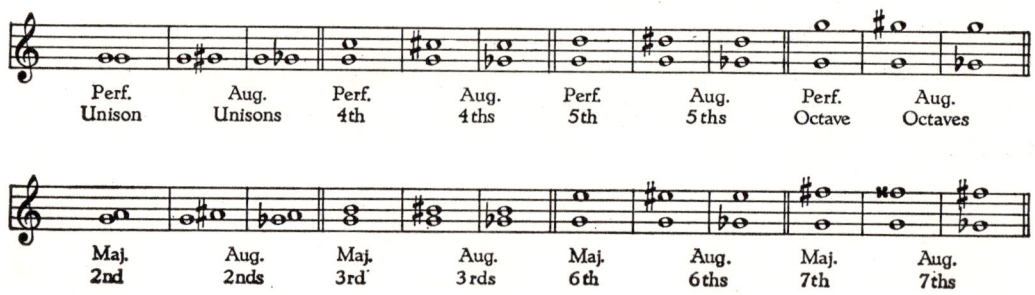

INTERVALS

Perfect and minor intervals can be made a half step smaller to form *diminished* intervals. This is effected through chromatic alteration either by lowering the top tone a half step or by raising the bottom tone a half step. Because it is impossible to form an interval smaller than a prime there can be no diminished unison.

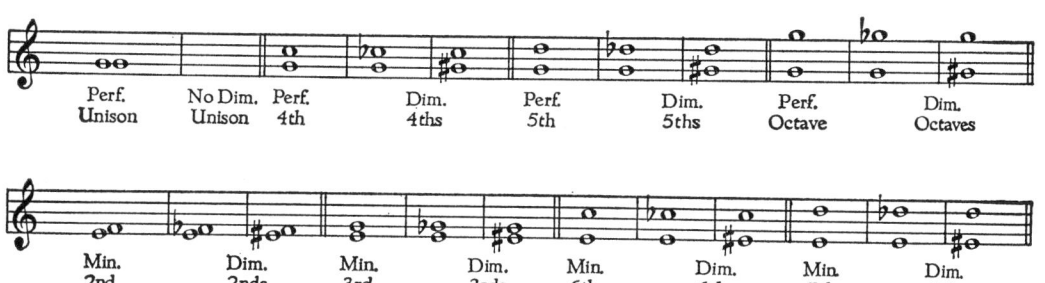

Augmented intervals invert to diminished intervals, while diminished intervals invert to augmented intervals.

Sample Inversions

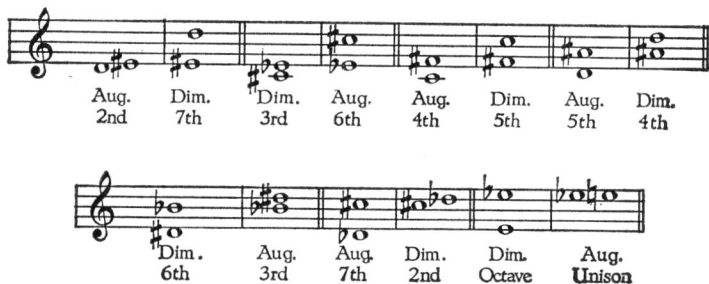

Summary

Alteration of Intervals

Through half-step alteration

Perfect intervals can be made Augmented or Diminished
Major   "   "   "   "   Augmented or Minor
Minor   "   "   "   "   Major or Diminished

Inversion of Intervals

Perfect inverts to Perfect
Major inverts to Minor   Minor inverts to Major
Augmented inverts to Diminished   Diminished inverts to Augmented

INTERVALS

Exercise

Reverse the inversions on pages 144 and 145. You will see that the same kind of interval results whether the inversion be up or down. The only difference lies in the location of the pitches.

Tritone

With but two exceptions (F–B and B–F) all the white-key intervals are either perfect, major or minor. F–B is an augmented fourth (being a half step larger than a perfect fourth, F–B♭) while B–F is a diminished fifth (being a half step smaller than a perfect fifth, B–F♯). The interval of three whole steps (F–B) is known as a *tritone* and, for a long time, it was held to be the worst possible sounding interval. B♭ was introduced by musicians for the very purpose of avoiding the progression from F to B. In writing melodies in the Lydian mode (the white-key scale beginning on F—see Chapter 12) composers usually avoided the tritone or replaced the B with B♭.

ENHARMONIC INTERVALS

Different intervals may sound alike when played on a keyboard instrument but one must remember that *an interval is named from the way in which it is spelled* and not from the way in which it sounds. Intervals which sound alike but are notated differently are called *enharmonic intervals,* just as scales which sound alike but have different spelling are called enharmonic scales.

Sample Enharmonic Intervals

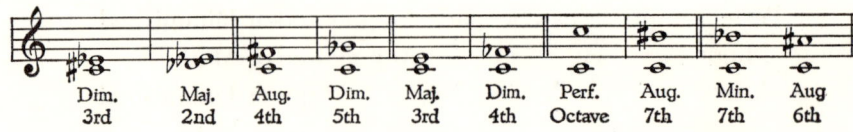

Dim. 3rd | Maj. 2nd | Aug. 4th | Dim. 5th | Maj. 3rd | Dim. 4th | Perf. Octave | Aug. 7th | Min. 7th | Aug 6th

INTERVALS

The study of intervals should be pursued *in* music. Every melody is a source for melodic intervals. Identify the melodic intervals that occur between the notes in the melodies of "Frère Jacques" and "Three Blind Mice."

Harmonic intervals occur whenever two tones are sounded together. Identify the harmonic intervals in the right-hand part of "Three Blind Mice" on page 85 and in the following simplified arrangement of "Silent Night."

Since Chapter 10, work at the piano has been devoted to transposing the three basic pieces (Chapter 11); to two-hand playing of modal melodies (Chapter 12); and to the practice of scales (Chapters 13 and 14). Now we shall learn a new piece for two hands, "Silent Night." The tempo is slow, the dynamics are soft, the meter indicates six pulses to the measure. Review the practice instructions given in Chapter 10 before proceeding with this carol.

Silent Night

Joseph Mohr　　　　　　　　　　　　　　　　　　　　　　　　Franz Gruber

HISTORY OF INTERVALS

As defined in Antiquity, consonance is a blending of two tones, a higher and a lower; dissonance, on the contrary, is a refusal of two tones to combine, with the result that they do not blend but grate harshly on the ear. For the Greeks the consonant intervals were those whose arithmetical ratios were simple: the octave, 2 : 1, the fifth, 3 : 2, the fourth, 4 : 3, and compounds of these, such as the double octave, the octave and a fifth, and the octave and a fourth.

In the Middle Ages, theorists tried to draw up distinctions between the levels of consonance and dissonance. To do this they employed the terms *perfect* and *imperfect*. A perfect consonance was an interval completely satisfactory to the ear; an imperfect consonance was an interval not completely satisfactory to the ear. A perfect dissonance was extremely harsh; an imperfect dissonance was less harsh.

Although at that time the terms perfect and imperfect were applied to all kinds of intervals, the use of the term *perfect* is reserved, today, for the unison, fourth, fifth, and octave. This reflects the early Greek category of intervals with simple ratios.

Major and *minor*, as the names imply, refer to the size of the intervals: large and small. Today, the second, third, sixth, and seventh are classified as major and minor intervals. The application of the terms major and minor to the areas of scales and keys (where the interval 1–3 is a major third in the major mode and a minor third in the minor mode) is probably not older than the eighteenth century.

We classify as consonances the perfect unison, fifth, and octave; the major and minor thirds and sixths. With the exception of the perfect fourth, all other intervals are always considered as dissonances. The perfect fourth is a special case. In Antiquity and the Middle Ages, when theorists tended to think of music in terms of mathematics, that interval which we define today as a perfect fourth (two tones and a half) was classified as a consonance because its arithmetical ratio is simple. In this sense we continue to regard it as such. In certain harmonic environments, the perfect fourth does have a dissonant quality and, in this sense, we continue to regard the perfect fourth as a dissonance.

As fascinating as the subject is, it belongs to the study of harmony and must be dealt with there. Nevertheless, the student should not be surprised to find the perfect fourth classified both as a consonance and as a dissonance. One need always remember that the classification depends upon how it occurs in specific usage.

CHAPTER 16

CHORDS

A *chord* is a compound sound created by combining two or more intervals.

TRIADS

The simplest chord, a *triad*, consists of three tones. One of the three tones serves as a fundamental tone for two intervals built upon it—a third and a fifth. These two intervals, sounded together, form a triad.

On the staff this involves three consecutive lines *or* spaces. The three tones of a triad are named *root* (the fundamental or generating tone of the series), the *third* (from the interval of a third), and the *fifth* (from the interval of a fifth).

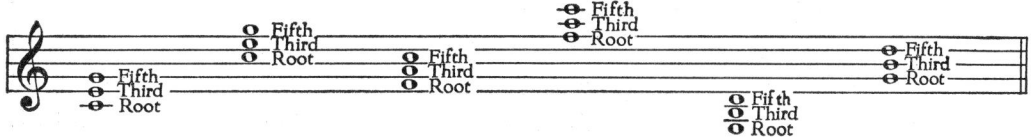

Any degree of the diatonic scale may serve as the root of a triad. The name of the scale degree, or the appropriate Roman numeral, is used to

CHORDS

identify the triad built upon it. Thus, the name of a triad depends upon its location in a tonality. For example, in the key of C major, C–E–G is called the I (One) chord or tonic triad because it is built on C, the tonic in the key of C; in the key of G major this same triad is the IV (Four) chord or subdominant triad because it is built on C, the subdominant in the key of G; and, in the key of F major it is the V (Five) chord or dominant triad because it is built on C, the dominant in the key of F.

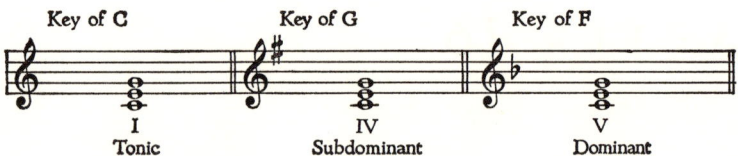

Triads of the major mode

The triads built on the seven degrees of the C major scale are:

Play these triads and listen to the quality of each. I, IV, and V have the same quality, the same kind of sound, because in each case the interval 1–3 is a major third and the interval 1–5 is a perfect fifth. A triad consisting of a major third and a perfect fifth is called a *major triad*.

Triads II, III, and VI also have a common quality, but it differs from that of the major triads. The difference lies in the kind of third. Here the interval 1–3 is a minor third. However, as in the major triad, the interval 1–5 is a perfect fifth. A triad consisting of a minor third and a perfect fifth is called a *minor triad*.

One triad, the one built on the seventh degree of the major scale, is neither major nor minor. In this triad the interval 1–3 is a minor third, but the interval 1–5 is not a perfect fifth—it is a diminished fifth. This diminished fifth is the distinguishing factor of the triad built on the seventh degree of the major scale. A triad consisting of a minor third and a diminished fifth is called a *diminished triad*.

Thus, a triad built on a degree of the major scale is either major, minor, or diminished.

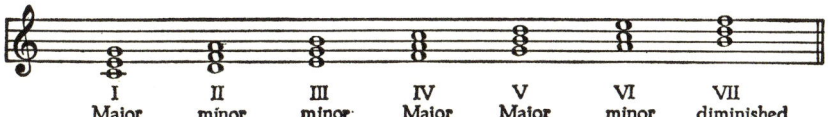

Triads may also be recognized by the kinds of thirds present in them. In the major triad, the interval 1–3 is a major third; the interval 3–5 is a minor third. In the minor triad, the interval 1–3 is a minor third; the interval 3–5 is a major third. In the diminished triad, both the thirds, 1–3 and 3–5, are minor.

Triads of the minor mode

Some of the triads built on the seven degrees of the minor scale vary with the kind of minor scale. It is not necessary to examine those that might be built on the degrees of the melodic minor scale because, as its name implies, this scale derives from the characteristics of melodies in the minor mode and not from any harmonic structure. But the triads built on the degrees of the natural and harmonic minor scales have important harmonic implications. Therefore, these triads need to be analyzed and compared.

Play the following triads and listen to the quality of each. The triads common to both scales are printed in white notes; those which vary, in black notes.

c *natural minor* (3 flats)

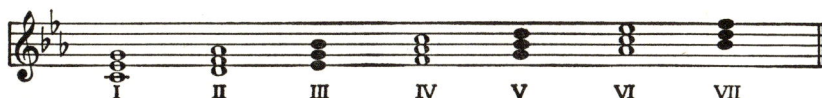

c *harmonic minor* (3 flats with raised seventh: B-natural)

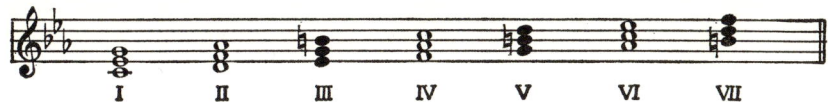

Of the common triads, I and IV are minor (minor third and perfect fifth); II is diminished (minor third and diminished fifth); and, VI is major (major third and perfect fifth).

Because the seventh (B) is common to the triads built on III, V, and VII, it is the fact that the seventh of the natural minor scale is unraised and the seventh of the harmonic minor scale is raised which accounts for the differences in these chords. In the natural minor, III and VII are major triads;

CHORDS

V is minor.

In the harmonic minor, each of these three triads is different.

One triad, the one built on the third degree of the harmonic minor scale is neither major, minor, nor diminished. In this triad the interval 1-3 is a major third, but the interval 1-5 is an *augmented fifth*. A triad consisting of a major third and an augmented fifth is called an *augmented triad*. It also may be recognized by the fact that both the thirds, 1-3 and 3-5, are major thirds. The other two triads are V, a major triad, and VII, a diminished triad.

All the triads of the harmonic minor, except the III, are more or less abundant in music of the minor mode. The III triad, in its augmented form, is rarely found in music before the late nineteenth century.

A triad, then, built on a degree of the minor scale is either major, minor, augmented, or diminished.

c *natural minor (3 flats)*

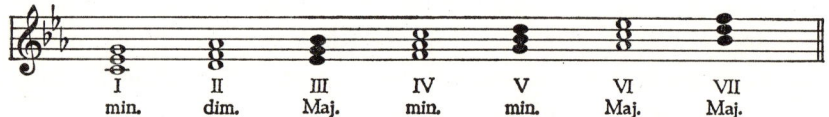

c *harmonic minor (3 flats with raised seventh: B-natural)*

The major and minor triads are consonant because they contain all consonant intervals—a perfect fifth and a major or minor third; the augmented and diminished triads are dissonant because each contains a dissonant interval—an augmented or a diminished fifth.

Summary: four kinds of triad

Major Triad	*Minor Triad*	*Augmented Triad*	*Diminished Triad*
Perfect Fifth	Perfect Fifth	Augmented Fifth	Diminished Fifth
Major Third	Minor Third	Major Third	Minor Third
Root	Root	Root	Root

CHORDS

The four kinds of triad found in the major and minor modes:

Kind	Major Mode	Harmonic Minor Mode	Natural Minor Mode
Major triad	I IV V	V VI	III VI VII
Minor triad	II III VI	I IV	I IV V
Augmented triad		III	
Diminished triad	VII	II VII	II

The quality of each triad in the major and minor modes:

Triad		Major Mode	Harmonic Minor Mode	Natural Minor Mode
I	(Tonic)	Maj.	min.	min.
II	(Supertonic)	min.	dim.	dim.
III	(Mediant)	min.	Aug.	Maj.
IV	(Subdominant)	Maj.	min.	min.
V	(Dominant)	Maj.	Maj.	min.
VI	(Submediant)	min.	Maj.	Maj.
VII	(Leading Tone)	dim.	dim.	Maj.

SEVENTH CHORDS

A *seventh chord* consists of four tones. Do not confuse the *tetrachord* (pp. 90 and 99) with the seventh chord. A tetrachord consists of four scale degrees sounded successively (C-D-E-F or G-A-B-C); a seventh chord consists of four disjointed tones (tones which do not occur next to each other in the scale). It is formed by adding the interval of a seventh to a triad. On the staff this involves four consecutive lines *or* spaces. The four tones of a seventh chord are called the *root, third, fifth,* and *seventh.* All seventh chords are dissonant because they contain the interval of a seventh, which is always dissonant.

Seventh chords built on the degrees of C major scale

CHORDS

In the next two examples, the seventh chords common to the natural and harmonic minor scales are printed with white notes; those which vary, with black notes.

Seventh chords built on the degrees of c natural minor scale

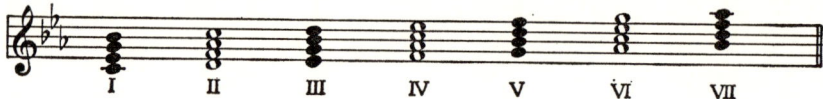

Seventh chords built on the degrees of c harmonic minor scale

The seventh chord built on the fifth degree of the scale commands special attention. Common to the major and harmonic minor scale, this chord—the *dominant seventh chord*—has been used more frequently in the music of the eighteenth and nineteenth centuries than any other, with the exception of the tonic triad. Note it well. It plays a very important part in the music that is presented in this book.

ADDITIONAL CHORDS

Three additional chords can be formed: by adding the interval of a ninth to a seventh chord; by adding the interval of an eleventh to a ninth chord; and by adding the interval of a thirteenth to an eleventh chord. The study of these chords lies beyond the scope of this text, but samples are given for the purpose of comparison.

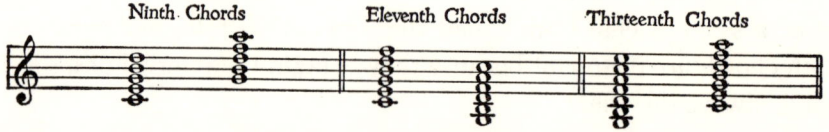

Theoretically a fifteenth chord could be formed. Why isn't it?

Mozart is credited with composing, at the age of six, a minuet that has lost none of its charm in these two hundred years. This delightful little piece is not difficult. It will serve the student as an addition to the repertory and as a study of intervals and implied chords.

CHORDS

At the end of the eighth bar there is a double bar with two dots in each staff. This is a *repeat sign*. It indicates that the preceding passage is to be repeated.

155

Minuet No. 2

W. A. Mozart 1756–1791

* This musical symbol ⌒ is called a *fermata* (Italian, stop). It is a pause of indeterminate length. It indicates that the note is to be held as long as the performer wishes.

CHAPTER 17

INVERSIONS

A chord has two distinguishing qualities: its *kind* and its *position*. The kinds of chords are major, minor, augmented, and diminished. The position of a chord is determined by that tone of the chord which is lowest in pitch at a given time. When the root of a chord is the lowest tone, the chord is said to be in *root position*. It makes no difference how many tones may be repeated in the chord or how far apart the tones of the chord may be; so long as the lowest tone of the group is the root of the chord, the chord is in root position.

Root Positions

Triad Built on C   *Seventh Chord Built on G*

When any tone other than the root is the lowest tone, the chord is *inverted*.

INVERSIONS

Inversions of a triad

A triad has three positions: *root, first inversion,* and *second inversion.* When the *third* (the first tone of the chord above the root) appears as the lowest tone, the chord is in its first inversion; when the *fifth* (the second tone of the chord above the root) appears as the lowest tone, the chord is in its second inversion.

Major Triad Built on C

First Inversions   *Second Inversions*

Inversions of a seventh chord

A seventh chord has four positions: *root, first inversion, second inversion,* and *third inversion.* As in the case of a triad, a seventh chord is in root position when the *root* appears as the lowest tone; it is in its first inversion when the *third* appears as the lowest tone; and it is in its second inversion when the *fifth* appears as the lowest tone. Since a seventh chord has four tones, it can have four positions. When the *seventh* (the third tone of the chord above the root) appears as the lowest tone the chord is in its third inversion.

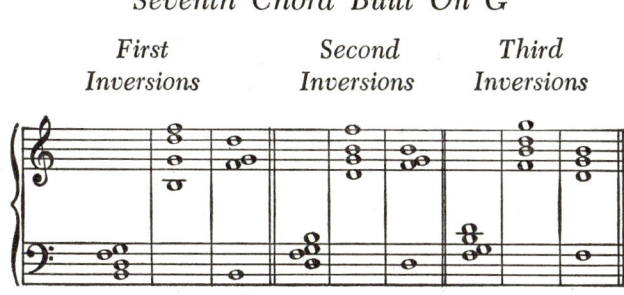

Seventh Chord Built On G

First Inversions   *Second Inversions*   *Third Inversions*

Figured bass

In the early Baroque period, composers indicated the positions of triads and seventh chords by placing numerals above or below the notes in the bass part. Reading these numerals, which indicated the intervals reckoned from

INVERSIONS

the bass upward, the organist or harpsichordist knew what additional tones had to be supplied in order to complete the required harmonies. This technique, this music shorthand, is known as *figured bass*.

Roman numerals are used in two instances: (1) to indicate the degrees of the scales (see p. 98) or (2) to indicate the location of the root of chords in the tonality in which they are found (see pp. 149–150). *Arabic* numerals are used to indicate the intervallic relationship between the lowest tone and each of the other tones of the chord.

Triad in root position

A *triad in root position* is indicated in three ways: (1) by a Roman numeral.

(2) By the Arabic numerals $\frac{5}{3}$, 5, or 3. (The Arabic numerals show the triadic relationship of the tones, particularly the top and bottom tones.)

(3) By nothing at all. (When no numeral attends a bass note it is understood that the bass note is the root of the triad.)

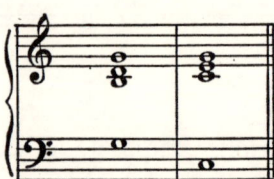

Seventh chord in root position

A *seventh chord in root position* is indicated: (1) by a Roman numeral plus an Arabic $_7$.

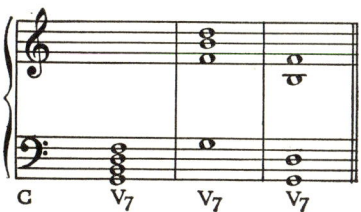

(2) Simply by the Arabic $_7$

In both cases the $_7$ shows that this is a seventh chord—a chord of four tones—and that the interval of a seventh exists between the first tone of the chord (root) and the fourth tone of the chord (seventh). Let it be said again: the position of a chord is determined by the tone that is lowest in pitch; the distribution of the other tones has nothing to do with the name of its position.

Figured inversions of a triad

In choosing the number or numbers to show the inversions of a triad, one must at all times use the number that locates the root of the chord.

A triad in its first inversion has its third as the lowest tone. Between its third (the lowest tone) and the root is the interval of a sixth; between its third (the same lowest tone) and the fifth of the chord is the interval of a third. Thus, the first inversion of a triad is indicated by the Arabic numerals $^6_3$.

The $_3$ may be omitted from the figuration of the *first* inversion of a triad because it is the $_6$ that locates the root. So, a triad in its first inversion is called a *six-three chord* or a *six chord*, and is indicated by the numerals $^6_3$, or simply by $_6$.

INVERSIONS

C Major Triad—First Inversion

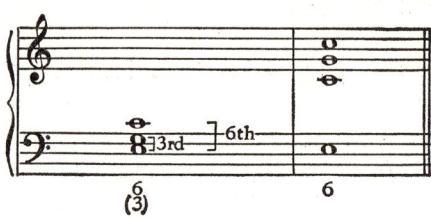

A triad in its second inversion has its fifth as the lowest tone. Between its fifth (the lowest tone) and the third of the chord is the interval of a sixth; between its fifth (the same lowest tone) and its root is the interval of a fourth. Thus, the second inversion of a triad is indicated by the numerals $^6_4$.

In the figuration of the second inversion of a triad the $_4$ is necessary because *it* locates the root. So, a triad in its second inversion is called a *six-four chord* and is indicated by the numerals $^6_4$.

C Major Triad—Second Inversion

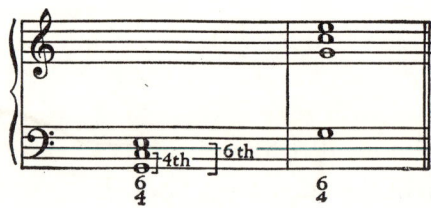

To show both the location of a chord within a tonality *and* its inversion, Roman and Arabic numerals are used together. For example, the first inversion of the C major triad is indicated by I_6 in the key of C major; by IV_6 in the key of G major; and, by V_6 in the key of F major.

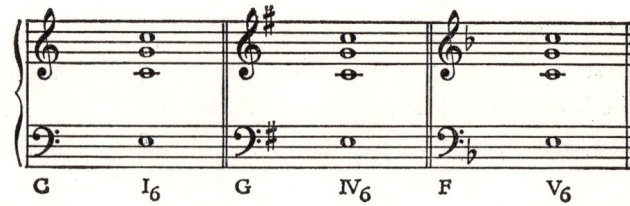

The second inversion of the C major triad is indicated by I^6_4 in the key of C major; by IV^6_4 in the key of G major; and, by V^6_4 in the key of F major.

INVERSIONS

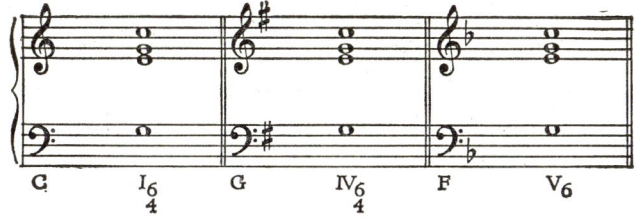

Figured inversions of a seventh chord

In choosing the number or numbers to show the inversions of a seventh chord, one must at all times use the numbers that locate the root and the seventh, except when the seventh itself is the bass note.

A seventh chord in its first inversion has its third as the lowest tone. Between its third (the lowest tone) and the root is the interval of a sixth; between its third and its seventh is the interval of a fifth; and between its third and its fifth is the interval of a third. Thus, the first inversion of a seventh chord is indicated by the numerals $^6_5{}_3$.

The $_3$ may be omitted from the figuration of the first inversion of a seventh chord because it is the $_6$ that locates the root and the $_5$ that locates the seventh. So, a seventh chord in its first inversion is called a *six-five-three*, or simply a *six-five chord*. A dominant seventh chord (built on the fifth degree of the scale) in its first inversion is indicated by both the Roman and Arabic numerals: V^6_5.

Dominant Seventh Chord—First Inversion

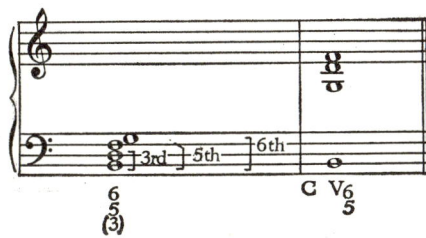

A seventh chord in its second inversion has its fifth as the lowest tone. Between its fifth (the lowest tone) and its third is the interval of a sixth; between its fifth and its root is the interval of a fourth; and, between its fifth and its seventh is the interval of a third. Thus, the second inversion of a seventh chord is indicated by the numerals $^6_4{}_3$.

INVERSIONS

The $_6$ may be omitted from the figuration of the second inversion of a seventh chord because it is the $_4$ that locates the root and the $_3$ that locates the seventh. So, a seventh chord in its second inversion is called a *six-four-three*, or simply a *four-three chord*. A dominant seventh chord in its second inversion is indicated by both the Roman and Arabic numerals: V_3^4.

Dominant Seventh Chord—Second Inversion

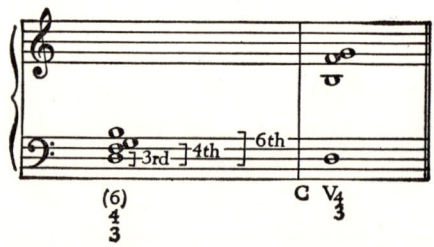

A seventh chord in its third inversion has its seventh as the lowest tone. Between its seventh (the lowest tone) and its fifth is the interval of a sixth; between its seventh and its third is the interval of a fourth; and between its seventh and its root is the interval of a second. Thus, the third inversion of a seventh chord is indicated by the numerals $_4^6\atop2$.

The $_6$ and $_4$ may be omitted from the figuration of the third inversion of a seventh chord because it is the $_2$ that locates the root. The seventh, itself, is the written note. So, a seventh chord in its third inversion is called a *six-four-two*, a *four-two*, or simply a *two chord*. A dominant seventh chord in its third inversion is indicated by both the Roman and Arabic numerals V_2^4 or V_2.

Dominant Seventh Chord—Third Inversion

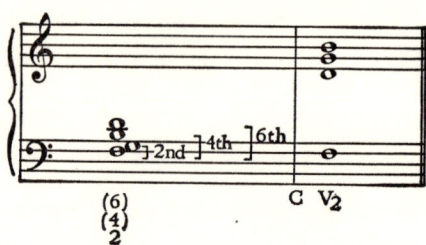

Summary

TRIADS

1st inversion is called a *six-three* ($_3^6$) or *six* ($_6$) *chord*.
2nd   "   "   "   " *six-four* ($_4^6$) *chord*.

INVERSIONS

SEVENTH CHORDS

1st inversion is called a *six-five-three* ($^6_5_3$) or *six-five* ($^6_5$) chord.

2nd " " " " *six-four-three* ($^6_4_3$) or *four-three* ($^4_3$) chord.

3rd " " " " *six-four-two* ($^6_4_2$), *four-two* ($^4_2$), or *two* ($_2$) chord.

In indicating the inversions of chords it is not always necessary to use all the Arabic numerals involved. However, the figured inversions of the *triad* must have, in each case, the number that *locates the root* of the chord. The figured inversions of the *seventh* chord must have the numbers that *locate the root and the seventh,* except when the seventh itself is the bass note.

Figured bass illustrated

The employment of figured bass may be seen in the organ part for one of Bach's settings of the famous chorale (hymn), "O Sacred Head Now Wounded." (This is the same melody as the one given on page 95 in chapter 12, "Origins Of Our Scales.") In Bach's time, the organist could harmonize the chorale with nothing before him but the following figured bass line.

The bass line just presented contains some figurations which have not been explained. Examine the realization of this figured bass in the following choral arrangement made by Bach for his Passion oratorio, "The Passion According to Saint Matthew." The solution to the few new figures can be found in the upper voices. Look at the chorale carefully; then play it on the piano.

INVERSIONS

O Sacred Head Now Wounded

J. S. Bach

164

CHAPTER *18*

BASIC CHORDS AND CADENCE PATTERNS

Harmony is a discipline which deals with the artistic arrangement of different musical pitches sounded simultaneously—the agreement of united sounds. As this book is intended only to provide a working knowledge of fundamental music principles, the discussion of harmony will be limited to a few basic chords and their function in the accompaniment of simple melodies.

The chords most frequently found in music of the major and minor systems are the tonic, dominant, and subdominant. Since very much of this music is oriented to the tonic and dominant, a command of these two chords alone will enhance one's understanding of a melodic line—its direction, its climax, and its denouement.

How does a melody begin? No one can answer this question. As with all created things, it is possible to see how a melody grows, reaches a high point, and finally comes to an end. But the "how" of its beginning is a mystery locked in the genius of the creator. If one has the talent to create a melody he will get it off the ground, but how well it will soar will depend upon his craftsmanship, his mastery of the art of musical composition.

But even though we may not dream of composing music, we do like to

BASIC CHORDS AND CADENCE PATTERNS

sing and play the compositions of others. There can be no intelligent performance without an understanding of the music. The expressions, "plays musically," "caught the spirit of," "knows the composer's intent" all indicate the public's expectation and appreciation of a sensitive performance. We can begin to prepare ourselves to achieve this end by studying melodies which have met the test of time, melodies which have won for themselves—simple as they might be—a place in the artistic world of music.

Look again at some of the melodies we have sung and played. Listen to them to find the places of greater and lesser tensions and repose, where dominant and tonic harmonies are implied. To play an accompaniment to these melodies, the places of activity and repose will have to be matched with harmonies of like degrees of dissonance and consonance.

Play "Mary Had A Little Lamb."

In this piece, the tonic triad sounds well with the melody in bars 1, 2, 4, 5, 6, and 8; while the dominant seventh chord is better in bars 3 and 7. Let us see how these two chords are implied in the melody.

In bars 1, 2, and 4, as well as 5, 6, and 8, every *accented* tone is common to the tones of the tonic triad (C–E–G). Wherever a D occurs in these bars it functions simply as an embellishment activating the melodic flow. This kind of melodic enrichment, called a *passing tone,* consists of a nonharmonic tone (in this case the D) passing on to a chord tone. It does not demand a change in the harmony.

However, in bars 3 and 7 the D takes a commanding position and calls for another kind of harmony, other chord tones than the C–E–G of the tonic triad. Here, the tones of the dominant seventh chord (G–B–D–F) are needed. Refer to page 79 where this piece is arranged with a chordal accompaniment. Analyze the chords and write below each the appropriate Roman and Arabic numerals.

CADENCE

Play the melody of "Mary Had A Little Lamb" again. Observe how, in bars 3–4 and 7–8, the implied harmonic progressions of the dominant seventh to the tonic divide the melody into two sections. Such a progression, called a *cadence* (Latin *cadere*, to fall), tends to shape a melodic line in much the same way as punctuation marks shape a written sentence, or as inflection shapes the expression in speech. The cadences outline the elements of contrast and symmetry. By noting cadences, one can understand the shape or *form* of a piece of music. The awareness of form is as important to the thorough appreciation of a musical composition as is the perception of melody, rhythm, harmony, and the other elements which combine to make an artistic musical whole.

In writing, there are many kinds of punctuation marks—period, comma, semicolon, etc. In music, there are many kinds of cadences. Our concern is limited to two basic ones.

Authentic cadence

The most common cadential pattern embodies the movement from the dominant to the tonic. It is the progression of V or V_7 to I which concludes the nursery tunes, "Mary Had A Little Lamb," "Three Blind Mice," and a host of other melodies. This cadence, characterized by great tension and release from that tension, is called an *authentic cadence*.

Plagal cadence

Another common progression, from the subdominant (IV) to the tonic (I), is called a *plagal cadence*. Less dynamic than the authentic cadence, it is nicknamed the "Amen Cadence" because of its use as the final harmonic expression in many hymns.

The terms *authentic* and *plagal* are used to describe cadences in much the same way as they are used to designate the kinds of Church modes (Chapter 12). *Authentic* is the name given to the progression where the tension is great and the final is definite. *Plagal* is the name given to the progression where the final is just as definite but the tension leading to it is less strong.

Cadences in the major mode

Two very common cadential patterns are given in the following example: the authentic, with movement from the tonic to the dominant seventh and back to the tonic (I–V_7–I); and the plagal, with movement from the tonic to the subdominant and back to the tonic (I–IV–I).

BASIC CHORDS AND CADENCE PATTERNS

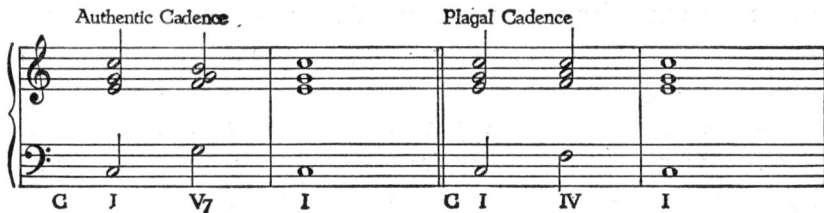

Voice leading

A satisfactory musical texture is obtained by what is called *good voice leading*—the smooth progression from one tone to the next. Sometimes it is necessary to eliminate a less important tone of a chord in order to effect good voice leading. *Every tone of a chord need not be represented with every use of that chord.* In the discussion of figured bass it was pointed out that the significant tones of a triad are the root and third; of a seventh chord, the root, third, and seventh. In both chords the fifth is of lesser importance. In the authentic cadence above, the D (the fifth of the V_7 chord) has been omitted to secure a smooth progression of the tones of the chord. The following example repeats the cadences given above. Sing the progression indicated in each of the voices in these two cadences.

Play the authentic and plagal cadences just illustrated. Transpose them *at the keyboard* into the keys of G, D, F, and B♭ major. Practice them until you can play them from memory. Finally, write the four transposed cadences.

Cadences in the minor mode

The same authentic and plagal cadential patterns may be employed in the minor mode. Remember, in the harmonic minor, the seventh degree of the scale is raised a half step. The third of the dominant seventh chord is this same raised-seventh scale degree. Play these examples and transpose them *at the keyboard* into the keys of e, b, d, and g minor. Practice them until you can play them from memory. Finally, write the four transposed cadences.

BASIC CHORDS AND CADENCE PATTERNS

Authentic cadence including the IV chord

A cadence may be enriched by placing the subdominant (IV) chord between the tonic (I) and the dominant (V), or dominant seventh (V_7).

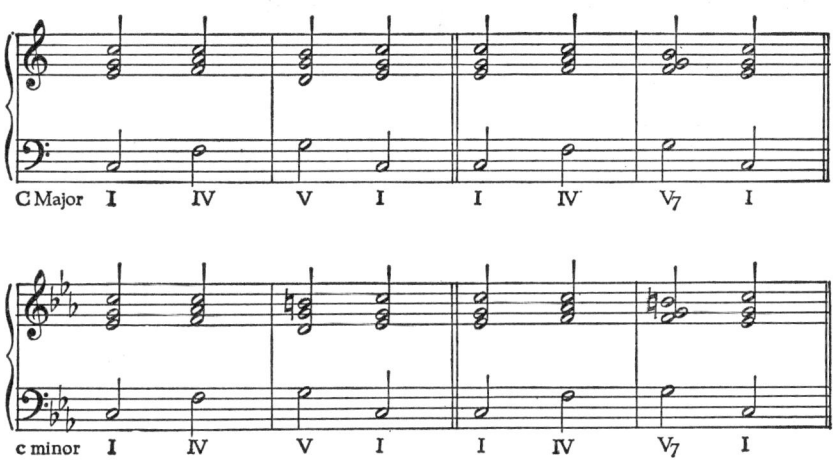

Play these cadences, I–IV–V or V_7–I, and transpose them *at the keyboard* into the major and minor keys of D, E, F, G, and A. Practice them until you can play them from memory. Finally, write the transposed cadences.

Authentic cadence including the I_4^6 chord

A cadence may be extended by inserting a tonic six-four (I_4^6) chord between the subdominant (IV) chord and the dominant (V) or dominant seventh (V_7). The dissonance of the perfect fourth in the second inversion of the tonic triad finds resolution in the consonant third of the dominant harmony. At the same time, it is a prelude to the greater tension of the dominant seventh and postpones the complete resolution that eventually attends the root position of the final tonic triad.

BASIC CHORDS AND CADENCE PATTERNS

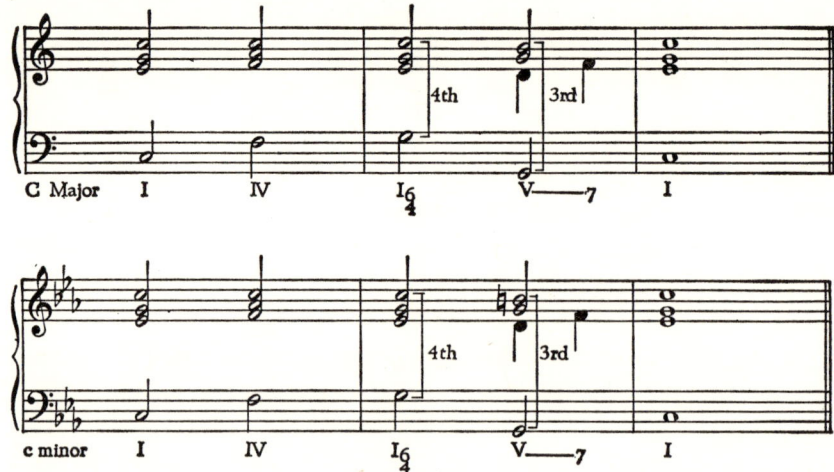

Play these I–IV–I$_4^6$–V–V$_7$–I cadential patterns and transpose them *at the keyboard* into the major and minor keys of D, E, F, G, and A. Practice them until you can play them from memory. Finally, write the transposed cadences.

Authentic cadence including the II$_6$ chord

Another common and useful cadential pattern employs the first inversion of the supertonic (II$_6$) chord just before the dominant.

Play these I–II$_6$–V$_7$–I cadential patterns and transpose them *at the keyboard* into the major and minor keys of D, E, F, G, and A. Practice them until you can play them from memory. Finally, write the transposed cadences.

BASIC CHORDS AND CADENCE PATTERNS

The secondary dominant

The harmonic progression within a melodic line may be enhanced by the introduction of the dominant seventh of a tone other than the tonic. For example, the dominant of C is G; the dominant of G is D. The dominant seventh chord built on D is D–F♯–A–C. In certain cases, the dominant seventh built on D might be played before the dominant seventh built on G, the true dominant seventh in the key of C. Such a sequence of chords does not destroy the existing tonality nor set up a new tonal center. It is usually an embellishment of the moment. Sometimes such a *secondary dominant* is necessary to the proper harmonic support of a melodic line; at other times it is not necessary but does serve to beautify the musical texture. A secondary dominant may be indicated as follows: V of IV, or V₇ of IV; V of V, or V₇ of V; and so on. The V or V₇ of V is also referred to as the *dominant of the dominant*.

Cadence Including the V₇ of IV

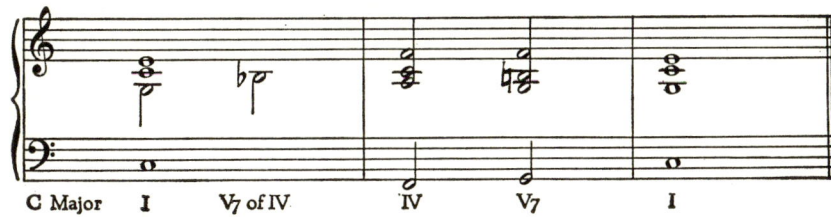

Cadence Including the V₇ of V

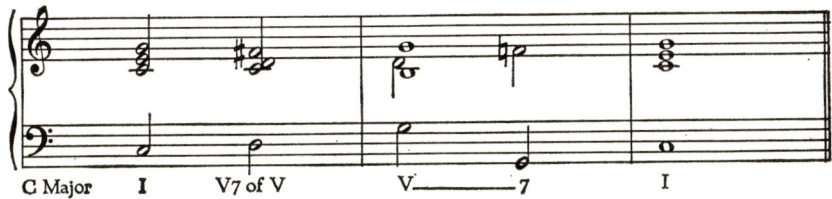

An effective use of two secondary dominant seventh chords can be seen in this arrangement of "Old Folks At Home." Sing the melody as you play the chordal accompaniment on the piano. (The *right hand* plays the notes with the *stems up;* the *left hand*, with the *stems down.*)

BASIC CHORDS AND CADENCE PATTERNS

Old Folks At Home

S. C. F.

Stephen C. Foster

CHAPTER 19

CHORDAL PATTERNS AND ACCOMPANIMENT FIGURES

People can be stimulated to sing with enthusiasm in a number of ways. One of the most successful is to accompany the singers at the piano. This is possible without an advanced piano technique. It can be done by playing, with assurance, some simple chordal patterns.

The beginning piano student usually has the problem of hand coordination. In playing a song it may be too difficult for him to play the melody with the right hand and the accompaniment with the left. However, when there are singers to carry the melody, an adequate and completely satisfactory accompaniment can be had by omitting the melody at the piano and playing the basic harmonies and rhythms with both hands. The result is similar to the kind of accompaniment one gets with a ukulele, mandolin, guitar, or similar instrument.

The following three chordal patterns are basic to this purpose. They contain the two most common chords: the tonic (I) and the dominant seventh (V_7). Each chord is in root position because the lowest note, which is given to the left hand, is its root. However, the arrangement of the notes given to the right hand are varied. In Example I, the right hand plays the tonic triad with the fifth on top; in Example II, the tonic triad has the root on top; and, in Example III, it has the third on top. Play all three examples

CHORDAL PATTERNS AND ACCOMPANIMENT FIGURES

several times to find the pattern that feels most comfortable under your fingers.

When you have found the pattern which suits you best, practice it with the indicated fingering until the change from one chord to the other comes easily and smoothly. Do likewise with the other examples. Then, transpose all three into nearby higher and lower keys.

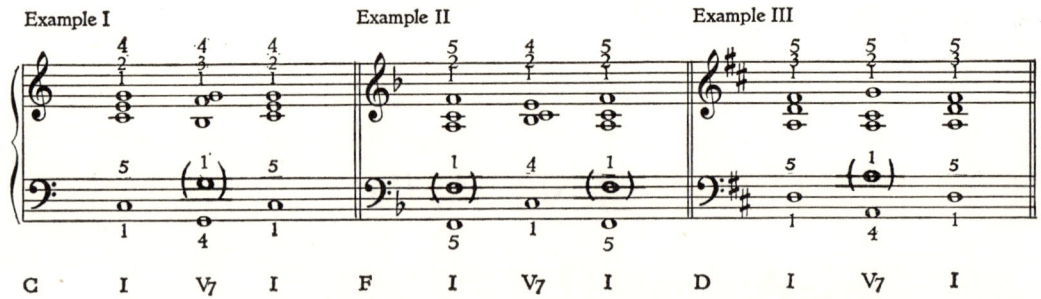

These chordal patterns are useful in that they can supply the harmonic background for simple melodies. However, even simple melodies need rhythmic as well as harmonic support. This important element of music may be added effectively by arranging the basic chordal patterns within the frame of different meters. Study the following accompaniment figures. Practice them until they can be played easily; then, transpose them up and down in different nearby keys.

Accompaniment Figures for Two Hands
$(I - V_7 - I)$

CHORDAL PATTERNS AND ACCOMPANIMENT FIGURES

Success in playing accompaniments to songs depends upon one's ability to choose one which is appropriate to the piece. Six exercises have been designed to show how a variety of accompaniment figures can be secured through chordal and rhythmic changes. Practice them in the following way.

1. Select a key.
2. Adopt one of the three hand positions given on page 174.
3. Play the patterns according to the indicated chords (I and V_7) and the rhythmic outlines.

After an exercise has been learned and can be played smoothly and without hesitation, change the key, the hand position, or both. Practice in this manner until all the exercises have been played in several ways.

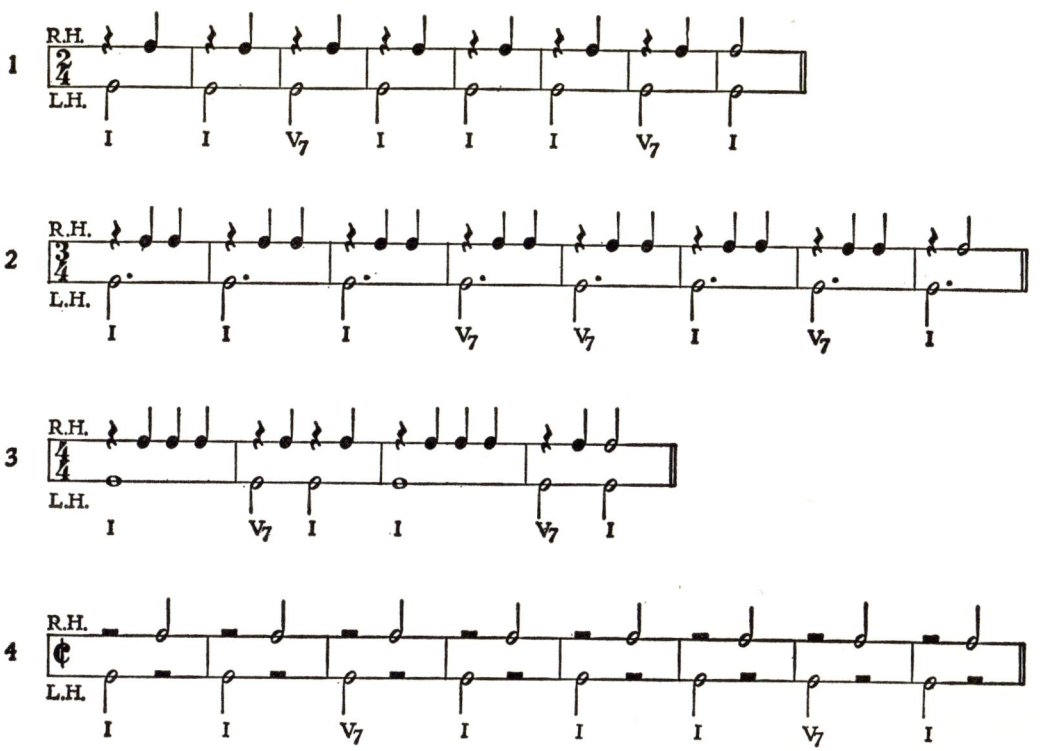

CHORDAL PATTERNS AND ACCOMPANIMENT FIGURES

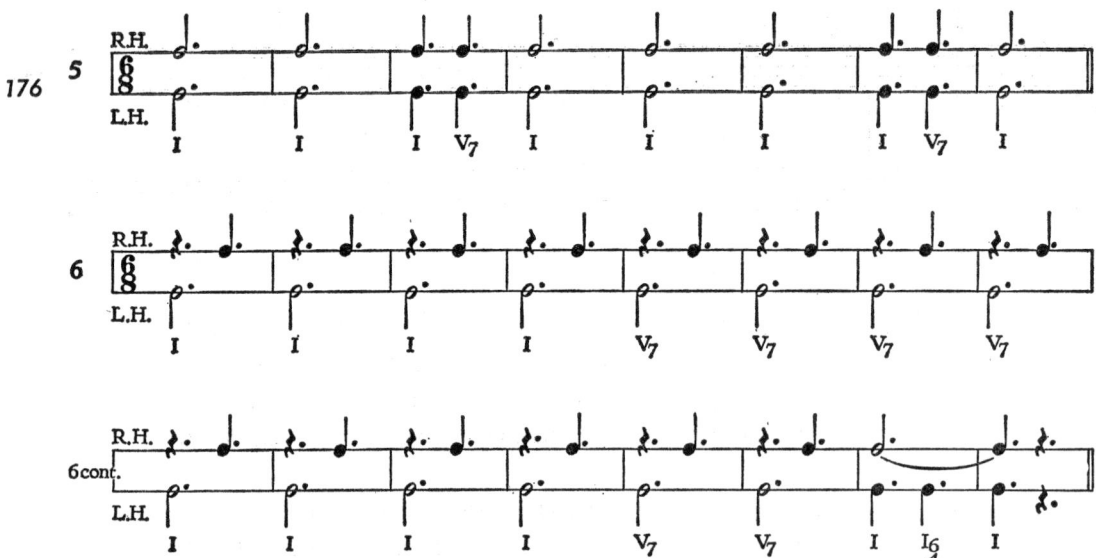

When one can move easily from one chord to another in different rhythmic patterns he is ready to match an accompaniment with a melody.

ACCOMPANYING BY EAR

Since every melody has implied harmonies, the correct chords can be selected by listening carefully to the melody. To choose and play chords in this manner is to accompany by ear.

In the following songs, the melody implies chords of the tonic (I) and dominant seventh (V_7). Suitable chordal patterns have been given in the opening bars of each piece. The figures under the bass staff are a guide to the changes in harmony. In the act of completing the accompaniment, continue with the rhythmic design suggested in the beginning.

Sing the songs as you accompany yourself. Do this several times before filling in the empty bars with the proper notation. Then sing and play the songs transposed into different nearby keys.

CHORDAL PATTERNS AND ACCOMPANIMENT FIGURES

177

$I - V_7 - I$
Mary Had A Little Lamb

Traditional

CHORDAL PATTERNS AND ACCOMPANIMENT FIGURES

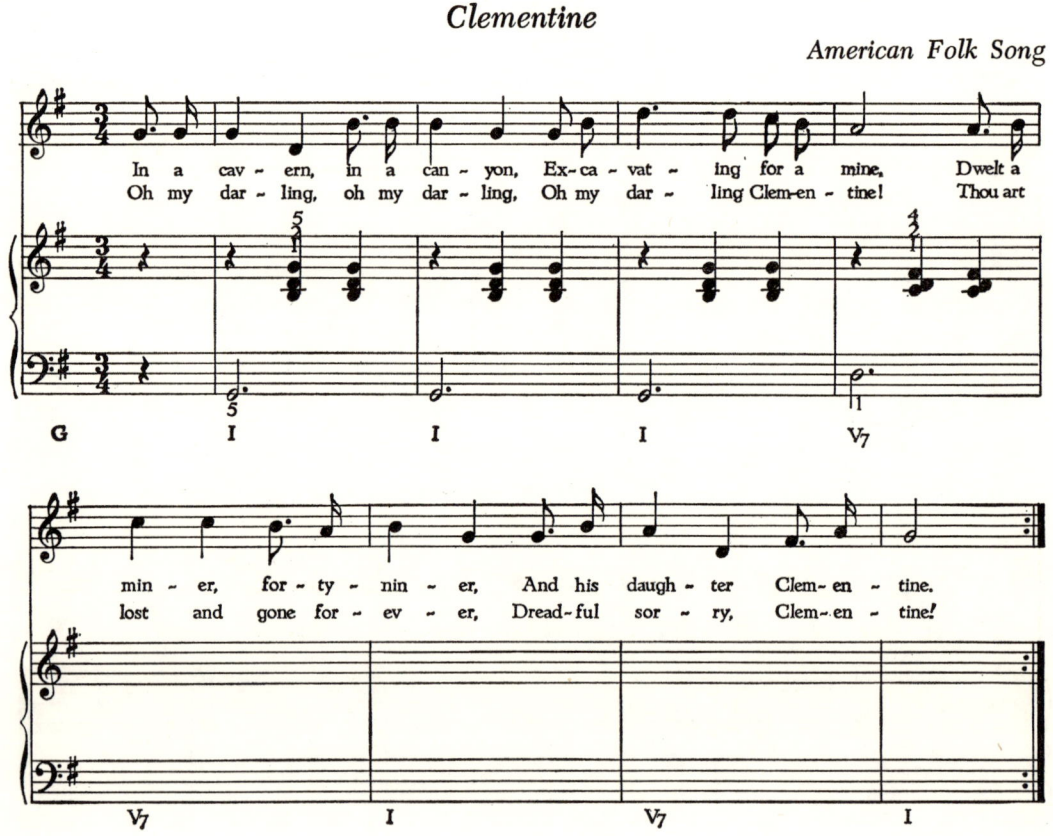

Clementine

American Folk Song

CHORDAL PATTERNS AND ACCOMPANIMENT FIGURES

179

Alouette
(The Lark)

French Folk Song

* D.C., an abbreviation for *Da Capo al Fine* (Italian, from the head to the end), is a direction to perform the piece again from the beginning to the place marked *Fine*, the end.

CHORDAL PATTERNS AND ACCOMPANIMENT FIGURES

London Bridge
English Game Song

CHORDAL PATTERNS AND ACCOMPANIMENT FIGURES

181

Sing Together

Traditional Round

CHORDAL PATTERNS AND ACCOMPANIMENT FIGURES

182

Hail, Hail, The Gang's All Here!
Sir Arthur Sullivan

CHORDAL PATTERNS AND ACCOMPANIMENT FIGURES

SELECT YOUR OWN ACCOMPANIMENT

Many songs (particularly folk, nursery, and game songs) can be accompanied adequately with simple figures using only the tonic and dominant seventh chords. Here are a few. Study the melodies to see where the I and V_7 chords are well suited. Place the numerals I and V_7 at those places where the harmony changes. Choose an appropriate pattern to accompany each song. Sing the songs as you play the accompaniment on the piano.

CHORDAL PATTERNS AND ACCOMPANIMENT FIGURES

184

Sing A Song Of Sixpence

Mother Goose
J. W. Elliott

Sing a song of six-pence A pock-et full of rye; Four and twenty black birds Baked in a pie; When the pie was o-pened, The birds be-gan to sing; Wasn't that a dain-ty dish To set be-fore the king? The king was in the par-lor, Coun-ting out his mon-ey, The queen was in the kitch-en, Eat-ing bread and hon-ey; The maid was in the gar-den, Hang-ing out her clothes; There came a lit-tle black-bird, And pecked off her nose.

Did You Ever See A Lassie?

(German?)
Traditional Game Song

Did you ev-er see a las-sie, a las-sie, a las-sie, Did you ev-er see a las-sie go this way and that? Go this way and that way and this way and that way, Did you ev-er see a las-sie go this way and that?

CHORDAL PATTERNS AND ACCOMPANIMENT FIGURES

Rig-A-Jig-Jig

American Chanty

Find other tunes that can be accompanied with tonic and dominant seventh chords. Try to sing the melodies from memory as you accompany them by ear.

TEACHING A SONG

There are a number of ways to teach a song to others. The two most common, of course, are to sing the melody for them and to play it on an instrument. Even when one has adequate vocal equipment there are advantages in playing the melody on the piano. When one sings with others it is difficult for him to listen carefully to their intonation and rhythm. This problem does not exist when the piano is used to guide those who are learning a melody. In fact, the timbre and exact pitch of a well-tuned piano are better suited for this purpose than most voices. In addition to playing the melody, the teacher can play a simple accompaniment. In this way the melody is further enriched by the harmonic and rhythmic support it receives from the accompaniment.

CHORDAL PATTERNS AND ACCOMPANIMENT FIGURES

ACCOMPANIMENT FIGURES FOR LEFT HAND ONLY

In playing a song on the piano the right hand usually has the melody while the left hand has the accompaniment. An accompaniment figure need not be complicated. To be effective it has to contain the harmonic and rhythmic elements but they can be arranged very simply.

The following examples show a variety of simple accompaniment figures for the left hand. They use the I and V₇ chords in duple, triple, quadruple, and sextuple meters. *Notice:* The chords are not restricted to root position. The positions have been chosen with regard to voice leading and easy progression from one chord to another. Learn these patterns; then transpose them into other keys. When you have developed facility in playing these accompaniment figures alone, choose an appropriate one for each of the melodies presented on pages 178–185. Play the melody with the right hand and the accompaniment with the left.

Left-hand patterns

Duple Meter

CHORDAL PATTERNS AND ACCOMPANIMENT FIGURES

Triple Meter

Quadruple Meter

CHORDAL PATTERNS AND ACCOMPANIMENT FIGURES

CHAPTER 20

EXTENDED CHORDAL PATTERNS

Many melodies imply more than tonic and dominant harmonies. A command of additional chordal patterns will be found useful to devise appropriate accompaniments.

The following pages contain chordal patterns and accompaniment figures featuring the IV, I_4^6, II_6, and two secondary dominant seventh chords: V_7 of IV and V_7 of V. *Learn to play the patterns as written.* Then sing the songs while you *play and complete* the suggested accompaniments. Finally, sing and play the songs transposed into other keys.

Note the effectiveness of a bass line not restricted to the roots of chords and the variety of accompaniment figures that can be invented with a bit of imagination.

EXTENDED CHORDAL PATTERNS

190

USING THE IV CHORD

Pattern

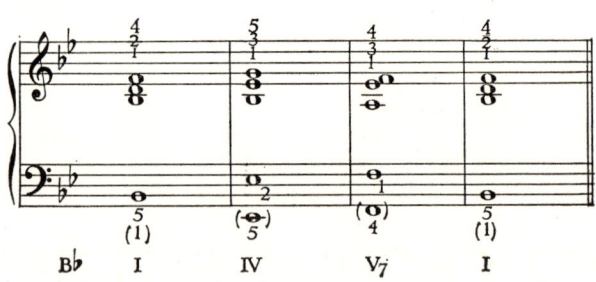

The Muffin Man

Traditional

EXTENDED CHORDAL PATTERNS

191

Pattern

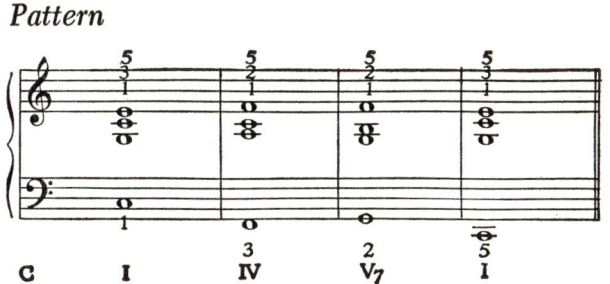

C   I   IV   V₇   I

Silent Night

Joseph Mohr
Franz Gruber

Si - lent night, Ho - ly night, All is calm, all is bright
C   I   V₇   I

Round yon Vir - gin Moth-er and child. Ho - ly In - fant so ten - der and mild,
IV   I

Sleep in hea - ven - ly peace. Sleep in hea - ven - ly peace.

EXTENDED CHORDAL PATTERNS

192

Pattern

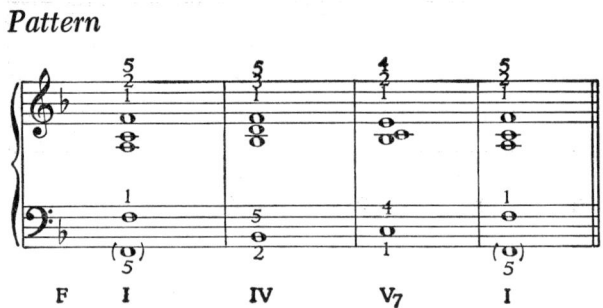

Auld Lang Syne

Robert Burns   Scotch Air

EXTENDED CHORDAL PATTERNS

EXTENDED CHORDAL PATTERNS

Pattern

Baa, Baa, Black Sheep

Traditional

EXTENDED CHORDAL PATTERNS

195

Pattern

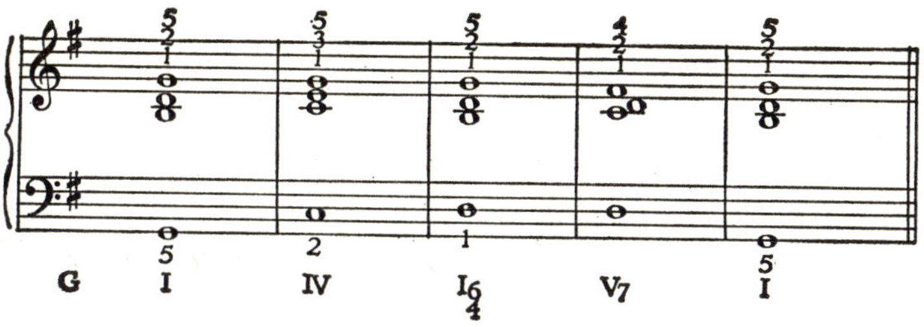

G: I   IV   I$_4^6$ V$_7$ I

Yankee Doodle

Doctor Shuckburg *English Game Song / Traditional*

Yan-kee Doo-dle went to town a-rid-ing on a po-ny, He stuck a feath-er
Fath'r and I went down to camp, A-long with Cap-tain Good-'in, And there we saw the

G: I   V$_7$

REFRAIN

in his hat and called it mac-a-ro-ni.   Yan-kee Doo-dle keep it up,
men and boys As thick as has-ty pud-din.

IV

Yan-kee Doo-dle dan-dy, Mind the mu-sic and the step, And with the girls be hand-y.

I$_4^6$ V$_7$

EXTENDED CHORDAL PATTERNS

Pattern

Rockabye Baby

Traditional

Rock-a-bye, ba-by, on the tree top. When the wind blows the cra-dle will rock;

When the bough breaks, the cra-dle will fall, And down will come ba-by, cra-dle and all.

EXTENDED CHORDAL PATTERNS

USING THE II₆ CHORD

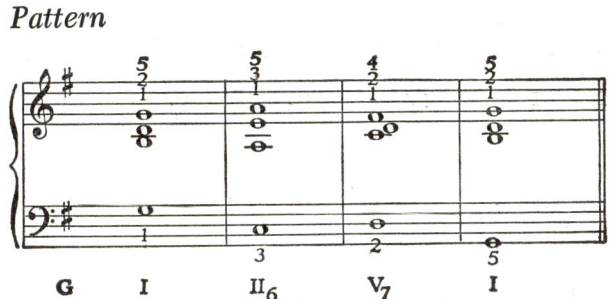

Skip To My Lou
Mountain Dance Tune

EXTENDED CHORDAL PATTERNS

Pattern

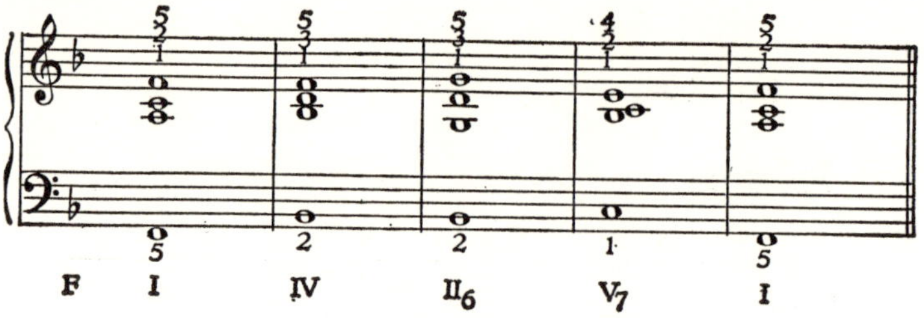

F I IV II₆ V₇ I

Away In A Manger

Unknown   Unknown

A-way in a man-ger, no crib for a bed. The lit-tle Lord
Je-sus laid down His sweet head; The stars in the sky looked down where He
lay, The lit-tle Lord Jes-us, a-sleep on the hay.

F I IV I V₇ I II₆ V₇ I

EXTENDED CHORDAL PATTERNS

Pattern

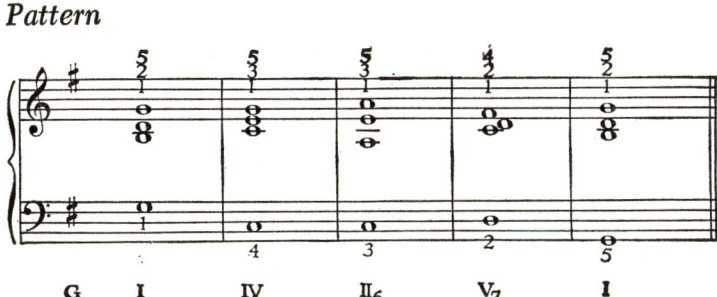

Jack Horner

Mother Goose   J. W. Elliott

EXTENDED CHORDAL PATTERNS
USING SECONDARY DOMINANTS

200   V₇ of IV patterns

EXTENDED CHORDAL PATTERNS

Good Night, Ladies

College Song

V_7 of V patterns

C I IV V7 of V V7 I
G I IV I V7 of V V7 I

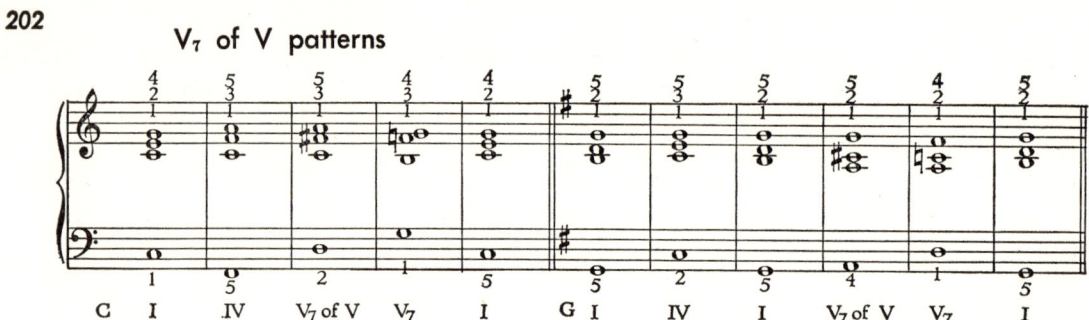

Dixie

Minstrel Song

Dan Emmet

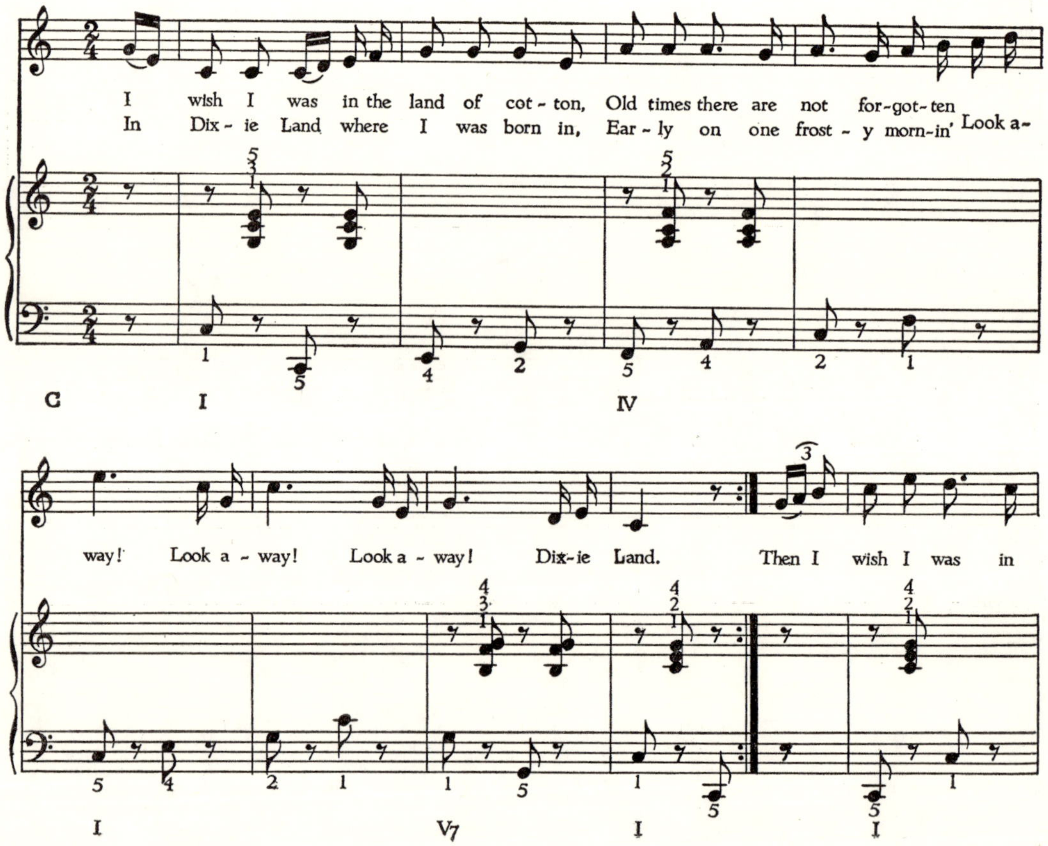
I wish I was in the land of cot - ton, Old times there are not for-got-ten
In Dix - ie Land where I was born in, Ear - ly on one frost - y morn-in' Look a-
C I IV
way! Look a - way! Look a - way! Dix-ie Land. Then I wish I was in
I V7 I I

EXTENDED CHORDAL PATTERNS

203

EXTENDED CHORDAL PATTERNS

EXTENDED CHORDAL PATTERNS

Devise your own accompaniment for the following songs

Jingle Bells

J. Pierpont

* The signs ⌐1⌐   ⌐2⌐   are called *First and Second Endings*. They are used when a repetition is exact except for the very end. After the first ending, the repetition is made as indicated up to the first bracket. At this point, the notes under the first bracket are omitted and the notes under the second bracket are played.

EXTENDED CHORDAL PATTERNS

My Bonnie Lies Over The Ocean

Scotch Air

EXTENDED CHORDAL PATTERNS

207

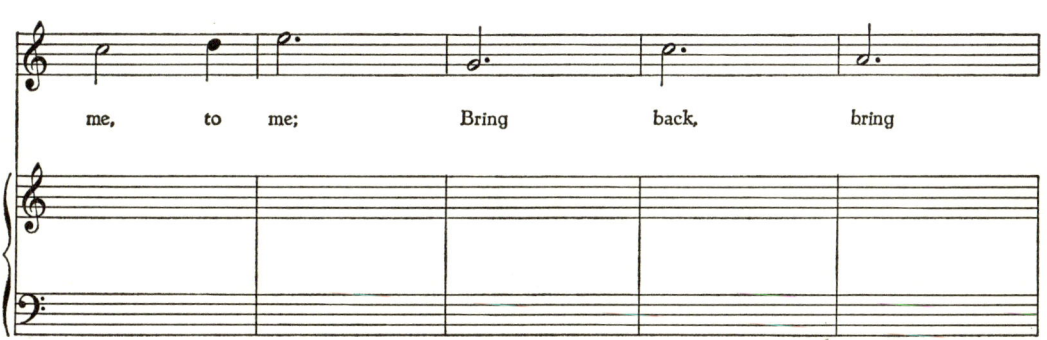

CHAPTER 21

USE OF THE DAMPER PEDAL

Reread the discussion of the piano pedals in Chapter 3.

The damper pedal is a most useful device. If applied wisely and correctly, the performer can be assured of smoothly connected musical lines, even when notes are so far apart that the hand cannot encompass the keys they represent. The increased resonance which obtains from its use gives warmth and color to the sounds. However, if applied without discretion, melodic lines may lose their shape, harmonies may become blurred, and the sounds unpleasant.

In using the damper pedal, the pianist must listen intelligently to the effects in order to get the best results. The most important consideration is this: avoid holding down the pedal when the harmonies change from one to another. Sometimes a composer might wish to secure a special effect by using the damper pedal to blend chords of different quality, but this is unusual, and in such a case he would give specific directions to the performer.

Normally the pedal is depressed a split second after the notes are played, but often this is done simultaneously with the striking of the keys. It is released and depressed again very quickly at a change in harmonies, or whenever it may be necessary to keep the sound clean—that is, to avoid blurring the melody or the harmony.

USE OF THE DAMPER PEDAL

In practicing the following pieces, depress the pedal at the letter P and release it at the asterisk (∗). For contrast, play the pieces without using the damper pedal.

Jack And Jill

Mother Goose   J. W. Elliott

USE OF THE DAMPER PEDAL

USE OF THE DAMPER PEDAL

Little Boy Blue I

Mother Goose   *Traditional*

In the first arrangement of "Little Boy Blue," the damper pedal is used to sustain the accompaniment and hold together the harmonies. It is not indispensable, however, because both hands play this simple accompaniment and they can manage easily the wide skips in the broken chords. A pedal effect can even be simulated by holding the notes in the left hand a little longer than their true value. Play the piece in this manner.

USE OF THE DAMPER PEDAL

212

In the following arrangement, where the melody is played by the right hand and the accompaniment is played entirely by the left hand, the damper pedal must be used. Without it, the tones of the broken chords are disconnected; with it, the effect is quite as good as when the accompaniment is played by both hands.

Little Boy Blue II

CHAPTER 22

SUIT THE ACCOMPANIMENT TO THE TUNE

Accompaniments can be as varied as the melodies themselves. The inexperienced pianist may believe that a good accompaniment figure depends upon the harmonic texture. This is seldom true. Chordal patterns that make effective simple accompaniments are relatively few and we have examined the most common ones.

An accompaniment comes to life through its rhythmic features. When there is little movement within the melody itself, as in "Silent Night," the accompaniment must supply the flow. When the tune is sprightly, as in "Jingle Bells," the accompaniment may assume a quieter form. Each of the next three songs is in the key of D major. Three simple chords, I, IV, and V_7, supply the harmony, but no one rhythmic pattern suits all the three pieces.

"Marching To Pretoria" has so much movement in the melody that little is needed in the accompaniment. But an occasional breaking of the "left-right" pattern is desirable where the melody comes to a stop (bar 15) and where the tune implies successive changes in harmony (bars 29–32).

"Joy To The World" becomes more effective with an accompaniment that flows with the melody and punctuates its rhythmic drive. Since the last four

SUIT THE ACCOMPANIMENT TO THE TUNE

bars of this melody are akin to the first four, the accompaniment in these final bars should resemble that of the beginning.

"Drink To Me Only With Thine Eyes" offers other possibilities. Although this piece is more temperate rhythmically than "Marching To Pretoria," it can be served well by a similar accompaniment: a "left-right" figure in bars 1–2, and a smoothly flowing one with both hands together when there are successive changes in the harmony. The real difference in this accompaniment lies in the manner in which the melody is outlined in the top notes of the part for the right hand. Coming as they do in a rhythmic variety of delays and concurrences, they create an atmosphere of informal charm. Not to be ignored is the bass line, which demonstrates the effectiveness of the frequent use of inversions.

Marching To Pretoria

English by Josef Marais South African Folk Song

Copyright, 1942, by G. Schirmer, Inc.

SUIT THE ACCOMPANIMENT TO THE TUNE

216 Joy To The World

Isaac Watts George F. Handel

SUIT THE ACCOMPANIMENT TO THE TUNE

One of the most distinguishing features of a fine accompaniment is an interesting bass line. In working out a bass line, avoid the constant use of

SUIT THE ACCOMPANIMENT TO THE TUNE

root positions. Experiment with various inversions—the melody will sound more lovely and the ear will be delighted with the movement generated by the bass. At times, a good bass line alone can be enough to complement a melody. Play the following two-voiced arrangement of "America." After you learn to play these two lines try to supply the complete harmonies.

America

Samuel Francis Smith

Henry Carey(?)

* P.T. Passing Tone. See page 166.

Consider the songs you have played in this book and others that you know. Following the example given in "America," compose, for the songs which lend themselves to such treatment, other bass lines not limited to the roots of chords. Write a melodic line in the bass itself and set it free from the commonplace style that contains no element of surprise and fails to challenge the imagination of the listener.

CHAPTER 23

INDICATIONS OF TEMPO AND EXPRESSION

Tempo (Italian, *time*, rate of motion) and expression indications, as we know them today, began to be favored by composers in the seventeenth century. Sensitive to the emotional implications and expressive qualities of their vocal music, composers awakened to a concern for the proper interpretation by performers other than themselves. At first the number of markings was small—the tempo was fast, medium, or slow; an occasional *f* for forte (loud) or *p* for piano (soft) sufficed to indicate the *dynamics* (the loudness or softness of tones). Later the indication for very soft became *pp*; for very, very soft, *ppp*; for very loud, *ff*; for very, very loud, *fff*. The composer's attitude had become so subjective by the late nineteenth century that he almost hid his notes in a maze of tempo and expression markings. Tschaikowsky asks for a dynamics range from *ppppp* to *fffff* (however soft or loud those may be), while Mahler, Strauss, and other composers of the late Romantic period choose words with the subtlest meanings to indicate a manner of performance: *dragging, roguishly, shadowy*, etc. Tempos, too, have been given narrow definitions: *fast, but not too fast; running, but not hurrying*, and so forth.

A full terminology was developed in Italy because the practice of indi-

INDICATIONS OF TEMPO AND EXPRESSION

cating tempo and expression began there. To this day, Italian is the universal language for musical terms. In the last century nationalistic feelings spurred some composers to use the language of their own country but publishers, realizing the necessity of accommodating an international public, often print the terms in Italian as well as in the tongue of the composer. A knowledge of these terms is imperative for every musician.

Tempo refers to the rate of motion at which the basic pulse, or beat, in music moves: quickly, slowly or somewhere in between. It is difficult to know the exact speed a composer intends when he uses words to indicate his desired tempo. *Fast* does not mean the same to everyone; nor does *slow*. But there is a point of reference that is helpful: the normal walking gait of man. A leisurely pace consists of about 76–80 steps per minute. It is this rate of motion which composers of Johann Sebastian Bach's time (1685–1750) called *tempo giusto* (just time) or *tempo ordinario* (ordinary time).

TEMPO MARKINGS

Andante (literally, going; fr. Italian, *andare,* to go) is used now to indicate the speed of a normal walking pace. Using this word as a midpoint, the following table gives the most common Italian words for various fast and slow speeds.

Prestissimo	Very fast
Presto	Fast
Allegro	Cheerful (quick)
Allegretto	Moderately fast
Moderato	Moderate
Andantino	Somewhat faster than andante
ANDANTE	A walking pace
Lento	Slow
Adagietto	Somewhat slower than lento
Adagio	Quite slow
Larghetto	Somewhat slower than adagio
Largo	Broad (very slow)
Grave	Solemn (very, very slow)

To appreciate the composer's great concern in the matter of tempo, one need only to play any piece in this book at an exaggerated rate of motion. A slowly played "Dixie" or "Jingle Bells," a rapid performance of "Silent

Night" or "Rockabye Baby," or any such distortion of tempo changes entirely the character of the piece. The danger of misunderstanding the tempo is not so great with vocal as it is with instrumental music because the text is there to guide the performer. But an instrumental piece without a descriptive title such as "Soldiers' March" or "The Merry Peasant Returning From Work" (sometimes called "The Merry Farmer") must have an accurate tempo marking if the performer is to approximate the intentions of the composer.

THE METRONOME

The nineteenth century saw composers developing attitudes of exactness in the notation of their musical conceptions. This is particularly true of Beethoven. Uncompromising in the matter of tempo, he welcomed a machine by which he could fix his tempos in terms of specific markings.

As a result of the inventiveness of Johann Nepomuk Maelzel and others, musicians have had, since 1816, the benefit of such a device, called the *metronome,* a clocklike instrument that ticks off rates of motion varying from 40 to 208 beats a minute.

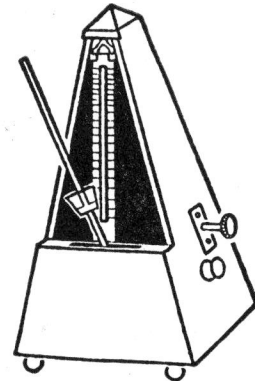

A Metronome marking is placed at the beginning of a piece of music or at a section where a new tempo begins. It is written as follows:

M. M. ♩ = 120

The "M. M." stands for Maelzel's Metronome. The ♩ indicates that the quarter note is the unit of pulsation. With the counterweight set at 120, the instrument produces 120 clicks per minute; the time from click to click represents the time value of the quarter note. Similarly, M. M. ♩ = 60 indicates that the half note represents the unit beat and that there are 60 beats per minute.

INDICATIONS OF TEMPO AND EXPRESSION

It would seem that the invention of the metronome solved one of the many problems confronting the composer—at last he had a means of indicating an exact tempo. But man is never satisfied. In the twentieth century some composers have felt it unwise to be too rigid. They prefer to rely on the performer for the proper speed. Schoenberg, in his *Fourth String Quartet* (1936), advises: "The metronome marks must not be taken literally—they merely give a suggestion of the tempo." Some American composers find it enough to use descriptive words such as *bouncy, free and easy, with a well-marked rhythm*, etc. Nevertheless, a *right tempo* is necessary for a fine performance. But what is a *right tempo?* Perhaps it best comes from the considered judgment of a talented and mature artist.

OTHER TEMPO DIRECTIONS

Accelerando	gradually quickening the speed
Affretando	hurrying; increasing the speed
A tempo	in time; a return to the original speed after some deviation
Comodo	(at a) comfortable (speed)
Con moto	with motion; rather quick
L'istesso tempo	in the same tempo as the previous section
Meno mosso	slower (less in motion)
Mosso	moved; in motion
Moto	motion
Più mosso	faster (more in motion)
Rallentando	gradually lessening the speed
Ritardando	retarding; gradually getting slower
Ritenuto	held back
Rubato	stolen; a term indicating flexibility of speed, quickening here and retarding there but without distortion of tempo in the larger context
Stringendo	pressing onward (tightening)
Tempo Primo (I°)	first tempo

Vivace	lively; sprightly
Vivo	lively; brisk

DIRECTIONS FOR BOTH TEMPO AND DYNAMICS

Allargando	broadening out; getting slower and louder
Calando	gradually getting softer and slower
Morendo	dying away
Perdendo Perdendosi	getting lost; a fading-away

TERMS INDICATING DYNAMICS

Crescendo	increasing; gradually getting louder
Decrescendo	decreasing; gradually getting softer
Diminuendo	diminishing; gradually getting softer
Forte	loud
Fortepiano	attack loudly; sustain softly
Fortissimo	very loud
Mezzo forte	moderately loud
Mezzo piano	moderately soft
Piano	soft
Pianissimo	very soft

TERMS INDICATING EXPRESSION

Affetto	tenderness; feeling
Affettuoso	tender
Amabile	amiable; graceful
Amorevole	loving; gentle
Animato	animated; spirited
Animo	spirit
Appassionato	passionate

INDICATIONS OF TEMPO AND EXPRESSION

Bravura	skill; dexterity
Brillante	brilliant; sparkling
Brio	pep; spirit; animation
Calmo	calm; quiet; tranquil
Calore	warmth; animation
Cantabile	in a singing style
Capriccioso	capricious
Deciso	bold; determined
Dolce	sweet; mild
Doloroso	sad
Espressione	expression
Espressivo	expressive
Forza	force; strength
Fuoco	fire
Furioso	furious
Gaio	gay
Giocoso	playful
Gioviale	jovial; genial
Grazioso	graceful
Maestoso	majestic; stately
Marcia	march
Marziale	martial
Mesto	sad
Misterioso	mysteriously
Piangevole	tearful
Pomposo	pompous
Ponderoso	heavy
Preciso	precise; exact
Risoluto	resolute; firm
Scherzando	(in a) joking (or playful **way**)
Scherzo	joke
Secco	dry

INDICATIONS OF TEMPO AND EXPRESSION

Semplice	simple
Sentimentale	sentimental
Sentimento	sentiment
Sereno	serene
Serio	serious
Spirito	spirit
Spiritoso	spirited
Teneramente	tenderly
Tranquillo	tranquil

TERMS INDICATING TONAL PRODUCTION

A due corde	on two strings: with soft pedal depressed half way
A tre corde	on three strings: without soft pedal
A una corda	on one string: with full soft pedal
Forzato	forced; strongly accented
Legato	bound; smoothly connected
Leggero / Leggiero	light
Marcato	marked; with emphasis
Pesante	heavy
Pieno	full
Portamento	sliding from one tone to another
Sforzando	forcing out (the tone); strongly accented
Sforzato	forced; strongly accented
Sostenuto	sustained
Staccato	detached
Tenuto	held (the full value)
Trill	A rapid alternation of the printed note with the next note above

INDICATIONS OF TEMPO AND EXPRESSION

MISCELLANEOUS TERMS

Al fine	to the end
Al segno	to the sign
A piacere	at one's pleasure; freely
Da capo	(repeat) from the beginning
Da capo al fine	(repeat) from the beginning to the end; i. e., to the place where *fine* is written
Dal segno al fine	(repeat) from the sign to the end; i. e., to the place where *fine* is written
Fine	end
Giusto	just; exact
Mano destra	right hand
Mano sinistra	left hand
Ordinario	ordinary; customary
Poco a poco	little by little; gradually
Segue	follow; continue without pause
Subito	immediately

AUXILIARY WORDS

A, alla, etc.	at, in, to (etc.)	e.g., a tempo	(back) to the original speed
Assai	very	e.g., adagio assai	extremely slow
Ben	well	e.g., ben marcato	well marked
Con	with	e.g., con animo	with spirit
Di	of	e.g., tempo di marcia	speed of a march

INDICATIONS OF TEMPO AND EXPRESSION

E	and	e.g., dim. e rit.	gradually getting softer and slower
In	in, at (etc.)	e.g., in tempo	in strict time
-issimo	suffix meaning *very*	e.g., prestissimo	very fast
Ma	but	e.g., ma non troppo	but not too much
Meno	less	e.g., meno mosso	less motion; slower
Mezzo	half	e.g., mezzo forte	half loud
Molto	much	e.g., molto meno mosso	much slower
Non	not	e.g., non troppo	not too much
Più	more	e.g., più mosso	more motion; faster
Poco	little	e.g., poco meno mosso	little less motion; slower
Poi	then; afterwards	e.g., poi a poi	by degrees
Primo	first	e.g., tempo primo	first tempo
Quasi	almost; as if	e.g., quasi una fantasia	as if it were a fantasia
Sempre	always	e.g., sempre forte	always loud
Senza	without	e.g., senza rit.	without slowing down
Simile	like	e.g., simile	in like manner (referring to a previous marking)
Stesso	same	e.g., lo stesso tempo	the same tempo
Tanto	so much	e.g., allegro non tanto	not too fast
Troppo	too much	e.g., non troppo	not too much
Un, una	a	e.g., un poco più mosso	a little faster

INDICATIONS OF TEMPO AND EXPRESSION

ABBREVIATIONS

accel.	accelerando
cresc.	crescendo
D. C.	da capo
decresc.	decrescendo
dim.	diminuendo
f	forte
ff	fortissimo
fp	fortepiano
fz	forzato
mf	mezzo forte
mp	mezzo piano
p	piano
pp	pianissimo
rall.	rallentando
rit.	ritardando
riten.	ritenuto
sf / sfz	sforzando; sforzato
sub.	subito
ten.	tenuto
tr.	trill

INDICATIONS OF TEMPO AND EXPRESSION

SIGNS

¢ alla breve (representing $\frac{2}{2}$ or $\frac{4}{2}$ meter)

} Arpeggio. This sign is placed in front of a chord to indicate that the notes are to be played quickly, one note after the other from the bottom to the top; harplike

C common time (representing $\frac{4}{4}$ meter)

< crescendo

> decrescendo; diminuendo

|1. |2. endings (first and second)

⌒ *fermata*, a hold of indeterminate length

forzato; sforzato; forzando

legato sign, called a slur. Not to be confused with the tie. Cf. footnote page 65.

marcato; stressed and sustained

‖: :‖ repeat marks

𝄋 segno (sign), used as a point of reference in D.C., al segno, etc.

staccato

CHAPTER 24

YOU—THE PERFORMER

The language of music has been explained; the piano has been explored; and you have taken your first steps in the role of performer and interpreter of great music.

A command of the materials presented in this book is sufficient to enable you to meet any simple musical demand, but, if you have developed a taste and love for music, you will want to pursue the subject to greater lengths.

The painter paints for all the world to see. He does not want his masterpieces to face the wall. The composer composes for all the world to hear. He does not want his masterpieces to lie silent on paper. Unlike the painter, however, the composer needs a performer—a liaison between him and his public. You may become a composer; but, most certainly, you have become a performer. As such, it is now your privilege to rouse the dormant strains, to give final meaning to the composer's intent.

A responsible performer wants to play in a style that is musical. A person who plays musically plays not only the correct notes in the correct time but in a manner that demonstrates a sensitivity to the phrasing, dynamics, expression marks, form, and all the other characteristics that determine the style of a composition. Your next goal is to develop this ability.

We leave you with two charming piano pieces—one of the last century and one of the present. By means of music symbols and language, the composers, Robert Schumann and Béla Bartók, have given directions designed to help you understand and interpret their artistic expressions. Learn to observe and obey such instructions from the moment you prepare to touch the keys.

Note: in the Bartók piece the *accidental signature* contains only a C♯. Why? Why is this not a *key signature?*

You now stand on the threshold of great music. Continue your studies so that you can cross it into a world of beautiful sounds. With Music as your constant companion the journey cannot be but joyous. Bon voyage!

Minuetto
Mikrokosmos, No. 50

Béla Bartók

(27 sec.)

Copyright 1940 in U.S.A. by Hawkes & Son (London), Ltd. Reproduced by permission of Boosey & Hawkes Inc.

APPENDIX I

TABLE OF PITCHES

For the piano, the following is a common method of indicating by letter the pitches of the notes in the various C octaves.

LETTER SYMBOL							NAME		LOCATION
c'''''							Five-lined Octave		4th octave above middle C
c''''	d''''	e''''	f''''	g''''	a''''	b''''	Four-lined	"	3rd " " " "
c'''	d'''	e'''	f'''	g'''	a'''	b'''	Three lined	"	2nd " " " "
c''	d''	e''	f''	g''	a''	b''	Two-lined	"	1st " " " "
c'	d'	e'	f'	g'	a'	b'	One-lined	"	MIDDLE C OCTAVE
c	d	e	f	g	a	b	Small	"	1st octave below middle C
C	D	E	F	G	A	B	Great	"	2nd " " " "
C,	D,	E,	F,	G,	A,	B,	Contra	"	3rd " " " "
					A,,	B,,	Sub-contra	"	4th " " " "

APPENDIX II

THE C CLEF

In addition to the G and F clefs there is another one commonly used today: the *C clef*. The C clef—unlike the other two—is movable; it may be placed on any line or space, but wherever it is placed it locates middle C. Its usefulness lies in the fact that it is not restricted to any one line or space and, therefore, may be moved about the staff to define different ranges within the limitations of certain voices and instruments. For example, the viola, an instrument like the violin but somewhat larger and lower in pitch, has as its lowest pitch the C below middle C. This is located on the second space of the bass staff. If this staff with the F clef were used for viola music the bottom two lines of the staff would serve no purpose; if the treble staff were used, four ledger lines would have to be added below it to indicate the lowest pitch of the viola.

But, by taking the heart of the eleven lines of the grand staff and using a clef to locate middle C on the third line, a staff is made available which is well suited to the range of the viola. The lowest pitch of the viola is thus indicated with one ledger line.

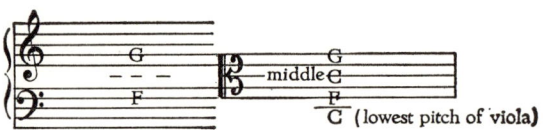

When the C clef is used to identify the third or middle line it is called the *Alto Clef*. This name derived from its use in vocal music. The alto voice seldom sings lower than the F below middle C and the use of this clef was found to be most suitable for this range. In learning the names of the lines and spaces of the alto staff it is helpful to remember that the bottom line, F, is the same F which is indicated by the F clef on the bass staff; and the top line, G, is the same G which is indicated by the G clef on the treble staff.

Today, the shape of the G and F clefs has been standardized. The C clef still enjoys a variety of designs.

The C clef identifies the first line of the staff for the soprano range; the fourth line for the tenor range.

Staff with *Soprano Clef*   Staff with *Alto Clef*   Staff with *Tenor Clef*

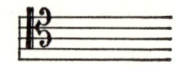

Now obsolete are the *Mezzo-soprano Clef* (the C clef marking the second line) and the *Baritone Clef* (the F clef marking the third line).

The following is a comparison of the location of the same pitch (middle C) using the various clefs:

INDEX

Accidentals, 103–104
    History of, 113
    See Chromatic signs
Accompaniments, 173–218
    By ear, 176, 183–185
    Left hand only, 186–188
    Two hands, 173–182, 189–207, 213–218
Alberti bass, 80
Alla breve, 59, 67, 229
All'ottava, 14

Bar, 57–60
    Bar line, 57
    Double bar, 57

Cadences, 165–171
    Authentic, 167
    Authentic including:
        I_4^6 chord, 169–170
        II_6 chord, 170
        IV chord, 169
        V_7 of IV chord, 171
        V_7 of V chord, 171
        In major mode, 167–168
        In minor mode, 168–169
        Plagal, 167
Chordal patterns
    Simple, 173–175
    Extended, 189–202
Chords, 149–154, 165
    Eleventh, 154
    Ninth, 154
    Seventh, 153–154, 156
        Dominant, 154
        Inversions, 157–162
    Secondary Dominant, 171
    Thirteenth, 154

Triads, 149–153, 156
    Augmented, 152–153
    Consonant, 152
    Diminished, 150–153
    Dissonant, 152
    Inversions, 157–162
    Major-Minor, 150–153
Chromatic Signs, 18, 100–106
    Double flat, 104–106
    Double sharp, 104–106
    Flat, 18–19
    Natural, 104–106
    Sharp, 18–19
    Use of flat, 101–104
    Use of sharp, 100–104
Circle of fifths:
    Major scales, 109–110
    Major and minor scales, 119
Clef, 12–13, 236
    Alto, 236
    Baritone, 236
    Bass, 13, 236
    C, 235–236
    F, 12–13, 236
    G, 12–13, 236
    Mezzo soprano, 236
    Soprano, 236
    Tenor, 236
    Treble, 13, 236
Common time, 59, 67, 229
Consonance, 144, 148
Counting, 69
Cristofori, Bartolommeo, 21

Da capo al fine, 179
Dissonance, 144, 148
Dominant, 98, 166
    See Chords

INDEX

Dominant (*continued*)
    See Scale degrees
Dot, 51–52, 56
Duplet, 66
Dynamics, 4, 223

Enharmonic change, 106
Enharmonic intervals, 146

Fermata, 95, 155, 229
Figured bass, 157–164
Fingering, 23, 69
    Harmonic minor scales, 126–127
    Major scales, 106–108
    Melodic minor scales, 131–132
    Natural minor scales, 122–123
First and second endings, 205, 229
Five C's, 34
Form, 167

Gregorian chant, 53, 90–92
Gregory the Great, 90
Guido of Arezzo, 15

Harmonic series, 7
Harmony, 77, 165
Homophony, 138

Intervals, 139–148
    Altered, 144–145
    Classification of, 141
    Compound, 140
    Enharmonic, 146
    Harmonic, 140
    History of, 148
    Inversions, 141–145
    Kinds, 142
    Melodic, 140
    Tritone, 146
Inversions
    See Chords
    See Intervals

Key, 97
Keynote, 97
Key signatures
    Major, 111–112
    Minor, 120

Ledger lines, 14
Legato, 80

Measure, 57, 59–60
Melody, 8, 165
    Played by two hands, 73
    Rhythmic representation, 58
    Written on staff, 33–37
Meter
    Compound, 62–63
    In poetry, 44–45
    Patterns in compound meters, 63–64
    Patterns in simple meters, 60–64
    Signatures, 57–58
    Simple, 62
Metronome, 221
Modes, 90–93
    Authentic, 91–92
    Church, 90–95
    Greek, 90
    Plagal, 91–92
Monochord, 15, 17
Monophony, 15

Neumes, 53
Notation, History of, 52–54
Notes, 49–51

Octave, 5–7, 19–20
Order of sharps and flats
    Major, 108–110
    Minor, 118–119
Overtones, 5–7

Partials, 5–7
Passing tone, 166, 218
Pedals, 20
    Use of damper pedal, 208–212
Performance directions in Italian
    Abbreviations, 228
    Auxiliary words, 226–227
    Dynamics, 223
    Expression terms, 223–225
    Miscellaneous terms, 226
    Signs, 229
    Tempo, 220, 222–223
    Tonal production, 225
Piano, 16–21
    Black keys, 18
    Compositions
        Minuet No. 2, Mozart, 155
        Minuetto, Bartók, 233
        Soldiers' March, Schumann, 232
    History of, 20–21
    Relation to staff, 34, 37–42
    White keys, 17
Pitch, 4–15, 53–54
    Table of pitches, 234
Polyphony, 15, 54, 81
Practice hints, 69

Quadruplet, 66
Quintuplet, 66–67

Repeat sign, 95, 155, 229
Rests, 51
Rhythm, 43, 58
    History of, 47–48
Round, 81–82

Scales
    Chromatic, 136–137
    Diatonic, 96
    Degrees (Names), 97–98
    Fingering; see Fingering

INDEX

Harmonic minor, 124–128
    History of, 138
Major, 92, 96–103, 106–108
Melodic minor, 129–132
    History of, 138
Minor, 92, 114–135
Natural minor, 114–117, 121–124
Origin of, 90–92
Other scales, 137
Parallel major and minor, 133–135
Patterns
    Harmonic minor, 124–125, 129
    Major, 98–99
    Melodic minor, 129–130
    Natural minor, 115–117
Pentatonic, 92, 94
Relative major and minor, 115–117
Whole tone, 137

Scansion, 44–45
Sextuplet, 66–67
Signature
    "Accidental" signature, 231
    Key signature, 110–111, 120
    Meter signature, 57–58
    Time signature, 57–58
Signs, 229
    Octave sign, 14
Slur, 65, 76, 229
Songs
    Alouette, 179
    America, 60,* 218
    America The Beautiful, 44 *
    Auld Lang Syne, 192
    Away In A Manger, 198
    Baa, Baa, Black Sheep, 194
    Clementine, 178
    Cradle Song, 76
    Did You Ever See A Lassie? 184
    Dies Irae, 93
    Dixie, 65,* 202
    Drink To Me Only With Thine Eyes, 217
    Drunken Sailor, The, 94
    Frère Jacques, 9–10,* 27–29, 36,* 38–39, 61,* 71, 81–82
    Good Night, Ladies, 62,* 201
    Haenschen-Klein, 89
    Hail, Hail, The Gang's All Here, 182
    Hickory, Dickory, Dock, 76
    Home On The Range, 204
    Jack and Jill, 209
    Jack Horner, 199
    Jingle Bells, 205
    Joy To The World, 216
    List To The Bells, 74–75
    Little Boy Blue, 211, 212
    London Bridge, 180
    Looby-Loo, 183
    Lux Aeterna, 92
    Marching To Pretoria, 214
    Mary Had A Little Lamb, 8–9,* 24–26, 35,* 37, 38, 45–47,* 55–56,* 58,* 70, 78–80, 177
    Mister Frog, 94
    Muffin Man, The, 45,* 59–60,* 190
    My Bonnie Lies Over The Ocean, 206
    North Wind Doth Blow, The, 45,* 210
    Old Folks At Home, 61,* 172
    O Sacred Head Now Wounded, 95, 163–164
    Rig-A-Jig-Jig, 185
    Rockabye Baby, 196
    Row, Row, Row Your Boat, 75
    Silent Night, 147, 191
    Sing A Song Of Sixpence, 184
    Sing Together, 181
    Sing Your Way Home, 44,* 200
    Skip To My Lou, 197
    Three Blind Mice, 10,* 30–32, 36,* 37, 40–42, 72–73, 83–85
    Twinkle, Twinkle, Little Star, 44 *
    When Johnny Comes Marching Home, 93
    Yankee Doodle, 195
Staff, 11
    Bass, 13
    Grand, 13
    History of, 15
    Meaning of, 11–12
    Related to piano, 34, 37–42
    Treble, 13
Step
    Half, 86–87
    Whole, 86–87
Syncopation, 61–62

Teaching a song, 185
Temperament, 7
Tempo, 69, 219–223
Tetrachord, 90, 99, 153
Tie, 51–52, 65, 76
Timbre, 4–7
Time
    Alla breve, 59, 67
    Common, 59, 67
    History of, 67
    Imperfect, 67
    Perfect, 67
    Signature, 57–58
Tonality, 97
Tone
    Semitone, 86–87
    Whole tone, 86–87
Tonic, 97, 166
    See Chords
    See Scale degrees
Transposition, 86–88
Triplet, 65–66
Tritone, 146

Upbeat, 59

Voice leading, 168

---

* Words only.